Wendy Soliman grew up on the Isle of Wight and started writing stories from a young age. She has also had published her novels *Lady Hartley's Inheritance* and *Duty's Destiny*.

THE SOCIAL OUTCAST

Eloise Hamilton, the illegitimate daughter of a wealthy banker, knows that society will never open its doors to the likes of her. So when Lord Richard Craven, heir to the dukedom, singles her out, she harbours no false illusions about the outcome. Her neighbour, the formidable rakehell Harry Benson-Smythe, is not only suspicious of her high-born admirer but inexplicably jealous too. It is only as Eloise and Harry work together to solve the mysterious abductions of local girls that Richard's true purpose becomes apparent. As do Harry's feelings for Eloise, which go beyond the merely neighbourly . . .

Books by Wendy Soliman
Published by The House of Ulverscroft:

LADY HARTLEY'S INHERITANCE
DUTY'S DESTINY

WENDY SOLIMAN

THE
SOCIAL
OUTCAST

Complete and Unabridged

ULVERSCROFT
Leicester

First published in Great Britain in 2007 by
Robert Hale Limited
London

First Large Print Edition
published 2007
by arrangement with
Robert Hale Limited
London

British Library CIP Data

Soliman, Wendy
The social outcast.—Large print ed.—
Ulverscroft large print series: historical romance
1. Illegitimacy—Fiction 2. Aristocracy (Social class)
—Great Britain—Fiction 3. Great Britain—History
—George IV, *1820 – 1830*—Fiction 4. Love stories
5. Large type books
I. Title
823.9'2 [F]

ISBN 978–1–84617–978–5

Published by
F. A. Thorpe (Publishing)
Anstey, Leicestershire

Set by Words & Graphics Ltd.
Anstey, Leicestershire
Printed and bound in Great Britain by
T. J. International Ltd., Padstow, Cornwall

This book is printed on acid-free paper

For my mother, Peggy,
and my late father David —
with my love to you both

1

Surrey 1820

The branch of the knarred oak tree beneath Eloise Hamilton's feet demonstrated an alarming tendency to flex quite without warning whenever she shifted her weight. With her entire attention focused upon her purpose however, she was quite indifferent to the precariousness of her situation, pondering instead upon how best to persuade the stranded kitten to come lower. She must have been in the tree for more than twenty minutes already and at last the silly creature was starting to trust her.

In the same unthreatening tone she had employed throughout her mission of mercy, brow wrinkled in concentration, Eloise strove to convince the kitten that she represented no danger to its well-being. Eventually, with an agility that belied its supposedly trapped status, it relented and leapt onto the branch immediately above Eloise's head, from which it regarded her speculatively through piercing green eyes.

'Good kitten!' she exclaimed with satisfaction.

'Now come on, come with me and I will take you back to the stables.'

Eloise reached up and fleetingly her fingers made contact with its fluffy pelt. Then, quite without warning, the ground started to tremble violently. Taking fright, the kitten fled upwards again, back to the relative safety of the tree's leafy canopy.

'Well!' Full of righteous indignation Eloise straightened up, her expression one of outrage. Forgetting where she was she took a step backwards, the better to bestow a frustrated scowl in the general direction of the kitten's escape route. 'Of all the ungrateful, devious . . . ahh!'

The branch shook violently and Eloise was unceremoniously deposited on the ground beneath it, landing with a hefty thud on her derrière. A string of the most unladylike profanities escaped her lips as she looked up at the cause of the earthquake. A magnificent black stallion had been brought to a halt mere feet from her landing place. It snorted its irritability at having its flat-out gallop brought to such an abrupt end and reared up defiance, hoofs flailing inches from Eloise's face. The man on the horse's back cursed even more roundly than Eloise had been able to manage as he fought to regain control of his mount.

'Eloise, I might have guessed! What in the name of Hades were you doing in that tree? Are you all right?' The man jumped from the horse, intent upon assisting Eloise to her feet, but she shook off his hand irritably.

'Harry.' She offered him a withering glare in lieu of a greeting. 'I should have known it would be you. Why did you have to come crashing along at just that moment? I was trying to rescue that wretched kitten. It has taken me ages and I almost had him; until you blundered upon us and frightened him off, that is.'

Eloise continued to glare her displeasure from her landing place at Harry's feet. Receiving nothing from him by way of an apology, other than an amused chuckle, she threw him a look of lofty scorn and climbed nimbly to her feet. She was relieved to discover that she had sustained no lasting injuries as a result of her tumble, saving her the trouble of inventing explanations to satisfy an eagle-eyed sister who was ever on the lookout for an opportunity to scold Eloise and lecture her about her want of propriety. It appeared that the mossy landing had cushioned her fall and the only damage was an unsightly grass stain on the back of the breeches she had appropriated from her brother's closet for her afternoon's excursion, together with a rather more abiding wound to her pride. Impatiently shaking off Harry's continued efforts to assist her she casually brushed grass and twigs from her bottom, wincing slightly at the contact and resigning herself to the inevitable bruise.

'Oh hello, Sampson darling!'

Eloise, ignoring Harry's attempt to give her a welcoming kiss, headed for his horse instead and, eyes sparkling with anticipated pleasure, flung her arms around his neck. She placed a delicate kiss on his soft muzzle and whispered heartfelt endearments to the magnificent creature. The stallion, who only minutes ago had been demonstrating his foul temper by attempting to deposit Harry on the ground, was now as docile as a lamb. He dropped his head in response to Eloise's petting and snorted into her hand.

Harry Benson-Smythe watched his neighbour and lifetime friend of his sister and made no attempt to disguise his amusement. He had been away from home for some months, but it was clear that not much had changed in that time with Eloise. He had been rescuing her, and by association his sister Jane, from multifarious scrapes for as long as he could remember. The girls were both seventeen now — old enough to be married and surely beyond climbing trees?

Harry actually smiled as he watched Eloise characteristically heading straight for Sampson and completely ignoring him. He was a rake with an awesome and hard-won reputation: not accustomed to engaging anything other than the complete attention of any lady he chose to favour with his attention. He dealt with his own wounded pride by reminding himself that she was still a child, unused to the ways of the world.

Jacob, Eloise's dog, chose that moment to trot up, tail spiralling in enthusiastic circles, and pushed his scruffy blond head beneath Harry's hand.

'Hello, old chap,' said Harry, scratching the dog's ears affectionately. 'Glad to see someone is pleased to see me.'

Jacob thumped his tail against Harry's shiny boots and grinned lopsidedly.

'Sampson is looking fit,' remarked Eloise.

'Naturally. But where have you hidden Molly?'

A pathetic whinny from behind a nearby stand of trees rendered any answer on Eloise's part unnecessary. Sampson, recognizing the call of his lady-love, instantly lost all interest in Eloise. Instead he pranced dramatically on the spot, arching his neck and pawing the ground impatiently. Harry had difficulty in holding his reins and eventually gave up the struggle, tying them instead to a strong lower limb of the oak tree Eloise had just so dramatically vacated.

Free of the demands placed upon him by an irascible stallion, Harry was able to look at Eloise properly for the first time. Apart from Thomas's grass-stained breeches, which clung to coltish limbs, outlining a neat bottom and slender hips, she wore an old plaid shirt that had seen better days and which was several sizes too large for her, beneath a serviceable leather jerkin. Her head was uncovered and several very long strands of hair had escaped the ribbon that was doing a poor job of holding it back, and trailed down her back in a riot of mahogany curls. Her face was smudged with dirt and she looked about twelve. There was, however, no mistaking the anger that flashed in her silver-flecked eyes as she turned her attention back to Harry.

'Why did you have to come along at that precise moment, Harry, making such a racket? Can't you ever do anything quietly? It had taken me twenty minutes to persuade that kitten to come down to me. I almost had him, but look what you've done now: he's gone right to the top again.' She offered him a quelling glance that would have floored a lesser man, or one who did not know Eloise

6

so well. 'What do you intend to do to put matters right?' She glared an injured challenge at him, hands on hips, foot tapping impatiently.

'And good afternoon to you too, odious brat,' replied Harry, his eyes brimming with laughter, 'I trust I find you well?'

Mindless of her famous temper, he took advantage of the fact that she was too exasperated to be on her guard and swooped, placing a kiss firmly on her lips, which caused her to scowl at him even more ferociously.

'Never mind all that, Harry,' she countered, making a *moue* of distaste. 'Concentrate your mind instead upon the matter in hand. The kitten,' she added, through tightly compressed lips, when he showed no sign of taking the situation seriously.

'Where did it come from?' he asked her, resigned at last to helping her since her anger showed no signs of abating.

'Our stable yard, I suppose. I was riding along when Jacob suddenly started barking at the bottom of the tree. I looked up and saw the kitten.'

'So you instigated a rescue mission?'

'Naturally! What else could I have done?'

'Left it to its own devices?' suggested Harry languidly. 'It doesn't look as though it needs rescuing to me.'

They both looked up and watched the kitten as it gracefully descended the tree with all the lithe grace and agility of . . . well, of a cat, and ran off in the direction of the stables.

'Well,' complained Eloise hotly, 'of all the ungrateful, contrary creatures!'

Laughing heartily at Eloise's discomfort, Harry, his dark eyes alight with mirth, defied her to continue taking the situation seriously. She tried to do so but it was hopeless and she gave up the effort with good grace, joining in with Harry's laughter, her anger falling away as quickly as it had arrived, as she too found diversion in the situation.

Wrapping a strong arm around shoulders that were still shaking with laughter, Harry asked her where she had learnt to swear so graphically, making it apparent that he had heard the expletives she used when she fell from the tree. Eloise shrugged, perfectly unconcerned at being overheard, and informed him that her brother Thomas was to blame for not moderating his language whilst in her hearing.

'Knowing you, Eloise, I would wager it was your behaviour which caused Tom to lose his patience in the first place. I dare say you left him with little alternative, other than to administer a well-deserved thrashing, than to resort to the use of base language. But pray tell me, where were you riding to at such a late hour, before you started rescuing kittens in distress that is?'

'Nowhere in particular: I was bored. The house is in uproar, what with Charlotte about to be presented, and I took the opportunity to escape. Not,' she added carelessly, 'that I am likely to be missed. Anyway, it is not that late.'

Harry produced a handsome half-hunter from his waistcoat pocket and told her that it wanted but fifteen minutes to four o'clock.

'Oh Lord, I must go, I am supposed to be at home! The vile Miss Standish has invited herself to tea and if I am not there you can be sure that Charlotte will make Papa aware of the fact.' Eloise scuttled away in Molly's direction.

'And who, pray, is the vile Miss Standish?'

'No one of import.'

'I cannot believe that. Anyone capable of reducing you to such a state must be worthy of note,' remarked Harry, extending his long legs and effortlessly catching up with Eloise.

'She is a miserable old busybody who has just moved into the village,' Eloise explained in a tone of mild derision. 'She made Charlotte's acquaintance, apparently by acci-dent, but I have my own opinion on that subject. Anyway, she bombarded her with flummery, assuring her that she is bound to make a splendid match during her forthcoming season,' she added, rolling her eyes in disgust. 'Needless to say Charlotte was completely taken in and we are now stuck with the wretched woman. She has her sights set on Papa and is also trying to take over the supervision of my musical studies.'

'I imagine she will be unsuccessful in her endeavours,' remarked Harry indolently. She would not be the first lady to bat her lashes in the direction of Eloise's wealthy father and he doubted that she would have any more success than her hapless predecessors. Mr Hamilton had no intention of becoming leg-shackled for a second time; Harry had good reason to know.

'Of course not! But it is most vexatious, being obliged to have anything to do with her at all. And it is all Charlotte's fault,' she added accusingly.

'What age is this old harridan?'

'A-hundred-and-four, I shouldn't wonder,' responded Eloise, with perfect indifference. 'Harry, I must go!'

Eloise had reached Molly, her beautiful palomino Arab mare, but before Harry could help her to mount she sprang, with an agility and grace almost equal to the kitten's, onto Molly's back. Harry's lips quirked. As always with Eloise, when she wore her brother's clothing, she had eschewed a saddle in favour of riding bareback. Digging her heels into the mare's sides she set off at a brisk canter, anxious to reach home and usurp the spiteful intentions which were doubtless already incubating in her sister's brain. She might not like Miss Standish but her father was a stickler for good manners, and if she was late, and the noxious Charlotte tattled on her, an argle-bargle was bound to ensue and her father could well reprimand her by preventing her from attending her first ball. After all, he had not yet entirely forgiven her for blacking the eye of the village bully when she encountered him tormenting a helpless puppy.

She could normally cajole her doting father into granting her every wish, but just recently he had been uncharacteristically strict, banning her from riding out alone, and harping on about the necessity to behave with decorum. Any further misdemeanours on her part could well result in her banishment from Sir Graham's assembly. Much as she pretended indifference to her forthcoming launch into local society, she had a strong yearning to see for herself just what went on at these gatherings and was not prepared to forego the opportunity simply to avoid the vile Miss Standish.

'I will escort you back to Staverley,' offered Harry, remounting Sampson and drawing level with her. 'Just in case some other cause, worthy of your attention, should present itself and delay your arrival.'

'Thank you, Harry,' responded Eloise, with such uncharacteristic sweetness that Harry wondered what he had done to elicit such ready acquiescence. Eloise was in fact reasoning that if she was observed returning home in Harry's company then Charlotte could not report to their father that she had defied his dictate yet again and ridden out alone. After all, she thought piously, Papa had not made any mention of her riding with a saddle, or about the attire she should adopt whilst on horseback either, for that matter.

'Sarah and Gerald arrive tomorrow.' Eloise shouted this information across the distance that separated her from Harry as they thundered along, side by side, at a spanking pace. She was referring to her married sister and favourite sibling, who was ten years her senior and Harry's contemporary. 'Charlotte is to go to London with them and will be chaperoned for the season by Sarah. Sir Graham Grey is giving a ball on Thursday evening and Charlotte is beside herself with excitement. She is treating it as a prelude to her season and imagines she will be the centre of attention, which,' continued Eloise, with an uninterested shrug, 'I imagine will be the case.'

Eloise fell momentarily silent as she made the now familiar comparison between herself and her beautiful but tediously dull, immaculately behaved sister. Why did she find it so impossible to emulate Charlotte's example: they were, after all, sisters? But Eloise already knew the answer and did not care to dwell upon the lamentable circumstances that made their difference in character inevitable.

'Shall you attend the ball?' she shouted to Harry, dragging her mind back to the present.

Harry raised a brow, amused at Eloise's ability to hold a one-sided conversation, encompassing several topics simultaneously, whilst cantering bareback on a frisky mare at a thunderous pace. 'I shall be delighted to see Sarah again and shall certainly make an appearance at Sir Graham's and dutifully admire Charlotte.'

'Your appearance is bound to find favour with her,' predicted Eloise prosaically. 'She will consider that you have put yourself out to return home particularly for her benefit.'

'Perhaps she will be right.' Harry winked at Eloise, amused that the subject of Charlotte could still so easily rouse her to anger. 'But why are they permitting a brat such as you to attend and risk embarrassing the beauty of the family?' he asked, adroitly steering himself and Sampson well clear of Eloise's raised crop as he said the words.

'I am supposed to use the occasion to gain a foretaste of good society and, as Papa put it, take the opportunity to learn how to behave.' Eloise's impish grin told Harry all he needed to know about the likely success of such an impossible scheme.

'Heaven forbid!' he mocked, his expression horrified.

They slowed the horses to a brisk walk, the better to negotiate a narrow path, and were thus able to continue their conversation in a more moderate tone.

'Tell me,' requested Harry innocently, raking her scruffy male attire with his eyes and allowing his amusement to show, 'since you are being permitted to consort with the gentry for the first time, do you have anything suitable to wear that will not lay you open to ridicule and embarrass your lovely sisters?'

Eloise resorted to type and stuck out her tongue at him. 'Harry Benson-Smythe, you are without doubt the most loathsome creature it has ever been my misfortune to be acquainted with and I sincerely hope

Charlotte does not accept you when you offer to dance with her!'

'That is a disturbing prospect, but I am not easily deterred, especially when the prize at stake is Charlotte's intimate and exemplary society for half-an-hour together,' he added, intent upon provoking his companion, 'and so I shall take my chances.'

'Huh, then I wish you good fortune!' responded Eloise, with evident insincerity. 'Who else is to attend this splendid occasion?'

'Thomas, of course, and his friend, Lord Craven.'

A fleeting frown creased Harry's brow which went unnoticed by Eloise. 'Ah yes. Craven has been working on your father's behalf, I am given to understand.'

'Yes, indeed. Papa is engaged upon raising finance for some sort of diamond-mining venture in Southern Africa and requires aristocratic backers. Thomas mentioned that his lordship might be amenable to a consultancy of that nature and Papa considered him the perfect candidate for his purposes.'

'Indeed.'

Harry's smile was ironic, bearing testimony to his appreciation of Mr Hamilton's astuteness. Harry was aware that his neighbour, a hugely successful merchant banker, had long ago ceased to resent the gulf that divided him from his betters and had learned instead to use it to his advantage. Richard Craven, the second son of the impecunious Duke of Esher, had all the breeding and connections that Mr Hamilton could possibly require if he was to succeed in attracting affluent backers for his scheme. The fact that almost everything Mr Hamilton touched turned to gold was unlikely to make much impression upon the plutocracy; unless, of course, they were offered the opportunity to become involved by one of their own.

'And what is your opinion of his lordship?' enquired Harry lightly.

'I have not yet made his acquaintance. You know how Papa can be when it comes to matters of business. It is not a suitable topic of conversation in front of ladies,' she said, mimicking her father's voice so accurately as to make Harry laugh aloud.

'Quite right too, brat!'

'Charlotte met him when she was in London with Sarah a few months ago and is completely besotted. He flattered her and told Thomas afterwards that she was quite the beauty and now she sees herself as the next Lady Craven.' The disgust in Eloise's voice made Harry smile. 'Naturally, such a connection would never be countenanced, but Charlotte is blind to all reason. She considers her beauty and fortune sufficient weapons to overcome any objections as to her suitability. You and I know better, of course.'

Harry looked at her with new respect. 'And pray what occasioned you to form such decided opinions upon a matter you are ill-qualified to comprehend?'

Eloise shrugged. 'I use my ears and I read the society columns in the newspapers. Charlotte may well attract some young aristocrat who is in need of a wealthy wife and prepared to overlook her lack of breeding because of it, but, however much Lord Craven might require the blunt, we both know he would never be permitted to marry so far below himself. I gather that his older brother is quite unwell and that Richard will most likely be the next duke. That only makes it more impossible.'

'Such cynicism in one so young,' repined Harry with a dramatic sigh, designed to disguise his continuing surprise at her perspicacity.

'I do not share Charlotte's attitude and choose not to look at the world in an unrealistic manner. It can only lead to disappointment.'

'I wonder that Craven chooses to grace Sir Graham's little assembly,' remarked Harry.

'His presence will be quite a coup for Lady Gray. But what inducement can have persuaded him to attend, apart from the lovely Charlotte, do you suppose?'

'Well, Esher Castle is not so very far from here and besides, his lordship is already acquainted with Sir Graham. Anyway, I imagine his friendship with Thomas and your brother James might explain it. You cannot have forgotten that the three of them were all up at Oxford together and were inseparable throughout their sojourn there.'

'Of course I had not forgotten.'

What Harry also knew, but did not say, was that when the three of them graduated James and Craven undertook their grand tour together. Thomas was not invited to be one of their party, being considered not quite up to the crack. Thomas, one of the most even-tempered and engaging people of Harry's acquaintance, took this entirely in his stride, understanding without having to be told that no disrespect was intended and it was simply the way things were. He was right, of course, but Harry wondered if Thomas appreciated the irony of the situation: considered unsuitable company as a travelling companion for the son of a duke but eminently qualified to recommend him for gainful employment.

* * *

Half-an-hour after Harry had seen Eloise safely into the Staverley stable yard she was demurely clad in a modest afternoon gown, her hair neatly pulled into a knot at her nape, all traces of dirt removed from her face. She was seated at the pianoforte in the elegant drawing-room at Staverley, her face determinedly averted from their unwelcome visitor, leaving it to Charlotte to play the role of hostess.

Eloise executed a complicated Bach sonata, demonstrating a passion and skill that belied her tender years, and was unrecognizable from the wild hoyden who had fallen from an oak tree less than an hour before.

2

Harry was still smiling as he turned Sampson back towards the spinney and in the direction of Boscombe Hall. Eloise's company, even as a child, had always been engaging; her incessant questions — the product of a lively imagination and enquiring mind — making it impossible to disregard her. Mr Hamilton and Eloise's long-suffering governess, whom Eloise had habitually led a merry dance, appeared to be combining forces in a belated attempt to curb her wilder instincts now that she stood on the brink of womanhood. They had his sympathy but, perversely, he rather hoped that their efforts would prove to be in vain. The *outré* bent to her developing mind, glimpses of which she had so artlessly displayed during their ride home, had been a refreshing fillip for his jaded spirit. Sparring with the adult Eloise, it appeared, would require him to keep his wits about him more closely then ever. The prospect was not altogether unwelcome.

Harry turned his mind to his forthcoming reunion with his father and wondered again why he had been summoned home from the management of the family estate in Shropshire so summarily. He had been hoping to procrastinate and live out at least part of the season in the country. Life there suited all of his appetites well: everything he could require for his entertainment was readily to hand and the few matrons in the area, in possession of daughters of marriageable age, were easily avoided.

Harry accepted grimly that his father was losing patience with him, wished to see him well settled and that escape from the madness of the annual marriage-mart was not likely to be so easily achieved this season.

Entering the house, the first person Harry encountered was his sister Jane. Her plain, moon-shaped face split into a beauteous smile of welcome and she hurled her dumpy self into Harry's outstretched arms.

'Harry, you're home at last!'

Harry hugged his favourite sister wondering, as he did so, how she would react to the news he had to impart with regard to her likely future. Jane was dutiful and obedient to a fault, with a sunny disposition and compliant nature that led one to overlook her want of beauty. But would persuading her into a marriage with that irascible old goat, Lord Bingham, cause her to rebel against her father's determination to see all of his children splendidly married regardless of their own feelings about his choice of partners for them? Harry, feeling like a first-rate cad at being the one who must push Bingham's suit and inflict unhappiness upon his compliant sibling, gently detached her arms from around his neck and linked her arm through his.

'How have you been, Jane?'

'Perfectly well, Harry, but glad to see you home again. So much has happened!' She frowned. 'James is causing us some little concern. He appears unsettled but we cannot discover that there is anything of consequence to make him so.'

Harry already knew this, from correspondence with his father. 'I dare say he will come round.'

'I do hope so. Charlotte Hamilton is to be presented this season and Ella and I are to attend our first ball on Thursday.'

'So I comprehend,' responded Harry, smiling at her excitement. 'I met Eloise in the woods on my way home.'

'Shall you attend, Harry?'

'I would not miss it for the world.'

They had reached the door to the library. Hearing voices, Sir Henry emerged and greeted his elder son with a warm handshake.

'Welcome home, Harry!' He led his son

into his inner-sanctum, his pleasure at seeing him again plainly apparent, and waved Jane away. 'Inform your mother that her son is home and will shortly wait upon her,' he said, closing the door as Jane turned to willingly do his bidding. 'Now, Harry, how are things in Shropshire?' asked Sir Henry, as he poured glasses of Madeira for them both.

'All under control now, Father. The repairs to the outbuildings at Home Farm are complete, I have managed to find additional markets for the excess harvest and have appointed a new cleric to the living in the village. An excellent man, with a compassionate nature commensurate with his calling and, mercifully, a tendency to preach short sermons.'

Sir Henry smiled. 'Excellent, Harry, I knew I could rely upon you.'

'Why the urgency to have me home, Father? Your correspondence was vague upon that point.' Harry decided to grasp the bull by the horns, suspecting there was more to it than his father's impatience to see him well married.

'Several matters have arisen that I feel the need to acquaint you with. Firstly, James.'

'Ah yes, I gather he is feeling unsettled. Perhaps we should find something worthwhile for him to do?'

Sir Henry rubbed his chin thoughtfully. 'That was my initial reaction. I felt assured that nothing more serious than the want of occupation could be the cause of his discontent. But for the past few months things have become progressively worse: in fact his whole personality appears to have undergone a marked change. He is short-tempered; drinking to excess; uncommunicative, and given to disappearing for long periods without explanation.'

'That does not sound at all like my easy-going brother. Do you suppose that a lady might be at the root of the problem?'

'That was precisely my conclusion,' said Sir Henry, 'but he will reveal nothing to me, which makes me suspect that if a petticoat is involved then James must imagine that I will consider her to be unsuitable. You and he have always been close and I hope that he will be more forthcoming if you broach the subject with him. If he has become unsuitably embroiled then we must put a stop to it immediately.'

Harry, draped elegantly in a winged chair, one booted leg crossed casually over his other knee, took in the stubborn set to his father's chin and nodded grimly. For the second time within half an hour he was reminded that Sir Henry would countenance no misalliances between his children and partners of inferior lineage. His own father before him had compelled his children to marry persons of influence and Sir Henry was intent upon continuing to raise the family's influential standing in society by following that example. Harry, as Sir Henry's heir, would be expected to make the best match of all. His two elder sisters were already settled with partners of Sir Henry's choosing and Jane would be required to follow suit. His father would be cheered by the news of Lord Bingham's interest in her.

'I will take the earliest opportunity to speak with James, Father.' He stood to refill their glasses, then refolded his six-foot frame into the chair he had just vacated. 'I should tell you that Edward Bingham called upon me last week.'

'Indeed, for what purpose?'

'He wishes to pay his addresses to Jane.'

As he had known would be the case, this intelligence cheered Sir Henry no end.

'Indeed? This is excellent news. A marquis for my little Jane, how splendid!'

'She may be reluctant,' cautioned Harry. 'Bingham is a good deal older than she, and a widower to boot.'

'That is of no import. Jane is a good girl and knows where her duty lies,' countered Sir

Henry emphatically. 'Bingham is well below the hatches, and also wants for an heir. Jane's dowry and youthful person will amply satisfy both of those requirements,' he added, displaying a rare bout of vulgarity.

'Bingham is an acquaintance of Sir Graham's and will be at his ball on Thursday.'

'Excellent! He has my full permission to pursue his suit.'

'I have already informed him so since I anticipated your answer.' Harry pondered the question for a moment, still reluctant to force Jane into a match with such a disagreeable man. 'Perhaps Bingham's estate being so close to ours in Shropshire will help to persuade Jane?'

'Undoubtedly. And if we can bring this match about it will save me the trouble and expense of giving Jane a season next year.'

Harry understood it was not the expense of Jane's season that concerned him: to a man of Sir Henry's wealth that counted for nothing at all. But for young ladies such as Jane, lacking in beauty and any immediately obvious charms, a season very often proved to be more of an agony than a pleasure. Girls of Jane's ilk were courted only for their fortunes, made to understand they were lucky to receive any attention at all and then obliged to step aside, mere spectators, as their fairer sisters enjoyed the lion's share of the entertainments. Sir Henry's intuitiveness on the point found favour with Harry.

'That had not occurred to me but you are right, Father, it could well be for the best.'

'Should I inform her of her good fortune in being noticed by Bingham before Thursday, I wonder, and make her understand that I wish her to encourage his attentions?'

'No, Father, it would be better, I think, if his approach appeared to be spontaneous.'

'Perhaps you are right. Now, Harry, I must acquaint you with my main reason for bringing you home. Some disturbing occurrences have arisen in the locality recently and I would appreciate your advice.' The seriousness of Sir Henry's tone forewarned Harry to expect more than a simple tale of poaching, drunkenness or the usual fallings-out amongst the tenants. 'About four months ago, the fifteen-year-old daughter of one of the tenants disappeared mysteriously. She was a pretty girl, but somewhat simple, and at first it was assumed that she had just wandered off and got lost.'

'Unlikely, if she has lived here all her life. She would know her way around well, simple-minded or not.'

'Exactly. Anyway, after three days she

reappeared but seemed more remote than ever. She could offer no explanation for her disappearance, put seemed frightened of her own shadow. She will not now leave her mother's side and never ventures out of the cottage; whereas before she loved the outdoors and worked happily in the fields all day long.'

'If she is a simpleton perhaps she was accosted by one of the villagers? It is just the sort of behaviour that some of them would consider to be good sport?'

'Indeed. However, after her safe return her father did not wish me to pursue the matter and so I let it drop.' Sir Henry leaned forward and Harry sensed that he was reaching the crux of the matter. 'Two weeks ago, another fifteen-year-old disappeared. This time it is more serious since it is the daughter of the blacksmith.'

'I believe I have seen her. Mary, is it?' Sir Henry nodded. 'A remarkably pretty girl, if memory serves, with an outgoing disposition.'

'Quite so, but unlike the first case she has not returned and nothing has been seen of her since. Her parents are beside themselves.'

'I daresay. What efforts have been made to discover her whereabouts?'

'I initiated a thorough search of all the cottages and outhouses. Men and dogs have scoured the fields, woods, streams and such like, and word has been spread to neighbouring villages; all to no avail. She appears to have disappeared into thin air.'

'Perhaps she has eloped? She is, after all, a pretty girl.'

'Unlikely. She was apparently a dutiful daughter and her parents knew of no particular attachment on her part to any young man. Besides, they are convinced that had she done so she would, at the very least, have sent them word.'

'I see.'

'The Hamiltons came to dinner last week and I discussed the problem with George over the port. What he had to tell me finally convinced me that these were more than just random disappearances and that I needed to talk it through with you.' Harry raised a questioning brow. 'It would seem that about two months ago an upstairs maid at Staverley disappeared as well. She went out on her afternoon off and did not reappear.'

'What, and Hamilton did not report her absence?'

'He was about to but, as in the first instance, she returned after two days.'

'And what was her explanation?'

'She too appeared confused and would not speak of it, other than to say that she had been taken and held somewhere against her will. She had been violated and then released some distance from Staverley. She was blindfolded the entire time and never heard her captors' voices.'

'Voices?'

'Ay, she claims there was more than one of the brutes.'

'Was her story believed?'

'Yes. Once again she is a pretty girl, who has worked at Staverley since the age of twelve. She was employed direct from the workhouse as a scullery maid and progressed to the position of upstairs maid through a combination of hard work and diligence. All of the staff, without exception, stated that she was a good, religious girl, who never gave a moment's bother. Some of the footmen admitted to trying to engage her as their inamorata but it would appear that she repulsed them all.'

Harry raised a brow in frank surprise. 'It is unusual to hear such a glowing testimony. I should have thought that if she was so pretty, and such a diligent worker, it would have raised jealousies amongst the other female staff, at least, and resentment amongst their male counterparts too, if she declined their respective advances.'

'That is a reasonable conclusion, and one

that I myself reached, but I am not in the happy position of being able to question the staff at Staverley and therefore am not qualified to draw any firm conclusions from first-hand knowledge.'

'Indeed. But did George not attempt to track down her abductors?'

'She begged him not to and, in truth, they had little to go on anyway. And then, a week or two ago, unhappily for the girl, she discovered her condition. George has sent her to an establishment in London. When the baby is born it will be adopted and George has agreed to keep her position at Staverley open for her.'

'That is very philanthropic of him.'

'Good servants are difficult to come by nowadays and I suspect he also feels partly responsible for what happened to her.' Sir Henry stood and paced the room. 'But, Harry, this can be no coincidence: three girls from the same area all disappearing within months of one another. What are the odds against that happening? Something sinister is at work here, if I am not much mistaken, and I need your help to discover what it is. That is partly why I called you home.'

'Of course, Father. Let me think on what it would be best to do and I will then discuss my strategy with you.'

'The other reason I wanted you here, Harry, is, I think, known to you.' Harry feigned ignorance. 'Harry, you are seven-and-twenty; it is high time you remembered your obligations, to your family and to me, and found yourself a suitable wife.'

'There is time yet, Father.'

Sir Henry ignored the interruption. 'Lady West is bringing her ward, Lady Hannah Price, to Sir Graham's ball. She came out two years ago, if you recall, and caused quite a sensation.'

'I do indeed recall,' drawled Harry carelessly, his voice devoid of any discernible emotion, or enthusiasm either.

'Then you will also recall that she is the daughter of the late Marquis of Devonshire. Her portion is substantial, her connections impeccable and her appearance pleasing.'

'She is also empty-headed, dutiful, dull and lacking in a single original thought,' added Harry contemptuously, his mind turning unbidden in the direction of his recent lively verbal clash with Eloise.

'What more could you require in a wife?' asked Sir Henry irascibly. 'Good God, Harry, you know only too well that you need but fill your nursery and can then live your life just as you please.'

'Do I recall Craven relentlessly pursuing

32

Lady Hannah during her season?'

'Indeed, yes, and I imagine her fortune was one of his primary interests. God alone knows the Esher estate is in desperate need of reinvestment, if only half of what I hear is correct. It was considered by those in the know that matters were all but settled between the two of them but then Craven went off on his Grand Tour and nothing came of it. Lady Hannah was, if the tabbies are to be believed, devastated by his desertion and felt she had been insulted and all but jilted. But since Craven never actually offered for her, nothing could be done. I imagine, having lined his pockets a little with the profits from George's diamond-mining venture, he is not in quite such desperate straights anymore and is holding out for a partridge with even fatter pockets.'

'Possibly.'

'Anyway, Harry, because of her history Lady Hannah is especially anxious to restore her self-esteem and I doubt that your suit will meet with too much resistance.'

'I am perfectly well able to make myself agreeable to a lady,' retorted Harry, stung, 'without first requiring that she be suffering from a disappointment in order to look kindly upon me.'

'Indubitably,' responded Sir Henry mildly,

'and that is why I expect you to single her out, at the very least, on Thursday evening.'

Annoyed at having been manipulated so skilfully by his father, Harry responded evasively. 'Thursday evening promises to be more entertaining than Sir Graham could have intended, what with Bingham embarking upon his suit with Jane; Craven putting in an appearance and, of course, Charlotte Hamilton about to embark upon her season.'

'And Jane and Eloise attending their first ball,' added Sir Henry, with a smile.

'Do you imagine Charlotte will succeed in snaring her prince this season?'

'Hard to say. She has the looks and fortune but, sadly, lacks the connections.'

Harry smiled again, both at his father's words and the fact that they so closely echoed Eloise's of a little earlier. 'It will be Eloise's turn next year, I suppose. God help the *ton!* Do you suppose it to be sufficiently robust to withstand the experience?'

'That won't happen, Harry. Eloise will not be presented.'

'Why not? Charlotte is taking her turn this year.'

'Think about it, Harry. Sarah never came out but was fortunate enough to meet Sir Gerald, who had no need of her fortune and married her because he fell in love, was free to marry wherever he chose and was not embarrassed by her lowly connections. It is only through his influence that Charlotte can be launched into good society. But Eloise is altogether a different matter. Do not forget that she is merely George's by-blow.'

'I always knew that she was half-sister to the other three, but I was never privy to the particulars.'

'George's marriage to Annabel was not a congenial one and so, not unnaturally, he turned to a mistress to provide the comforts he clearly did not enjoy at home. He made precious little secret of the fact that he was besotted by his ladybird and she became his wife in all but name, often acting as his hostess in Annabel's stead when he entertained his business connections.'

Harry frowned. 'Wasn't that dreadfully embarrassing for Annabel?'

'Probably, but she brought it upon herself by her own behaviour. She was less than discreet for many years, which put paid to any ambitions George might have entertained about being accepted into the upper echelons of society. It gave the tabbies just the excuse they were seeking to close their doors to the couple; however much they might have wished to tolerate their company for pecuniary reasons. As you know, it is quite acceptable for a married lady to behave as Annabel did, provided she is discreet. But Annabel did not understand the meaning of the word. She was very beautiful, but wilful, and determined to capture the attention of any gentleman who took her fancy, regardless of her married state.'

'I certainly recall that she was beautiful,' agreed Harry, 'and I can see her features replicated in Sarah and Charlotte. Poor Eloise! No wonder she feels the need to rebel. My schoolfriends and I were quite in love with Annabel, you know, and spent many a restless night pondering the question of her innumerable charms.'

'Yes, I can well imagine what the sight of her did to boys of your age! But it was her actions that eventually drove George into the arms of his doxy. I knew her slightly and could quite understand George's obsession with her. Although her beauty could not match Annabel's, she nevertheless had an innate elegance about her and was intelligent and amusing besides. She was also an excellent musician and skilled hostess, intent upon promoting George's interests rather than attempting to steal the limelight.

'About eighteen months after Annabel gave

birth to Charlotte, George's mistress presented him with Eloise. George adored the child at first sight and she has unquestionably been his favourite ever since. Annabel died not long after Charlotte was born and George's mistress went to her grave when Eloise was almost three. George took his favourite child into his household then and acknowledged her as his own. Sarah and Thomas accepted her unquestionably but Charlotte took exception to the fact that she was no longer the centre of attention at Staverley. The relationship between the two of them has, unsurprisingly, never been an easy one.'

'I see. And you are saying that even though George acknowledges her, the *ton* would not accept her?'

'Yes, it will be hard enough for Charlotte, but for Eloise it is impossible. What is more, I suspect she knows it. George has confided in me that he intends to settle an even larger portion upon Eloise than he has upon his other two daughters, but even that will be insufficient to persuade anyone of significance to admit such a person.'

'Yes, I daresay,' agreed Harry, disappointed for Eloise and reminded too of her cynical words of a little earlier. 'And so she will be an heiress of some significance, but an outcast in the eyes of good society.'

Sir Henry nodded his head. 'Charlotte has a small chance of success, since she is so beautiful, wealthy and in possession of pretty manners and an obedient, complying nature.' Sir Henry smiled. 'Even if Eloise were to be given a chance to shine within society I cannot imagine her adjusting her rebellious spirit and ready tongue simply to comply with its dictates.'

Harry smiled his agreement. 'Well, I cannot say that I am gladdened by what you say, it seems so unjust, but what you tell me at least explains the difference in the looks between the three sisters. Sarah and Charlotte are both radiantly pretty; Eloise is not only much taller but is also not blessed with their fine features. She has without doubt inherited her mother's musical talent and I for one find her lively mind and unconventional outlook a refreshing change.' Harry smiled for a second time. 'I encountered her on my way here. She had ridden bareback to the woods, was wearing Tom's clothing and when I came upon her she was up an oak tree, attempting to rescue a stranded kitten.'

Sir Henry laughed. 'That sounds like Eloise. George will be concerned to learn that she was riding out alone however. He has forbidden her to do so and she believes it is because he wishes her to behave with greater propriety. But his concern lies with these disappearances, about which Eloise knows nothing, and he is seeking to protect her.'

'I will find a way to warn her, without disclosing my reasons.'

'Yes, do that, Harry. You know in what great regard I hold the whole family, despite the fact that they are not our social equals, and I would not care to see any harm come to Eloise whom, I own, is a favourite of mine too.'

Sir Henry's voice became reflective. 'I find myself blaming George for not keeping her under stricter control and fear he may come to regret his laxity in that regard. It will be difficult enough for her to make a good match, as I have already indicated, but if her want of conformity is added to the equation, along with an intelligence she is unlikely to see any need to conceal and which is bound to make any gentleman who sets his cap at her feel inferior, then the outlook for her becomes bleaker still. I cannot easily imagine her bowing to the dictates of some future husband unless it suited her purpose to do so,' he added, smiling at the prospect in spite of his concerns. 'George adores her but is totally taken up with his business and social engagements and, as you are aware, is often not at Staverley for days at a time. He assumes that Miss Gregson keeps Eloise in line, much as she did Sarah and Charlotte before her, but we both know that Eloise is quite capable of running rings around her governess. How else could she have ridden out alone this afternoon?'

Harry laughed. 'Miss Gregson has my sympathy.'

'Quite so.' Sir Henry's relaxed expression underwent a sudden change and he fixed his son with a gimlet gaze. 'But enough of the Hamiltons. Your mother is in her sitting-room, Harry, and eager to see you again. But before you pay her your respects I need your assurance that you intend to oblige me on Thursday in respect of Lady Hannah.'

3

Charlotte's attitude towards having her younger sister present at Sir Graham's ball was one of resigned indifference, so confident was she that Eloise could never eclipse the centre-stage position she firmly intended to make her own. A gentleman of Lord Craven's standing would surely only deign to attend such a parochial assembly if there was a very strong inducement for him to do so? Charlotte had decided weeks ago that she was that inducement and, as a result, felt sufficiently kindly disposed towards Eloise as to offer her rare and unasked for advice as to her ball gown.

'Pray be guided by me, Ella, for I have experienced several country balls now, which you have not, and know just what you must expect. Pale muslin would be just the thing for you, I think, and perhaps a chemise of lustring and, of course, a modest fichu,' she added, with a spiteful glance in the direction of Eloise's ample décolletage. 'Yes, yes!' Charlotte clapped her tiny hands together as though the matter was all but decided. 'I declare, that will be quite lovely. We must consult Mrs Fields on the matter without delay.'

Eloise made no objection to her sister's dictatorial attitude, other than to pull a face at her when her back was turned, but was quite determined to make up her own mind about her gown. She consulted Mrs Fields when Charlotte was otherwise engaged, persuaded her to her point of view and swore her to secrecy.

Dressed ready for the long-awaited ball Eloise examined her reflection critically in her full-length pier glass and began to wonder if, perhaps, she should have heeded her sister's advice after all. Her gown was of rose-coloured damask, with a spangled overskirt, but otherwise perfectly plain and devoid of all the ribbons, flounces and furbelows that Charlotte would have considered indispensable. The simplicity of the gown, which was caught below her breasts with a sash, before falling unimpeded in gentle folds to her feet, whispered softly about her legs as she moved, only serving to emphasize their extraordinary length. The demure neckline could not begin to hide the fact that she still refused to bend to the dictates of fashion and wear a corset.

In advance of the event Eloise had enjoyed the thought of rebelling in such a drastic manner but now the time had arrived and the results of her impulsive action stared defiantly back at her from the mirror it seemed more like an immature attempt to shock and draw attention to herself, leaving her to dread her father's censure. She so wanted him to be proud of her but instead now feared that her behaviour would cause him to look upon her with disappointment.

Such musings were brought to an abrupt end by the arrival of Charlotte, who burst into Eloise's room without bothering to knock.

'Come, Ella, the carriage is . . . good heavens, what on earth do you think you are wearing?'

'My first ball gown,' responded Eloise sweetly, dismissing her abigail with a wave of her hand, signifying that she was satisfied with her hair, which was now piled on top of her head and fell about her face in shiny mahogany ringlets.

'But this is not what we agreed and, in any event it is entirely unsuitable. Papa will not approve at all!' cried Charlotte, her genuine dismay fuelled by jealousy as she looked in the glass at her own reflection, suddenly full of doubts where none before had existed, about her own fussy creation. 'You will have to change at once.'

'Certainly not! I did not agree to your

suggestions; you simply assumed that I would do as I was bid, and anyway I have no choice but to wear this gown, for I have no other.'

'But you cannot go to a ball so obviously not wearing a corset,' cried Charlotte, truly distressed, 'you will disgrace us all.'

'Nonsense!' Charlotte's outrage was all that was necessary to restore Eloise's confidence and she brought the discussion to a peremptory close by the simple expedient of picking up her fan and sweeping decisively from the room.

'Papa!' cried Charlotte, running behind Eloise as fast as her heavy brocade would permit, 'you must make Ella change immediately. She cannot possibly wear such a garment; it is altogether too shocking.'

'Come, come, girls, there is no time for changing, or for squabbling either. Come, Charlotte, where is your cape? And yours, Ella, my love? You must take care not to catch cold.'

Mr Hamilton, smiling benevolently upon Eloise and showing none of the disapproval she had so dreaded, offered an arm to each of his daughters and assisted them into the carriage. Charlotte sulked for the entire journey; the pleasure she had so eagerly anticipated already blighted by her irksome sister who would, in spite of her father's apparent unconcern, be bound to bring censure upon them as a family.

Eloise stood with Jane and observed Charlotte, who had already recovered her good humour due to the fact that she was surrounded by a group of young gentlemen, all vying to write their names on her dance card. Preoccupied with, and more than a little disgusted by, Charlotte's coquettish performance, Eloise did not observe her brother make his entrance, in the company of Lord Craven and James Benson-Smythe. Most of the matrons in attendance marked it keenly though and began plotting remorseless campaigns to bring their daughters to the attention of at least one of these fine gentlemen.

The trio greeted their hostess and made slow progress across the room, acknowledging acquaintances as they went and avoiding the scheming matrons with a skill born of experience. Eventually they drew level with Eloise and her companions and Thomas made the introductions.

'I believe you are already acquainted with Miss Benson-Smythe and my sister Charlotte?'

Lord Craven agreed that was the case, bowed to the ladies and kissed each hand in turn.

45

'And may I bring to your notice my younger sister, Eloise.'

Eloise examined Richard Craven from beneath thick, lowered lashes. He was as tall as Thomas, exquisitely attired, and in possession of a shock of blond hair that was wont to fall across his face quite without warning. He was undoubtedly handsome, his even features being enhanced by a pair of piercing green eyes which held a permanently amused, slightly bored and perhaps even vaguely cynical expression. Eloise supposed that when one occupied such an elevated position within society as his lordship then one had earned the entitlement to be as cynical as one chose. Even so, it was the one aspect of his character that instinctively earned her disapproval. With privilege came responsibility and Richard ought not to allow his derision for what must appear to him as a very provincial assembly to show.

No matter, mused Eloise collecting herself, everything else about him met with her complete favour, especially his punctilious manners, and she curtsied low as Thomas's introduction reached its end. Richard took her hand and she felt a fusion of excitement as his lips briefly brushed the back of her gloved fingers. She could understand now just why Charlotte was so enamoured with this young man; even if her expectations were destined to remain unfulfilled.

Charlotte, far from taking pleasure in the fact that so many men were surrounding her, now appeared irritated by their presence. Eloise watched, half-amused, as she less than subtly extricated herself from their midst and moved surreptitiously closer to Richard.

'You do us much honour appearing at this small gathering, my lord,' she remarked, batting her lashes at him.

'My dear Miss Hamilton,' he responded with a gallant bow, 'when I became aware that you and your charming sister were to attend, wild horses could not have kept me away.'

'You are too generous, sir.' Charlotte blushed prettily, ignoring Eloise's share of the compliment, naturally assuming it was all meant for her.

Eloise hid behind her fan and pulled a face at Jane, trying hard not to giggle at her sister's ridiculous performance. Thomas, standing with his hands clasped behind his back, bore it all with his customary equanimity.

Before Charlotte could embarrass her sister further the first dance struck up. Richard, seemingly aware of the duty owed to Charlotte's seniority, politely enquired if she was free. She was not, of course, and he appeared gratifyingly dismayed to discover that her card was completely full until after the supper interval. Eloise could not but feel sorry for her, in spite of her silliness. She knew just what a cachet it would have been for Charlotte to have been the first lady to stand up with Lord Craven, but Charlotte, in her anxiety to ensure that her card was full, clearly had not considered the matter until it was beyond remedy. Her partner for the first materialized at her side and she permitted him to bear her away with as much good will as she could muster.

Eloise wondered if Lord Craven would still dance and upon whom he would bestow that not inconsiderable favour. It was a moment before she collected herself and realized that he was bowing in front of her.

'Miss Eloise, may I have the honour?'

'Why, yes, thank you, sir,' she replied simply, employing none of the flummery that Charlotte would have deemed necessary on the occasion.

As they took their place at the bottom of the dance Eloise could feel Charlotte's eyes boring into her back. She turned in her direction and fleetingly observed genuine anger reflected in her eyes. Eloise smiled and offered her a miniscule shrug. She had no intention of stealing her sister's thunder and, anyway, Charlotte could hardly imagine her capable of outshining her, but what else was she supposed to have done when Lord Craven requested a simple country dance?

As the dance began, Richard examined her in a most disconcerting manner, eventually causing Eloise to enquire if anything was amiss.

'Oh no, Miss Eloise, pray excuse me. In truth I was merely trying to imagine how you would appear wearing your brother's breeches and racing across the heath astride your horse.' He spoke in a lightly flirtatious tone and smiled directly into her eyes in a most disarming manner. A lock of hair had fallen across his brow, seemingly unnoticed by him, and his flashing green eyes were alight with laughter. 'The vision this thought creates is altogether mesmerizing and I find myself quite disturbed by it.'

Eloise was at first dumbfounded by this bold — not to say fast — statement, but not for long. No missish reprimands sprang to her lips in the way they undoubtedly should have. Instead she responded by throwing back her head and laughing without inhibition, causing several other couples to glance in their direction and Charlotte to glare pointedly at her sister.

'I can only suppose that my brother has tattled on me,' she said, with mock severity, when she had recovered her composure.

'No, m'dear, I did not gain my intelligence from that source. It would appear that your fame has spread before you, for it was my sister who advised me of your passion for riding in the style of a man.'

'Indeed, that is quite remarkable. But if that be the case you might be better advised to describe it as my infamy, for I am entirely certain that I have never had the pleasure of making your sister's acquaintance. I did not realize that my conduct had generated so much public interest. Mind you, my sister will say that she had been telling me as much for a long time and, to save me from a tedious lecture, I should be very much obliged if you were to refrain from sharing your knowledge with her.'

'Your secret is entirely safe in my keeping,' he assured her and, for the second time in the space of a few minutes Eloise found sparkling green eyes smiling a provocative challenge directly into hers.

★ ★ ★

Harry Benson-Smythe entered the ballroom and appeared to dominate it effortlessly. He

50

was half a head taller than any other gentleman present and his elegant form, draped casually against the wall as he watched the dance in progress, was a magnet for half the females in the room. He glanced about him, spotting old acquaintances and acknowledging their greetings. He could see Eloise's sister Sarah across from him, looking as breathtakingly lovely as ever, in spite of the fact that she was now a mother three times over. And there was Charlotte, looking as beautiful as Eloise had predicted, dancing with the son of the local squire.

Harry's eye alighted upon Richard Craven and observed him dispassionately as he danced with an unfamiliar lady in pink damask. He frowned fleetingly. There was something about Craven that didn't sit happily with him, but he was unable to put his finger on precisely what it was. He shrugged, concluding that he was probably being unfair, deciding to give that gentleman the benefit of the doubt.

Harry stood a little straighter as the dancers changed position and he was afforded a better view of Richard's partner. Who was she? She must surely be newly arrived in the locality or she would be known to him, for no one that attractive would have escaped his notice. He relished the sight of

51

her slender and curvaceous body which, even from across the room, was spectacular. She had a natural style about her, wholly unpretentious, and her every movement, from the gentle swaying of her lips to the elegant way in which she moved her arms, was underlined with a sensuous grace which, he suspected, the lady herself was unaware she possessed.

The object of his scrutiny chose that particular moment to turn her head and, even allowing for the noise in the room and the distance that separated them, the sound of laughter that was far too loud and completely uninhibited was instantly familiar to Harry. All movement on his part was arrested as the truth dawned. Good God, it couldn't possibly be! But it was: Eloise — his Eloise, all grown up — and in all the right places too! He thought of her as she had last appeared to him a couple of days previously: up a tree, wearing Tom's clothing, her face smeared with dirt. It had been a worthy disguise, but even so, why had he not noticed the changes in her then?

As the dance came to an end Richard raised Eloise from her curtsy, holding on to her hand for a protracted period, and found Harry at his side.

'Benson-Smythe.'

'Craven.'

The gentlemen, displaying a mutual antipathy, greeted one another as briefly as politeness would permit and made no attempt to shake hands.

'Good evening, Harry.'

'Hello, brat.' Harry clasped her lightly to him by her waist and kissed her. 'Whatever has happened to you?' He twirled her round, taking in her appearance from all angles. 'You look a little better than when I was last exposed to the dubious pleasure of your company.'

Eloise raised her chin and wriggled out of his hold, unaware that Harry was still contemplating her tempting curves with incredulity. How could he not have noticed the changes in her the other day, he asked himself for the second time? He was supposed to be a rake, for God's sake, and it was his duty to notice such things. Perhaps he had considered Eloise as nothing more than another sister for so long now that he had not troubled to apply the rules in her case but, even so . . .

When Eloise complained that she could never compete with her sisters' beauty he supposed she spoke the truth. But if not beautiful, there could be no denying that she was striking; especially when the devil got in her, as it evidently had at that moment, and her enormous silver eyes sparkled with suppressed laughter at his shocked expression. And as to her attire, well, plain it might be but he found it a hundred times more pleasing than her sister's frothy ensemble. Charlotte lacked Eloise's height, which unfortunately caused her choice of gown to make her appear almost as wide as she was short.

'Come dance with me, Eloise,' he suggested.

A waltz was striking up and Harry made to take Eloise in his arms, but before he could do so Richard's voice stayed them.

'Not so fast, Benson-Smythe,' he admonished, regaining Eloise's hand and placing it on his arm in a proprietary manner. 'I will only release Miss Eloise into your care if she promises to save the supper waltz for me and allows me to take her in.'

'You drive a hard bargain, Craven,' remarked Harry, matching his light tone and doing his best not to frown.

'Be that as it may, those are my terms. What do you say, Miss Eloise?'

'Oh no, but I cannot!' expostulated Eloise with youthful impetuosity. 'You must ask Charlotte. She will expect it,' she added artlessly, in response to both gentlemen's astonished expressions.

Only Richard's impeccable manners could prevent him from smiling at her lack of restraint. 'Nothing would give me greater pleasure, I do assure you, but your sister's card was, lamentably, full until after the interval.'

'Oh yes, so it was. All right, sir, I accept your offer with pleasure.' A pretty frown creased her brow. 'But I think we should endeavour to find space at the same table as Charlotte, do you not agree, otherwise she will be most dreadfully angry with me?'

'Consider it done,' promised Richard, allowing his smile free rein as he surrendered her hand to Harry, who swung her effortlessly into the waltz.

'You are very good at this,' remarked Eloise after a few minutes, enjoying the feel of Harry's strong arms guiding her effortlessly into the steps, 'but is there not some rule about my waltzing when I have not been presented?'

'If we were in society it would not be possible, but a country ball is different. Even irritatingly odious children have to learn the art somewhere.'

'And you are the right person to teach them, I suppose?'

Harry offered her a speaking look. 'Who

else of your acquaintance possesses sufficient stamina to survive the experience?'

'This is fun, Harry,' she said, choosing for once not to respond to his taunting and laughing up at him instead, all spirit and flashing silver eyes.

Harry grinned at her non-contrived expression and felt, to his consternation, the first stirrings of desire. He made an enormous effort to pull himself together and disregard his tumescent state: it would pass soon enough. He reminded himself that it was Eloise whom he held in his arms, causing him problems of a very different nature to those which he was accustomed to expect from her. Desire was most definitely an emotion that had no place in his relationship with this inexperienced child.

'I see you managed to find something suitable to wear for the occasion,' he said, aiming for a languid tone but suspecting that admiration and a certain huskiness, resulting from the desire he was still fighting to suppress, took precedence.

'What,' she responded with a seraphic smile, 'this old thing? Do you like it, Harry?' she asked him anxiously, abandoning her haughty visage and offering Harry a timely reminder of the young Eloise with whom he was so much better acquainted.

'It is my first ball gown.'

'Hum, I have not yet made up my mind. Perhaps I prefer you in Tom's breeches?'

'Oh, you men are impossible! Lord Craven was just remarking upon the same subject.'

'Was he indeed! Anyway, I would advise caution where that gentleman is concerned; although he appeared quite taken with you.'

'And why should he not be? Not everyone regards me as their little sister, you know.'

'God help him then!' responded Harry, battling now with a new emotion that he was surprised to identify as jealousy. 'Anyway, darling, how are your bruises today?' He briefly dropped the hand that was supporting her back in the direction of Eloise's derrière.

'Behave yourself, Harry!' she expostulated, attempting ladylike hauteur. 'Anyway, what makes you suppose that I have sustained any injuries?'

'Lucky guess,' he assured her, laughter in his eyes.

'Oh, well, if I have it is all your fault!' she cried accusingly, abandoning her ladylike ambitions and reverting to type. 'If you and Sampson had not come crashing along at that precise moment all would have been well.'

'You have my apology, Eloise, and my assurance that I would be happy to try and put the matter right. Have you considered the application of witch-hazel to the afflicted area?'

She glared at him. 'Harry, I'm warning you — '

'Darling, I was merely thinking of your comfort. You surely cannot imagine that I would derive any pleasure from acting as your nursemaid?'

Ignoring his banter, which was causing her to feel breathless and more than a little out of her depth, Eloise tried another tack. 'Harry Benson-Smythe, I might have a bruised . . . well, bruises, but I'll wager that Molly and I can still beat you and Sampson over a mile on the heath.'

'I accept your challenge with great anticipation. Will tomorrow morning suit?'

'Provided I can find something suitable to wear.'

Harry felt as though he was wading through treacle. Eloise, whom he had known all his life, was growing up and causing him difficulties that were as unexpected as they were unwelcome. But there could be no denying that he was drawn towards her, however hard he tried to discipline himself to ignore his instincts. She was attractive, lively and demanding; and possessed in addition total disregard for the dictates of society: if nothing else her choice of attire demonstrated at least that much. In short she was different: her candid outburst when Craven requested the supper waltz offering all the proof he required on that score. He had always felt protective towards her, but the nature of that protectiveness had undergone a marked shift in the past half-hour. Harry forced his eyes away from her enticing body. With anyone else and he would have allowed his thoughts to roam in their usual licentious fashion: with Eloise he knew he could not risk that indulgence.

'You are not making life easy for me, Harry,' complained Eloise, her voice jarring him out of his introspective thoughts.

'God forbid, what have I done now?'

'Just observe Charlotte's face when she looks in our direction and you will understand the difficulty.' When Harry still appeared to be in ignorance, Eloise explained. 'First of all Lord Craven favours me and then you turn up, looking handsome enough, I suppose, to make half the women in attendance swoon; what with that thatch of black hair, those wide shoulders of yours, so ostentatiously displayed to their best advantage in that exquisite coat, and *you* ask me to dance as well. I suppose you realize that she will spend the rest of the week scolding me for that which is not my fault.'

'Why, Eloise, I had no idea that you considered me to be in any way handsome,' remarked Harry, treating her to a meltingly-gentle smile that was, in spite of his best intentions, anything but inquisitively innocent.

'Oh, of course you are, Harry,' she said, her irascible smile dimpling her cheeks in a most engaging manner, making it impossible for him to drag his eyes away.

'Thank you indeed, ma'am,' he said seriously, wondering why he had never before noticed her dimples. Did young ladies only develop them when they started to attend balls? Surely not.

'Who is Jane dancing with?'

Harry dismissed the matter of dimples from his mind and looked across at his sister, who appeared to be enjoying dancing with Bingham, for the smile on her face, he could tell at a glance, was far from artificial. They made an incongruous couple, Bingham being shorter than Jane and whip-thin, but such nugatory considerations did not appear to be troubling his sister.

'Lord Bingham,' said Harry. 'Jane appears to be enjoying his company.'

'Harry, surely you are not suggesting that . . . ' Eloise's voice trailed off, but the horrified expression which the sight of

Bingham and Jane together had brought to her face was not so easy to dismiss.

'Suggesting what?'

'You know very well! I appreciate that you must all improve your stock by marrying only into the rarefied upper echelons of society,' she said, her scathing tone making her opinion of such contrived behaviour clearly apparent, 'but, Harry, Bingham?'

'And what aspect of that gentleman's situation is so repugnant to you?'

'Everything! Quite apart from being a dwarf, he is at least a hundred years old. And I cannot believe that you — ' Her hand flew to her mouth. 'Harry, is that dreadful woman over there, the one in the mauve turban with the wilting plumes, his mother?' Harry inclined his head in acknowledgement. 'Then you cannot possibly abandon Jane to such a fate.'

'I was unaware that you were acquainted with her ladyship.'

Eloise pulled a face. 'She was in the lady's withdrawing room and complained, when I entered, most vociferously I might add, and all because I did not acknowledge her presence with the degree of respect which she obviously considers to be her due. You have my assurance that her ladyship's opinion upon the standard of behaviour amongst young girls nowadays is as pedantic as it is tedious.'

Harry's eyes twinkled with mirth. 'I am unsure that I wish to know, but I think you had best tell me how you responded, for I am persuaded that you did not permit her reproof to pass unchallenged, as you most assuredly should have done.'

'I did nothing inappropriate,' claimed Eloise hotly. 'I merely advised her ladyship, most courteously I might add, that my purpose in visiting the room was too urgent to allow for obsequious behaviour, offered her a brief curtsy, begged her pardon and went rapidly about my business.'

Harry's bark of spontaneous laughter drew the attention of other couples. 'Odious brat! Let us hope that you have not queered Jane's pitch.'

'So you *do* mean for him to take Jane!' cried Eloise aghast, her eyes flashing her disapproval. 'Harry, how could you?'

Having no wish to engage with Eloise upon a subject that disturbed him almost as much as it did her, Harry was pleased that a commotion at the door deflected her attention.

'Oh, Lord save me!' he groaned, not realizing he had spoken aloud.

'What is it, Harry? Who is that lady who

has caused such a commotion? Oh look, your father is approaching her.'

'That is Lady Hannah Price,' responded Harry flatly, observing a tiny creature who not only matched Charlotte in age but appeared intent upon rivalling her when it came to lack of restraint in the fashion stakes. But there the similarity ended. Charlotte was truly beautiful, and still biddable: Lady Hannah was passably pretty but, Harry had good reason to know, as silly as a goose.

Eloise, ever perspicacious, understood the situation in the blink of an eye. 'Does your father intend Lady Hannah for you, Harry?'

'That I cannot say,' responded Harry smoothly. 'But to be on the safe side, perhaps I had better offer for you instead. What do you say, minx?'

'Don't be ridiculous, Harry! I look upon you as a brother and how could I possibly marry my own brother? It would be incestuous,' she added indignantly, pretending to treat his proposal seriously.

'You are perfectly correct.' He sighed lamentably. 'I had not considered it in that light.'

'Besides,' continued Eloise, warming to her theme and enjoying herself enormously, 'I don't think I am quite what your father has in mind for you, and your family would never recover from the dishonour.'

'Ah yes, there is that, I suppose. Thank you for bringing me to my senses, brat.'

'I suppose we could elope,' mused Eloise, a devilish light in her eye, 'but I consider elopements to be exceedingly vulgar and I dare say my own father would take great exception to it.'

'Well, there you have me again,' conceded Harry. 'I am devastated.'

'Anyway, I have not the slightest intention of falling victim to the perils of matrimony.'

'Most of your sex would consider it to be anything but a perilous journey,' remarked Harry, much diverted. 'In fact I have yet to meet one above the age of fifteen who is not already preparing herself, with single-minded determination, for the marriage-mart.'

'Well, I have more intelligence, I trust, than to indulge in such ridiculous behaviour,' retorted Eloise, putting up her chin. 'I intend to stay at Staverley for the rest of my days and bear poor Papa company. I have no need of a gentleman, ordering me about and taking control of my every waking minute.'

'I doubt that a man has been born who would be equal to the task,' commented Harry with feeling.

'Good, because even if he has, I have no wish to make his acquaintance.'

'Speaking of your father, tell me, is that the vile Miss Standish?' he asked, nodding in the direction of George Hamilton, who had been pinioned in a corner by a lady unknown to Harry and was looking frantically about him for a means of escape.

'Yuk, yes!'

'You were right about her age, sweetheart,' Harry assured her, laughing, for the woman in question could not be a day over five-and-thirty. 'Perhaps you will introduce us later?'

'Why?'

'So that I can ask your vile Miss Standish to favour me with a dance. She looks as though she would make you an admirable stepmother and, God alone knows, you could do with someone with sufficient stamina to keep you in line.'

'Harry, if you do that, I will *never* forgive you.' Eloise glared at him, only to burst into laughter as he winked at her.

The dance came to an end and Harry escorted Eloise back to her sister.

'I do hope Charlotte restrains her lecture until you return to Staverley,' he whispered in her ear, winking conspiratorially, 'but just to be on the safe side I will append my name to her rapidly filling dance card. Will that help, do you suppose?'

'Indubitably.'

'And now, if you will excuse me, my dear, duty calls.'

'A duty that will, if I am not mistaken, prove to be less than arduous for someone of your stamp,' remarked Eloise drolly, following the direction of Harry's gaze until it alighted upon Lady Hannah, and grinning at his apparent discomfort.

'That, my dear,' responded Harry, kissing her hand and backing away from her with genuine regret, 'is just where you are wrong.'

4

In spite of retiring at such a late hour Eloise was still about early the following morning, dressed conventionally for riding, and ready to undertake her challenge with Harry.

She had spent much of the night reviewing the occurrences at the ball and, most particularly, the unexpected stir she had created. It would be asking a lot of any lady to dismiss as inconsequential the fact that two of the most handsome gentlemen in attendance had been reduced to almost fighting for her favours; which had been the case with Lord Craven and Harry. Eloise knew well enough that Harry was simply expanding his role of surrogate brother to encompass her launch into local society but, even so, it raised her spirits to see him, in all his sartorial glory, singling her out and causing other ladies to look upon her with envy.

Richard Craven was altogether another matter and a largely sleepless night had afforded insufficient time for her to settle upon an explanation for his apparent interest in her: especially when infinitely more attractive ladies — such as her sister

Charlotte, and Lady Hannah Price too, who could claim the added cachet of a position within the *ton* almost as exalted as Richard's own — awaited his pleasure. But Eloise, much to Charlotte's chagrin, had been the only lady whom Richard favoured twice. He had indeed danced with Charlotte, and Lady Hannah too, but Eloise couldn't help but observe that he treated those interludes more as a duty than a pleasure, earning her disapproval by permitting that look of disdainful boredom she had detected upon first making his acquaintance to occasionally grace his features.

When he stood up with other ladies Eloise could observe none of the spontaneity in his manner that had reigned during their time dancing together. The supper interlude, and the press of people about them, had inevitably brought an end to their embryonic intimacy. Charlotte's incredulous expression, swiftly superseded by a look of pure vitriol as she observed Richard escorting her sister, turned into a specious smile of acquiescence when Richard, with a swift, ironic glance in Eloise's direction, courteously begged permission to join Charlotte and her dull escort. Charlotte took over then, dominating Richard's attention for the duration of the interval and singularly ignoring her sister, except when throwing victorious glances in her direction when Richard appeared totally engrossed by what she had to say to him.

Eloise sat quietly, making little contribution to the conversation, allowing her sister to shine. She dwelt instead upon what had passed between her and Richard during the waltz immediately before supper, still unable to account for the singularity of it all. She had noticed a very great difference in his attitude towards her and, at first, felt an irrational stab of disappointment. He conversed with her in a conventional manner and refrained from making any outrageous comments, focusing instead upon her equestrian interests.

'Do you exercise your mare on the heath most mornings, Miss Hamilton?' he enquired.

'Oh yes, indeed I do. We only absent ourselves if the weather is inclement.'

'I hope to have the pleasure of encountering you there for myself before long. You have excited my curiosity and I must see Molly for myself.'

'Do you habitually ride the heath? I do not believe I have had the pleasure of seeing you there.'

'I have not often ridden your part of the heath in the past, but then, I have never been in possession of such a strong inducement to do so before now.'

His arm had tightened across her back as he spoke these outlandish words: the intense smile which he focused on her face did not waver. Eloise was glad he had taken a tighter hold of her because her legs seemed suddenly to lose all of their strength. Not one to lack courage though she had lifted her eyes to his and held his gaze, feigning ignorance as to his meaning, which she was quite sure would have been convincing had she not spoiled the effect by blushing quite so deeply.

Confused as his behaviour had made her, there could be no doubting that she had engaged his especial attention when he begged permission to introduce her to his sister as soon as a suitable opportunity presented itself. Eloise was unequal to doing more than absently smiling her agreement as she absorbed the full force of this singular compliment.

She found Richard at her side once again as Mr Hamilton shepherded his party towards the door. He spoke so quietly that only she could hear him.

'When we meet on the heath will it be breeches or a habit? You may be sure that I shall rest but little until I know the answer to this most tantalizing of conundrums.'

Charlotte claimed his attention at that moment, thereby saving Eloise the trouble of devising the pithy put-down that such a forward remark deserved, but she was still smiling to herself as she took her father's outstretched hand and climbed into the waiting carriage.

She wondered now as she headed for the stables if Richard had meant what he said and, if so, how soon it would be before he could reasonably be expected to ride in their direction. Realizing that she was in danger of becoming as absurdly smitten as Charlotte, she turned her attention, and a sunny smile, upon Thomas and her brother-in-law, who at that moment joined her, also intent upon riding out. She accepted their offer to accompany her with pleasure, resigned to the fact that her race with Harry must be postponed until another day. Even her brother, indulgent to a fault, would be unlikely to sanction such a reckless wager and Harry, she suspected, would be reluctant to undertake it in Thomas's presence anyway.

The air was crisp and fresh, giving notice of a fine day in prospect and Eloise took pleasure in the sight of the woods burgeoning into life. Harry and Sampson were already on the heath: a fact which was brought home to them by Molly who, sensing Sampson's presence, lifted her head and whinnied a joyous greeting.

'She has missed him,' explained Eloise, with dignity, to her amused audience.

After greeting the rest of the party and agreeing upon the best route to take, they set off together, Harry naturally falling in alongside Eloise. He cast an admiring glance over Molly and her mistress simultaneously, unable to decide which looked the sleeker or fresher. There was no question which was the more desirable. In daylight, the changes in Eloise were even more apparent. She wore a golden velvet habit and matching hat with a large feather that seemed in permanent danger of obscuring her vision. She had obviously grown since the habit had been made and it now fitted her very snugly indeed, outlining her breasts and narrow waist clearly. She sat poised and erect in her side-saddle, every inch the well-bred young lady. Harry knew he was staring but somehow couldn't find the strength to look away. It was fortuitous therefore that Jacob chose that moment to run up and clamour for his attention.

'Good morning, brat,' he said to Eloise, 'and how did you enjoy your first ball?'

'It was very interesting, Harry,' she responded, her tone perfectly conversational but at complete variance to the saucy look she cast him from beneath that ridiculous plume.

Harry chuckled. 'Is that the best you can do? Very interesting, indeed!' He threw her an amused glance, observing as he did so just how elegantly in tune her movements were with Molly's, just as they had been with his when they had waltzed together the previous evening.

'Well it was interesting,' she expostulated. 'We are not all hardened veterans of these occasions, you know. Anyway, you appeared to enjoy yourself. I noticed that you danced twice with Lady Hannah and took her into supper as well. I suppose you mean to marry her?'

'Well, sweetheart, you were my first choice, but you were so cruel as to turn me down, remember?'

'Well, of course I did, Harry. How else would you have me respond?'

'You do not like Lady Hannah, I fancy?' he remarked, choosing to ignore her question by answering it with one of his own.

'I hardly know her.'

'Come, come, minx, it's not like you to prevaricate.'

'All right then, Harry, since you have asked me for it I will give you my opinion. I spent a few minutes in company with her, that's all, but cannot pretend that I found her conversation particularly edifying. All she could talk about was fashion!' exclaimed Eloise accusingly. 'You would imagine that if the subject engages so much of her attention she would have a better idea of what becomes her by now. Oh, sorry, Harry, I didn't mean to denigrate your intended, but you did ask.'

'She is not my intended.'

'Oh, is she not? I thought — '

Thomas and Gerald were now some distance behind them and Harry, having no wish to dwell upon the unattractive proposition of Lady Hannah on such a lovely morning, much less be reminded of her virtues — or lack of them — decided it was as good a moment as any to raise the subject of Eloise riding out alone.

'I do not see your groom anywhere about?'

'I do not need a groom with me: I have Thomas and Gerald. And you.'

'Did you know that your brother and Gerald intended to accompany you?'

'Oh, Harry, don't be so stuffy. Had they not done so I only had a short distance to ride to meet you: no harm would have come to me.'

'It's not a question of harm coming to you, it is more — '

'Surely you do not imagine my father is

insisting that I don't ride out alone because he wishes me to improve my conduct? Harry, how can you be so dense! He is merely concerned about the disappearance of those three young girls and fears for my safety.'

'You know about that?' asked Harry faintly.

'Of course I do,' she responded in exasperation. 'One of them was employed at Staverley and the staff spoke of nothing else for days. My abigail was especially vociferous on the subject. And as for the blacksmith's daughter, well, it's all over the village.' She threw back her head and let out a long breath in exasperation, causing her plume to flutter across her eyes and her breasts to rebel against the tight confines of her bodice. 'Honestly, the way my father carries on, thinking I know nothing about the subject that's on everyone's lips: I would have to be not only deaf but a simpleton as well to remain in ignorance.'

'Then you must be able to comprehend his concerns for your safety.'

'Harry, those three girls did not enjoy the protection that surrounds, and sometimes threatens to suffocate, me. Anyway, how did you know about them?' Her confused expression gave way to one of comprehension. 'Is that why your father summoned you home, Harry: to look into the question of these abductions? I thought it was because he intended you to marry Lady Hannah.' She gave a sigh of satisfaction. 'At last! I knew the three occurrences could not be a coincidence. Obviously Sir Henry agrees with me. But, Harry, if you are to investigate you must allow me to assist you. After all, I — '

'Who said anything about investigating?'

'But you are, Harry, aren't you?' she said, her eyes sparkling with mischief. 'I just know it. And you will need my help. I can question Mary's family, and the family of poor Meg as well. And,' she added, improvising madly, 'I can please my family for once by going up to town with Sarah for a few days and taking the opportunity to call upon our maid, Rachel, in the mission Papa placed her in. They will all talk to me, Harry, but you would be unlikely to engage their confidence. You are far too large and, anyway, you are a man,' she concluded with satisfaction, convinced of the irrefutability of that argument.

Harry's lips quirked even as his brain sought ways to dissuade her from her hare-brained scheme. She was, he accepted resignedly, unlikely to give in easily. 'I am glad to learn that your powers of observation have not deserted you,' he remarked lightly.

'Be serious, Harry. Now, what do you say to my helping you?'

'A most decided *no*.'

His response, succinct and definite, was designed to discourage further discussion but appeared to have no affect upon Eloise whatsoever.

'Ah, so you *are* looking into it. Well,' she said, emphatically, 'whatever you might think now, you will soon realize that without my assistance you are doomed to failure. And then, if I *am* abducted, you will only have yourself to blame.'

'Anyone who might attempt to abduct you has my most sincere sympathy,' he told her with feeling.

'Humph, you say that now, but you would be sorry indeed if it were to happen, and all because you were too proud to seek my assistance.' Eloise threw him a look of pitiable scorn and cantered on ahead.

Their course took them about three miles across the heath at a brisk pace, through gorse, across streams and over natural obstacles, before they were obliged to slow down for a fallen tree. Eloise was all for putting Molly at the obstacle, assuring Harry that her mare was now jumping higher than ever.

'You imagine she will be able to clear that?' he asked, deliberately provocative: anything to divert Eloise from her desire to investigate the disappearance of young girls in dubious circumstances: circumstances which were likely to have resulted in damage to their respective persons, the nature of which she could hardly be expected to comprehend.

'Of course! What will you wager?'

'Our usual terms, I think, sweetheart. But will you be able to jump properly in that dress thing you are wearing?' Harry moulded his features into an expression of polite enquiry.

'It is not a dress thing, idiot, it is a grown-up riding habit. Anyway, I thought you wanted me to grow up.'

'Oh, I want you, darling, make no mistake about that,' responded Harry, surprising himself by putting into words concupiscent thoughts that he was aware should not even be in his brain, much less spoken aloud. 'Now, are you going to jump or do you intend to sit there all day discussing fashion?'

'Oh, never fear, I am going to jump. Come on, Molly darling.'

Without a backward glance Eloise set Molly on course for the tree. Thomas and Sir Gerald had been discussing the coppicing due to take place in a nearby thicket and had not heard Harry and Eloise strike their wager. Thomas saw her heading for the tree only when it was too late and cried out in alarm.

'Fear not, Thomas,' said Harry with a

placating wave. 'Molly can take that easily.'

'Harry, there is a wide ravine on the other side of that tree. I saw it when I was out this way last week. The spread is enormous and Molly won't see it until she is airborne.'

'God, we must stop her!' Harry was appalled at his own lack of judgement but realized it was too late to intervene and watched, helplessly, as Eloise and Molly took off.

Eloise looked supremely confident. She set Molly at the tree on a perfect stride and Harry knew she would be harbouring no doubts about her ability to clear the obstacle with ease. As they took off Harry could only imagine the thoughts that would pass through her mind as she first observed the yawning gap. He knew her too well to imagine for a moment that she would spare a thought for her own safety. Her only concern would be for the welfare of her beloved Molly: for her little mare's legs. Harry cursed himself roundly for his careless stupidity in goading Eloise into a wager he knew she would be unable to resist; already wondering how he could hope to justify his conduct to Mr Hamilton.

In his concern for Eloise, Harry failed to give any credit to her plucky little mare. Molly saw the gap beneath her just as she took off but because Eloise had set her up for the jump so well she extended her reach in mid-air and was just able to gain firm ground safely. Disaster had been averted by the merest whisker.

As Eloise sailed through the air on Molly's back; her seat elegant and light; her hands on the reins maintaining a gentle contact; her weight pushed forward in perfect harmony with her mount; so two riders appeared from the other direction. They drew rein and watched in fascinated admiration as Eloise took the jump. Richard knew at once who it was. They were not yet close enough for him to recognize Eloise, but from her detailed description of Molly the previous evening he instantly recognized the golden coat and flaxen mane and tail.

'Good gracious!' exclaimed Lady Emily Craven. 'What a superb horsewoman.'

'I think that is my friend Thomas's sister,' responded Richard, impressed out of his languor for once.

Harry's party cantered round the fallen tree and were there to greet Eloise. Each breathed a heartfelt sigh of relief when they saw her land safely and in one piece.

'I am so sorry, Eloise!' cried Harry, his habitual sang-froid giving way to blatant concern. 'I did not know about the ravine. Are you both all right?'

Eloise dismissed Harry's concern with a breezy smile and casual wave but he was not deceived. He knew only too well how frightened she must have been at the time and, equally, how determined she would now be not to reveal the fact. But her body gave her away. Instead of her face being flushed from the exercise she was deathly pale and he noticed that her hands were trembling slightly. He also couldn't help noticing how her breasts rose and fell against the confines of her tight-fitting habit as she fought to regain her composure. Resolutely he looked away, rather pleased with himself for displaying such self-restraint; only to look back again almost immediately. What harm could simply observing her do?

Lord Craven and his sister rode up and joined the party and the introductions were made. Harry and Eloise exchanged a wry smile. It was evident that Thomas was already acquainted with Lady Emily and he was making no effort to conceal his admiration for her. Before much conversation had been exchanged though Jacob pushed his way in between the horses and sat in front of Richard and Emily, front paw in the air, head on one side, examining them closely.

'Who is this delightful creature?' asked Emily, already clearly enraptured.

'That is Jacob, my sister's dog,' responded Thomas with alacrity, grasping this useful excuse to enter into private discourse with Lady Emily.

Jacob continued to consider the newcomers. Amiable to a fault, Eloise was astonished when he moved away from the vicinity of Richard's horse, tail uncharacteristically between his legs. He took up a position instead close to Emily, an appealing expression and lopsided smile on his face.

'Eloise, upon my honour, that mutt becomes more spoiled by the day,' declared Harry, amused, giving no indication that he, too, had observed Jacob's tactical withdrawal from Richard's presence.

'Ignore the horrible gentleman, Jacob darling,' retorted Eloise, deliberately putting her nose in the air and turning her back on Harry. 'He is only jealous because Molly and I took that jump so easily.'

Jacob responded by rolling on his back, squirming energetically, legs thrashing wildly in the air, eyes blissfully closed. Everyone laughed.

'The precocious brute has, I believe, just proved my point.' A smug-looking Harry ruthlessly drove home his advantage.

'Well, I think he is beautiful,' declared Emily resolutely. 'What is his history?'

Thomas rode close to Emily's side: far closer than was strictly necessary in Harry's amused opinion. 'He was found abandoned as a puppy by our head stableman, Jacobs, who took him in and nursed him back to health and intended to find a home for him as a hunting dog. That was three years ago. As soon as Eloise laid eyes upon him she declared her intention of adopting him and promptly named him after Jacobs. We all, especially my sister Charlotte, tried to tell her that young girls should have small lap dogs, not great hounds like Jacob, but it did us no good.'

'Well, of course it didn't!' exclaimed Eloise indignantly, surprised that anyone could possibly hold such an opinion. 'Who would want a silly lap dog when they can have Jacob?' She blew her dog a defiant kiss.

An invitation from Eloise to the new arrivals to return to Staverley for refreshments was enthusiastically accepted.

'Harry, will you join us too?'

'Sorry, sweetheart, I have an appointment.'

Harry now wished it were otherwise. The young widow he had gone to such pains to win was fast becoming a liability; demanding of his time, constantly craving his company. He would far rather have spent the rest of the morning in the company of his neighbours.

Besides, there was something about the way Craven looked at Eloise that didn't sit comfortably with Harry. Common sense told him that she must be safe. Richard could neither offer for her nor dally with her affections: she was not well enough born for the former but, perversely, too well connected for the latter. So what was it that he *did* want? It was obvious there was something and Harry intended to find out what it was. He dragged his eyes away from Eloise, enchanting in her tight-fitting habit, and made to ride away.

'Keep Molly on a tight rein, Eloise. You know how she loves Sampson and will follow him anywhere.'

'Don't be ridiculous, Harry.' She put up her chin once again, striving for a haughty expression. 'Molly is not that sort of horse.' But she tightened rein anyway. 'Shall we ride together in the morning?' she asked him in an undertone. 'We can discuss our strategy.'

'What strategy?' asked Harry, feigning ignorance.

'If you don't require my help then I shall look into the matter alone,' she informed him with a seraphic smile. 'I shall be at Staverley all alone soon: everyone else will be in London so who is to stop me?'

Harry knew when he was beaten and

agreed to the meeting with a reluctant nod of his head. With a final wave, he turned to ride away. Molly's head snapped up and she whinnied pitifully at Sampson's retreating hindquarters.

'Traitor!' hissed Eloise savagely.

Everyone laughed. Harry looked back over his shoulder, white teeth flashing a smile, whilst Eloise tried unsuccessfully for a scowl. Having ensured that Eloise had Molly safely under control Harry directed an exaggerated wink in her direction and cantered smoothly away.

★ ★ ★

As the rest of the party turned back towards Staverley, Richard fell in alongside Eloise.

'I did not anticipate having the pleasure of seeing you again so soon,' remarked Eloise in a conversational tone.

It took a moment for Richard to respond. He was looking at Eloise's profile but not really seeing her. Instead another, forbidden, image sprang uninvited into his mind. The young lady riding beside him in that image was mounted on a spirited Lippizaner, her head demurely covered by a veil that singularly failed to hide the passion in her eyes. They were riding slowly through her father's orange groves in Seville, accompanied by a ridiculous number of chaperons and grooms, which precluded intimate conversation of any type.

With an angry frown Richard dismissed the image, refusing to dwell upon his disappointments; his unfulfilled ambitions. With a supreme effort of will he refocused upon Eloise and smiled at her, deliberately flirtatious.

'I did warn you last night, Miss Hamilton, that I would not be satisfied until I received an answer to my question. You are very heartless not to express sympathy for the restless state in which you left me.'

It was Eloise's turn to maintain an astonished and confused silence. It amused Richard to imagine the thoughts filtering through her brain. She could not doubt that he was deliberately flirting with her here in broad daylight on the heath and sardonically imagined her to be already planning her trousseau, as seemed to be the custom with any young lady nowadays if he chanced to favour her with his attention for more than five minutes. Would they never learn! Suppressing such cynical thoughts he raked her face with sparkling green eyes and deliberately lowered his voice to an intimate drawl.

Richard was surprised to find himself charmed by her answering blush, even though he supposed himself to be long immune to such wiles, and reluctantly acknowledged that the beguiling combination of uncontrived innocence, guileless confusion and impetuosity still had much to recommend it.

'You have not disappointed me,' he assured her, admiring her tight fitting habit in his turn: the swell of her breasts not being lost on him either. Perhaps there would be unexpected advantages in the game that was taking shape in his mind.

'I am so pleased you are satisfied, my lord,' she responded sweetly.

Richard almost choked. She was an innocent — at the moment anyway — and could not possibly know what she was saying. He coughed to hide his reaction and, taking pity on her, changed the subject.

'You took that tree remarkably well but the spread was considerable. Was it safe?'

'I was unaware of the spread before I took off,' she admitted.

'What made you do it without looking first?'

'Harry dared me to and by the time I saw the ravine it was too late.'

'I really think Benson-Smythe should have — '

'Oh, don't blame Harry,' countered Eloise, automatically springing to her friend's defence. 'He was in ignorance also and was appalled when he found out.' She chuckled as she recalled his horrified expression. 'Anyway, it was of no consequence since Molly was brilliant.' She stroked her mare's sleek neck affectionately.

'Were you scared when you realized?'

'Terrified! But don't you dare tell Harry, for if you do I would never hear the end of it.'

'Your secret is quite safe with me.'

As they reached Staverley and entered the drawing-room it became immediately apparent that Charlotte must have obtained early notice of their visitors' arrival from an upstairs window for she was clad in a frothy ensemble that Eloise had not seen before and which, in her opinion, was not only unsuitable for morning visits but quite disastrously unbecoming too. But Charlotte was ecstatic, attributing the honour of Lord Craven's visit as a sign of his interest in *her*.

'Pray be seated, my lord,' she gushed, when the introductions to his sister had been completed. 'Ella, ring the bell for refreshment,' she added bossily.

Mr Hamilton appeared pleased to see their guests at Staverley and it was apparent to Richard that he had not only observed the particular attention he was bestowing upon Eloise but that he was gratified by all it implied. All Richard had heard about the regard in which Mr Hamilton held his youngest daughter was very evidently true since he made precious little effort to conceal it. Richard allowed himself the ghost of a sardonic smile: if he decided to make good his embryonic plan then it would be even easier to execute than he had originally anticipated.

Charlotte's tiresome voice reminded him of his duty and he bestowed a charming smile upon her blushing person. 'I beg your pardon, Miss Hamilton, but I missed what you just said.'

'I was merely assuring your sister that I hoped Eloise has not been regaling you with endless stories of her equestrian pursuits,' she said, casting a darkling glance upon the offending party, without any discernible effect. 'She has yet to learn the meaning of discretion,' she added spitefully, 'and thinks nothing of speaking about horses for above half an hour together.' Charlotte, who hated anything to do with horses, shuddered and smiled simultaneously at Richard, convinced that they were of one mind upon the subject.

'Indeed not, I do assure you. I was entirely impressed with her abilities in a hazardous situation,' responded Richard smoothly, disappointing Charlotte, since it had not been her intention to show her sister up in anything other than the most unfavourable light.

'What hazardous situation?' demanded Mr Hamilton, ever alert to Eloise's spontaneous character and lack of regard for her own safety.

Upon learning particulars of her dangerous jump he became apoplectic with rage. 'Really, it is too bad of Harry!' he expostulated. 'He should take more care. And I blame you too, Eloise. You and Harry are far too keen on striking wagers with one another. It is most unseemly and I shall certainly speak to Harry about the matter.'

'It was not Harry's fault, Father,' put in Thomas. 'He was not aware that the ravine was there.'

'Perhaps not, but he should not flippantly dare young ladies to jump such obstacles without first checking that it is entirely safe.'

'Oh, Molly managed easily, Papa, and I won five guineas from Harry as well.'

Mr Hamilton's frown gave way to a reluctant smile of admiration as he observed his beloved daughter's animated features. He patted her hand gently and, as usual, allowed her to escape without punishment. Charlotte, put out by the amount of attention being foisted upon Eloise, was determined to recapture the attention of the gentlemen and launched into an excited soliloquy about her forthcoming presentation.

'I assume you will be in town for the season,' she said to Richard.

'For part of the time, yes, but I also have duties at Esher Castle which cannot be ignored and employment on your father's behest to occupy me as well.'

'We are having a farewell dinner for Charlotte here at Staverley in two nights' time,' put in Sarah, taking pity on her sister and issuing the invitation that she knew Charlotte must be silently willing her to voice. 'Perhaps we could persuade you both to join us?'

The invitation was accepted with an alacrity almost equal to that at which Charlotte's good humour was restored.

'If you have a moment, Richard,' said Mr Hamilton, 'perhaps we could take this opportunity to discuss a few matters of business before you leave? One or two areas in which I crave your assistance have been brought to my attention and I had intended to request that you wait upon me at my office. But since you are here?'

'By all means, sir.'

When Richard left Mr Hamilton's library half an hour later, a cynical snarl twisted his lips, marring his handsome face. The old man thought he was such an astute businessman, even aspiring to treat him, Richard Craven, the next Duke of Esher, as an equal. But he knew nothing of the ways of society, not even realizing the extent of his *faux pas* earlier in inviting Richard to discuss business with him when this, his first visit to Staverley, was intended to be upon a purely social footing. It was simply not the thing to mix business with pleasure, as any true gentleman could attest. Richard permitted his grievances to flow through him unchecked, wondering, as he did so, how much more a man could be expected to take.

Blowing out his cheeks and composing his features before re-entering the drawing-room, Richard silently vowed to himself that he would, indeed, make good his half-formed plans for revenge. Mr Hamilton had just, unwittingly, played straight into his hands and Richard was far too full of resentment at the hand life had dealt him to let such an opportunity pass him by.

5

Harry was better prepared for the sight of Eloise the following morning, determined not to permit the beguiling air of unconscious sensuality which enveloped the child-woman he no longer recognized to affect him. It required just five minutes in her vivacious company for him to concede defeat. A hint of mischief crept into her already ebullient expression as she reminded him that they had yet to run their race. She had clearly learned nothing from the scare she received the previous day and Harry, sighing in frustration, accepted there was little he could say to deter her from her implacably reckless course.

'All right then, brat,' he said on a long sigh. 'If you are quite ready, Sampson and I will give you twenty seconds' start.'

'I only require ten in order to best you,' she assured him, turning to look over her shoulder and flashing him a smile by way of a challenge as, eyes brimming with laughter, she pushed Molly into a flat out gallop.

Harry allowed her to gain a substantial lead before giving Sampson his head and they reached the end of their agreed course side by side.

'You did that on purpose!' she cried indignantly, as soon as she could draw enough breath to speak. 'You deliberately waited twenty seconds instead of the agreed ten.'

'I was simply making it a more even contest,' he responded, his tone carelessly avuncular. 'It would have been no contest at all had I set off any sooner and you would scarce have tolerated my holding him back.'

'True, but still you should have made that plain at the beginning. Anyway, Molly might be small but she is agile and, even if she does have short legs, she still covers the ground very fast and can take corners more nimbly than Sampson.'

'True enough,' conceded Harry too readily.

'Humph!' she responded suspiciously, regarding him closely through coruscating eyes. 'Anyway, Harry, enough of that. For now,' she added in an ominous tone that reminded Harry, if any reminder were necessary, that the matter of their equestrian wager was far from settled between them in Eloise's mind, 'we had much better occupy our time discussing how best to look into the unfortunate disappearances of those poor girls, which is our reason for meeting this morning, in case you had forgotten.'

'As if I could,' he said, raising a brow and dredging up his most forbidding expression.

'So, Harry,' she said, dismissing his formidable countenance with a careless shrug, 'I thought I might visit poor Meg's family this afternoon. It would be the most natural thing in the world for me to do so. After all, I visit the tenants all the time — '

'Isn't that more properly a duty that should fall to Charlotte's lot?'

Eloise's expression was disdainful. 'Oh, she hates the village and can always find reasons not to go there.' Eloise removed one hand from her reins and held up her fingers as she counted off those reasons. 'The street is too muddy and she fears for her petticoats; the animals frighten her; the children cry too much, or get under her feet, or dirty her clothes with their grubby fingers; the cottages are too damp and she lives in constant dread of catching cold; or the chimneys smoke and make her cough — '

'All right,' said Harry, laughing, 'I comprehend her difficulties. And so you take on the mantle of lady of the manor and visit in her stead, I suppose?'

'Yes, I like most of the villagers — and they like and trust me. That is precisely my point. And what is more, Meg's oldest sister had her first baby last week, which gives me a perfect excuse to call upon the family; I was intending to do so anyway. I expect Meg's mama will be preoccupied with her grandson and so, if I am clever, I might be able to manage a few words with Meg on her own.'

Harry frowned. 'I don't like it above half, Eloise.'

'Oh fudge, Harry, do stop molly-coddling me so, nothing can happen to me!'

'If I had not taken it upon myself to molly-coddle you over the years, as you so eloquently put it, I doubt we would be enjoying this conversation today.'

'What, you mean because you happened to be about if I chanced to fall from my pony?'

'Falling is hardly the word I would use to describe your antics. You encouraged Jane to race with you across the heath at a breakneck pace and then put your ponies at hurdles which were far too high, without a second's thought for their welfare or your own, taking crashing falls as often as not, which I was obliged to extricate you from.'

'How else is one supposed to learn to ride effectively?' she enquired, smiling provocatively.

'And then,' continued Harry, warming to his theme, 'there was the occasion upon which I was privileged to rescue you both from drowning.'

'Oh, Harry, now you are simply being melodramatic. Jane and I were damming up the stream at Boscombe Hall, if memory serves, but we made something of a mess of it and managed to become stranded, that was all.'

'All, do you call it? I was obliged to wade in, procure one of you beneath each arm and carry you to safety.'

'For which, I dare say, I expressed suitable gratitude.'

Harry chortled. 'Gratitude, you little termagant, is that how you would describe your reaction? If memory serves you accused me of being an autocratic, interfering meddler and that you could well have reached safety without my assistance.'

'Don't be absurd, Harry, I was but ten years old. Such words do not form part of the vocabulary of a ten year old.'

'Of yours they most certainly did, brat. You inveighed against me for half an hour together and I soon heartily regretted rescuing you.'

'Well, Harry,' she declared with a gurgle of laughter, 'if I was indeed able to express myself so eloquently at such a tender age then Miss Gregson must surely be congratulated upon her proficiency as a governess.'

'Miss Gregson has my heartfelt sympathy,' responded Harry with feeling. 'A female of less robust constitution would have retired from the fray many years since, if only out of respect for her nerves.' Eloise contented herself with tossing her head but Harry could discern the light of devilment in her eye. 'And do not imagine that I have forgotten the occasion when you fell from that apple tree,' he continued, intent upon cataloguing her youthful misdemeanours.

'I did not fall!' she exclaimed, a note of ill-usage in her tone. 'Jane shook the branch and caused me to lose my footing.'

'But it was I who was obliged to summon the sawbones to set your broken limbs and explain the circumstances to your poor father,' he reminded her.

'It was nothing. Anyway, despite all you say, I am still quite determined to make my call upon Meg's family this afternoon. I shall take Jacob with me: Meg likes him and he her. Well,' conceded Eloise, after a pause, 'that doesn't count for much I suppose because, of course, Jacob likes everyone.'

'Except Lord Craven perhaps,' suggested Harry lightly.

Eloise frowned, recalling that when they had returned to Staverley the previous day,

Jacob had continued to avoid close contact with Richard, even though that gentleman had gone to considerable trouble to befriend the animal. Eloise thought she had detected a brief expression of irritation cross his face when Jacob continued to resist his efforts. Eloise couldn't understand it at all: had never known it happen before. Jacob liked everyone and Richard's sister had experienced no trouble in persuading him to sit at her side for the purpose of having his ears scratched.

'Perhaps Jacob could detect something of Richard's own dogs about him and did not care for them?' she suggested, not believing this unlikely explanation any more than Harry appeared to, given his sceptical expression, but unable to come up with a more tangible account for her dog's behaviour. 'Anyway, Harry, I think I will take the opportunity to go to the village this afternoon and then, at Charlotte's farewell dinner tomorrow evening, I will be able to inform you of my findings.'

'Well, all right,' he agreed reluctantly, 'but you must promise me that you will have your groom accompany you.'

'Yes, yes, Harry, don't fuss so! We will go in the gig and, just to demonstrate how co-operative I am prepared to be, I will even allow Green to drive.'

Harry smirked, knowing that for Eloise to give up the reins to anyone was a rare concession indeed. 'Good girl!'

'I am glad to observe that you appreciate the sacrifice,' she replied with lofty scorn.

'I have been thinking about your maid.'

'About poor Rachel,' responded Eloise, surprised by his sudden change of tack, 'what about her?'

'I understand she was — er — an object of admiration to some of your male employees,' he said, searching for a delicate way to voice his thoughts.

'Yes, but she would have none of them,' countered Eloise proudly.

'Are you sure?'

Eloise hesitated. 'Yes, I believe so. If she had developed a *tendre* for one of them I think it unlikely that it could be kept a secret from the rest of the staff. These things always have a way of becoming known, do they not? After all, there was that time last year when the undergardener took a shine to little Lizzie in the scullery and — '

'Yes, yes,' said Harry, hurriedly cutting her off, well able to anticipate how that little scenario played itself out but sincerely hoping that Eloise could not. 'It was just a thought. Do you happen to know if any one of your staff pursued her more determinedly than the rest?'

'No, but I could make enquiries.'

'Discreetly, if you please.'

'All right, Harry, but won't you tell me what is on your mind?' When he showed no signs of obliging her, she leaned perilously from her saddle and pushed her face close to his, magnetic eyes narrowed in warning. 'Just remember that we are partners in this investigation, Harry, and so you must share all of your thoughts with me. How else can we be expected to get to the bottom of things?'

'Find the information I need first and then I will tell you what is in my head.'

'Humph, you had better!'

$$\star \quad \star \quad \star$$

In spite of her earlier promise Eloise, feeling over-protected and stifled by the restrictions placed upon her movements, was seriously tempted to drive herself into the village. It was only because she would not put it past Harry to have a watch kept on her that she did as she had said she would and allowed Green to drive her the short distance in the gig, Jacob loping easily along beside it.

She was clad in one of her oldest afternoon

gowns, which she did not mind dirtying, and her hair was confined beneath a brightly decorated straw bonnet. She carried a basket on her lap which contained gifts for the baby and fresh produce from the kitchen garden, eggs and a lard cake for the family.

After dutifully cooing over the baby, discreetly avoiding any mention of its father, since there appeared to be some uncertainty as to his actual identity, Eloise asked after Meg, who was nowhere to be seen.

'Oh, Miss Hamilton,' responded Mrs Parsons, 'she is so much better now! For weeks she would not leave my side, and she is still nervous of strangers, but now she has taken to wandering into the yard and is happiest when she is with the animals. She is milking the cow at this moment, I do believe.'

'Perhaps I shall take Jacob out to see her. Do you suppose she would enjoy that?'

'Oh yes, miss, by all means, do. I am sure she would like it above all things.' Mrs Parsons dropped a hasty curtsy and opened the door to the mud-strewn yard, which led to a ramshackle barn adjoining the building, in which the animals lived side by side with their human counterparts. 'Shall you mind getting your feet muddy, miss?'

'Oh, heavens no, Mrs Parsons, have no fear on that score.'

Eloise was grateful to the baby for choosing that particular moment to commence bawling. Up until that point Mrs Parsons had been intent upon accompanying their distinguished guest but, the novelty of being a grandmother not yet having lost its charm, the baby's needs easily took precedence and Eloise assured the flustered woman that she could well find her own way.

Meg, seated on a three-legged stool, was indeed milking the cow and crooning quietly to herself as she did so. She started violently when Jacob dashed up to her, wagging his tail and barking a greeting, but recovered soon enough when she recognized Eloise and even managed to giggle at Jacob as he rolled his head foolishly in her lap.

'How are you faring, Meg?' asked Eloise gently, seating herself on a convenient hay bale, the easier to bring herself down to Meg's level.

Meg mumbled an incoherent reply and kept her eyes trained upon her work. Undeterred, Eloise tried another tack, telling Meg all about Jacob's antics and how annoyed the squire had been when his prize bitch recently whelped, producing not the valuable pedigree litter he had been confidently expecting but a motley collection of half-breeds that closely resembled Jacob. Meg smiled ponderously, assimilating this information slowly and with obvious difficulty.

'Why would the squire mind having Jacob's puppies?' she eventually asked in bewilderment.

Eloise smiled and continued to chat away, gradually putting Meg at her ease. But the moment she tried to turn the rather one-sided conversation in the direction of Meg's abduction the girl became violently agitated and clammed up completely. Fearful of oversetting her further Eloise was obliged to leave a short time later, frustrated because she had learned very little more than she had known an hour before.

As she journeyed home she reviewed what little information she had been able to glean, irrelevant thought it appeared. She was angry with herself for not having put more thought into the best way to question simple-minded Meg before actually attempting it. Harry, she could easily imagine, would tell her that he'd known all along there was nothing she could do to help and that she would be better advised to drop all thoughts of investigating and occupy her time more usefully by practising her performance at the pianoforte.

★ ★ ★

Harry, feeling equally frustrated, sat opposite his father and recounted the outcome of his recent interview with his brother James.

'I got nowhere, Father,' he conceded. 'At first, James would admit to having nothing on his mind of particular import and several times tried to change the subject. When I persevered he eventually mumbled something about having made an imbroglio of his personal affairs.'

'In what respect?' asked Sir Henry sharply. 'Was he referring to money, or to affairs of the heart?'

'I regret that I cannot say, Father. Naturally I asked him but his only response was to fly into a temper, demanding to know why people were always wanting things from him that he was unable to give and why they couldn't just let him be. Then he dashed out of the house and I haven't seen him since.'

'Hm, I am disappointed. I really thought he would talk to you but, if naught else, he has at least admitted to having problems. Should I send him away to Shropshire for a time, do you think? The change of scene could be beneficial to him.'

'I would not recommend it. I get the feeling that whatever ails him will not disappear just because he distances himself from it. Better to keep him where we can observe him. I think he will eventually talk to me when he feels ready.'

'Very possibly.' Sir Henry drifted into silent contemplation. 'All right, Harry, I will take your advice. For the present, at least. Now, about the missing girls.'

Harry told his father about Eloise's involvement, which earned him a sharp reprimand.

'George is trying to protect her from this business, Harry, not actively involve her. Whatever were you thinking of to even tell her about it in the first place, not to mention permitting her to investigate? Alone as well.'

Harry smiled satirically. 'It is clear, Father, that you have never had to deal with Eloise when she has her mind set upon a purpose.'

'That is hardly the point, Harry. Do you not realize just how dangerous — '

'Besides,' interposed Harry smoothly, 'she was already fully conversant with the disappearances and suggested that it would be far easier for her to question the families concerned in a general sort of way, without raising their concerns, than it would for me. Unfortunately that is a fairly irrefutable argument, since there can be nothing extraordinary about her going to the village for that purpose; she visits the tenants often enough already and is there this afternoon, speaking to Meg's family.'

'Let us just hope that George does not discover what she's about. Have a care, Harry; I don't like the idea of Eloise exposing herself to the slightest danger. Drop it altogether rather than put her at risk.'

'I will not allow any harm to come to her,' said Harry with such heavy emphasis and determination of purpose as to occasion Sir Henry to look at him askance.

★ ★ ★

Eloise deliberately chose a gown she had worn several times before for the occasion of Charlotte's farewell dinner: an apricot damask that was plain to the point of severity. Whilst having little in common with her sister, and frequently being the target of her jealous and spiteful tirades, Eloise was not vindictive and had no wish to upstage her. The fact that she had done so, unintentionally and completely to her surprise, had been brought home to her by Charlotte herself only the day before, when she had complained most vociferously that life was unfair.

'I behave exactly as I should. I never disobey Papa and try my best always to please him. You, on the other hand,' she said, fixing her sister with a gimlet gaze through eyes that were fast becoming blurred with self-righteous tears, 'do precisely as you please without reference to anyone; express your opinion far too readily; threaten to bring censure on us as a family with your wild ways and outrageous attire and yet Papa can see no wrong in you and favours you most decidedly; always taking your part. It is most unjust!'

'I know,' agreed Eloise meekly, head resting in her hand as she considered the matter from her sister's point of view and found herself surprisingly in sympathy with her. 'I do not mean to overset you, Charlotte, and often wonder myself why I should feel the need to behave in the way that I do.'

'Well that is something, I suppose,' conceded Charlotte with asperity, mollified by her sister's uncharacteristically docile attitude but determined to clear her breast of her grievances. 'And then, to cap it all, not only Lord Craven but Harry as well, appear to be fighting for your favours. I cannot understand it at all.'

'Lord Craven has no interest in me,' said Eloise in a small voice of regret, 'nor I him. And Harry, well, Harry and I have always been good friends.'

'He was not looking upon you in the

manner of a friend when he danced with you at Sir Graham's: I heard several people remark upon it.'

'Nonsense! Besides, surely you do not have any particular interest in Harry?' Eloise looked at her sister with incredulity.

'Well, no, not really, but you must own that he did look very handsome in his evening clothes and he has such charming manners, everyone at Sir Graham's said as much. And he is eligible too,' she pointed out reasonably. 'He must marry sometime soon since I dare say Sir Henry wishes to see him settled and, after all, he knows us so well that it would be a most convenient thing if he did happen to glance at me with favour.'

Charlotte inspected her image in the drawing-room mirror, patted her curls and viewed her beautiful profile with satisfaction, seemingly unable to imagine any gentleman being able to withstand her charms. She glanced at Eloise and blushed very prettily, managing to look stubbornly defiant and proudly confident at the same time; daring her sister to raise the thorny subject of their low standing within society.

Eloise imagined Charlotte had not intended to reveal her newfound amatory interest in their neighbour and only her indignation at what she saw as her sister's deliberately putting herself forward had caused her to blurt it out. Eloise sighed, feeling a combination of disappointment on her sibling's behalf and annoyance at her gullibility. In spite of it all Eloise also felt closer to Charlotte, and more in sympathy with her determination to behave decorously, than had ever before been the case. She had not fully appreciated until that moment just how marked her father's partiality for her was, or how adversely it played upon Charlotte's insecurity.

All these years Eloise had felt inferior to Charlotte, in terms of both birth and beauty, and had not stopped to consider that Charlotte might be harbouring resentment of her own; not just in respect of Eloise's standing in their father's eyes but, if her indignant outburst of a few minutes previously was anything to go by, her intelligence too, which afforded Eloise the opportunity to join in lively debates over the dinner-table, whilst Charlotte struggled to comprehend even the basic nature of the discussion and was ill-qualified to contribute towards them. Eloise's willingness to blithely disregard the proprieties was a long-standing resentment of Charlotte's but, for the first time, Eloise could understand why it aggrieved her sister so excessively.

As she explained gently why Harry, and Lord Craven, could never look seriously upon either one of them, Eloise vowed that she would do all she could to remain in the background on the evening of Charlotte's farewell dinner and do nothing to deliberately engage the attention of either of the gentlemen they had just been discussing. It would, Eloise generously decided, be her own particular gift to Charlotte on the brink of her season.

At first Eloise managed to stick to her resolve. There were upwards of thirty people present and Sarah and Charlotte between them donned the mantle of hostess. Eloise chatted amiably with some of their neighbours present and, most particularly, with Harry's sister Jane, who was full of the attention being paid to her by Lord Bingham. Eloise was appalled all over again by the very notion of it but, for once, managed to stay her tongue. It was not her business to interfere and if Jane could look with equanimity upon the possible alliance then she must do her best to appear pleased for her friend.

'What about his dragon of a mother?' Eloise could not help but say when Jane finally paused for breath.

'Ah yes, well, Harry thinks he knows how I can best her,' said Jane, sounding anything but sure about her ability to best anyone.

'And how does he suppose that can be achieved?'

'He has not yet advised me. But remember, Ella, Lord Bingham has not yet declared himself so it may all come to naught.'

'But he has requested an interview with your father tomorrow?'

'Yes.' Jane beamed radiantly, a circumstance that transformed her face and made it impossible for Eloise not to be happy for her.

'Well, there you are then.'

'Ella, I know what you are thinking,' said Jane quietly, demonstrating a perspicacity that surprised her friend, 'but, just remember, I have always known that I would have little say in my choice of husband. Bingham's estate is close to our own in Shropshire, which will be a comfort to me, and he is a kind man: I enjoy his society. If Harry can solve for me the difficulty of his mother then I shall be perfectly at my ease.'

'I am sure you will be, Jane, and I hope you do not imagine that I am disapproving.'

'I know you, Ella, and do not expect to change your opinion. Still,' continued Jane brightly, 'if this does come about then I will not have to go through a season next year and that will be a great relief to me.'

Eloise linked her arm through her friend's

and smiled. 'Then we shall both be denied the dubious pleasure of being presented,' she said softly, 'but for very different reasons.'

Dinner was announced and Eloise found herself seated between Harry's brother James and a neighbour of her own age whom she'd known for years. Richard was, of course, seated beside Charlotte and Harry was several places down from her on the other side of the table. She had not, as yet, exchanged a single private word with either of them; a fact which had not gone unnoticed, or unappreciated, by her sister.

The gentlemen did not linger over the port and upon rejoining the ladies prevailed upon them for entertainment. The vile Miss Standish, to whom Charlotte had insisted upon extending an invitation, was the first to take a seat at the pianoforte. Her performance was faultlessly proficient but sadly lacking in true passion. Upon its conclusion it was rewarded with mere polite applause.

Miss Standish was succeeded by Jane, whose choice was far lighter and varied, albeit far less technically demanding, but much easier on the ear.

Now it was Eloise's turn. She demonstrated all Miss Standish's technical proficiency but managed to combine it with an underlying passion and astute interpretation that shone through effortlessly. She lost herself in the music and played from the heart, naturally and without artifice. The applause, led by her father, was prolonged, causing Eloise to throw a guilty look, disguised as a plea for understanding, in Charlotte's direction. Fortuitously though her sister was engaged in a conversation with Lord Craven and, for once, appeared immune to Mr Hamilton's eulogy of his youngest daughter.

Since no other lady was prepared to take a turn, Eloise, with a mischievous smile, turned to her friend. 'Come on then, Jane,' she commanded.

The two girls sat at the instrument together and, after a brief consultation, struck up a duet of modern melodies. James and Sarah both had pleasant voices and were persuaded to sing and the whole atmosphere was informal and relaxed.

When Eloise eventually wandered away from the piano, leaving it to others, Richard materialized at her side.

'You are full of surprises, Miss Hamilton,' he remarked.

'Why so, my lord?'

'Well, my sister was right. You ride your horse at least as well as any man and now I find you play like an angel as well. I want to know what other talents you are hiding from me and how I am supposed to find them out.'

Eloise, annoyed that a fusion of excitement coursed through her in response to this presumptuous remark, was angrier still that she blushed so violently. She was also more than a little disturbed by this elegant sophisticate's desire to flirt with her so blatantly. If he wished to flirt with anyone at all it should be Charlotte, who was staring sullenly at them from across the room. All of Eloise's efforts at generosity towards her sister had been undone in one foul stroke, and it was not even her fault. She was too preoccupied to notice that her father was also observing her intimate conversation with Richard in a very different, seemingly satisfied light.

'I do not have the pleasure of comprehending your meaning, sir,' said Eloise in a tone designed to discourage any further outrageous disclosures on Richard's part.

'Oh, I think you do,' he responded mockingly. 'The question is, when — '

'What do you think you're about, Craven?' asked Harry, strolling up to join them, an urbane smile that didn't quite reach his eyes gracing his lips. Eloise had never been more grateful to have a conversation interrupted in her life, in spite of the fact that she now had both Richard and Harry deliberately seeking her out. 'Monopolizing our host's youngest daughter is hardly good form, you know.'

'Possibly not,' responded Richard lightly, 'but can you blame me for trying?'

'Just bear in mind, if you will, that I was put on this earth solely to ensure that no harm ever befalls Eloise.'

'Why should you imagine that I intend her any harm?' asked Richard, a hard edge creeping into his voice.

'Harry, behave yourself!' commanded Eloise, softening her words by reaching up and placing a soft kiss on his cheek.

'Me, m'dear?' Harry appeared all amazement. He slipped his arm around her waist and pulled her against him, smiling a proprietary warning at Richard as he did so. 'Don't I always?'

'Hmph, that will be the day. Gentlemen, please excuse me.' Slipping out of Harry's grasp Eloise bobbed them both a brief curtsy, breathing a sigh of relief as she made good her escape.

Harry sought her out again a short time later, having first ensured that Richard was safely ensnared in Charlotte's circle.

'No more new gowns for me to admire this evening then, minx?'

'No, Harry, this is Charlotte's moment and

what I wear does not signify.'

'Surely you do not imagine that you could outshine your lovely sister?' asked Harry insouciantly. 'You yourself have already acknowledged the impossibility of that.'

Eloise pouted. 'She accuses me of deliberately setting out to snare both you and Lord Craven.' Harry's burst of laughter caused Eloise to smile reluctantly. 'I know, I know, but I feel there is some validity to her grievances when she declares that Papa allows me considerable licence, and so I wore this old gown deliberately to make her feel more kindly towards me and now, here you are, talking to me all alone and undoing all my selfless work.'

Harry cast his eye over her attire in silent appreciation. The gown might not be the height of fashion but it fitted her very snugly indeed and did little to disguise her burgeoning charms, youthful freshness and naturally graceful movements. In a further effort to defer her emergence into womanhood she had left her hair loose, simply tying it back with a ribbon that matched her gown. It spiralled down her back in a riot of thick, wayward curls, ending just above her waist. Harry picked up a strand and ran it through his fingers.

'You have lovely hair,' he remarked in an

unusually tender tone, devoid of the light-hearted banter that usually underlined their exchanges.

'Stop it, Harry!' she spat at him, tugging her hair out of his grasp impatiently. 'People are looking at us.' She smiled at Sir Henry, who was observing them closely from across the room, and offered him a small wave. He acknowledged her greeting and turned his attention to his son James, who was enjoying a lively conversation with Richard Craven in another part of the room.

'Since when did you care for public opinion?'

'Since I decided to look kindly upon my sister,' she responded haughtily. 'Anyway, Harry, you have not asked how I fared in the village yesterday.'

'No, but I was about to.'

'It was all to no avail. I did manage to speak to Meg alone but could get no sense out of her regarding her abduction. She became very agitated and would only say one word, over and over again.'

'And that word was?'

'One that helps us not one jot. She just kept saying, 'Jem, Jem', becoming more and more agitated as she did so.'

'Who is Jem?'

'The village bully. He has been her

118

tormentor for years and she cannot abide him. I think that in her mind she must have confused the agony of her abduction with her fear of Jem.'

'The same village bully whose eye you blacked?' clarified Harry, laughter in his eyes.

'Yes,' said Eloise emphatically. 'I found him badgering a harmless puppy and gave him a piece of my mind he won't easily forget.'

'And the back of your hand?'

'That too! But, Harry, what do we do now?'

'We think some more about what we have discovered.'

'We have discovered precisely nothing,' said Eloise, almost stamping her foot in exasperation.

'Not necessarily. Ride with me in the morning, sweetheart, and we will talk more then: now is not an appropriate time for such cogitations.

6

Inclement weather prevented Eloise from riding with Harry the following morning. She employed her time instead by quizzing her abigail on the question of Becky's suitors; with frustratingly discouraging results. She had it confirmed that Becky worked hard and gave no trouble, but nothing was known about how she spent her afternoon off and it could not be confirmed that she was particularly intimate with any one member of staff above all the others.

Recalling Harry's stricture that she should make her enquiries discreetly precluded Eloise from widening her net and discussing the matter with the housekeeper, under whose ultimate auspices Becky would have fallen. As one of the longest serving members of the household, Mrs Parker would likely have more knowledge of the girl's affairs than anyone else at Staverley, but even Eloise had to acknowledge that it would appear very curious indeed for her to raise such a delicate subject, about which she was supposed to have no knowledge, without disclosing a very good reason for doing so. It would also, inevitably, be brought to her father's notice that she had been making inappropriate enquiries and, since he had adopted such an intransigent position about the whole affair and appeared determined to keep all details from her notice, she knew she could not take the risk.

The weather was insufficient to deter Jane from calling that afternoon to inform her friend in a breathless whisper that she was now formally engaged to Lord Bingham. She proudly displayed her engagement ring; a Bingham family heirloom which Eloise privately considered to be horrendously ostentatious. Keeping such opinions firmly to herself Eloise congratulated her friend with all the enthusiasm she was able to muster. Jane insisted that Eloise must be her principal bridesmaid and they spent a comfortable hour discussing styles and planning their assault on Lady Benson-Smythe's modiste at the earliest possible opportunity. An engagement party was to be held at Boscombe Hall in a sennight, at which Harry's mysterious plan to overcome the meddlesome Lady Bingham — a plan which Harry confidently predicted would precipitate her early departure to the dowager house — was to be put into operation. Eloise smiled at this disclosure, wondering just what it was that Harry had in mind. The woman was a harridan: she was known to bully her staff, terrify her acquaintances, and completely dominate her only child. Eloise was curious to know how Harry planned to banish her to the dowager house and prevent her from dominating the self-effacing Jane as comprehensively as she did everyone else.

Harry sent Eloise a brief note, informing her that he had been called to town on business and was unlikely to see her before Jane's party. He also warned her, in language impossible to misinterpret, against carrying out unilateral investigations in his absence. Uncharacteristically, she obeyed his dictate. Until she travelled to town and spoke to Becky herself there was little more she could do anyway.

Eloise was soon to discover that the absence of Charlotte, now happily ensconced in London with Sarah and already apparently enjoying the attentions of several worthy gentlemen, and Harry's own sojourn in that particular location, did not mean that her residence at Staverley was destined to be solitary. Nor did she lack for male company since Richard Craven was a regular visitor: a circumstance that Eloise was unable to account for.

The first occasions were the result of

definite appointments with her father, when they ensconced themselves in his library and discussed business behind the firmly closed doors for hours at a time. But afterwards Richard always sought her out; walking in the grounds with her, drinking tea in the family sitting-room or listening to her practise on the pianoforte. With each visit his flirtatious remarks became more explicit and increasingly difficult for Eloise to look upon as simply an elegant gentleman's notion of gallantry. It was equally impossible for her not to feel the full force of the compliment such singular attention implied.

Eloise could not help but wonder why Richard and her father should suddenly take to meeting at Staverley: Mr Hamilton had never been wont to conduct business from his home in the past, having a perfectly adequate office in the City which much better served that purpose.

On the third occasion when Eloise encountered Richard she was defying her father's instructions yet again and riding alone on the heath. He fell in beside her, offering no explanation for his sudden appearance, and showing no surprise when she informed him that both her father and Thomas were that day in the City and that she was at Staverley alone. Far from deterring him, this intelligence merely prompted a predatory grin.

'And so I have you to myself at last, Miss Hamilton.'

'Hardly that, sir,' she responded, 'the house is full of servants.'

'Who will not interrupt us if you instruct them that you do not wish to be disturbed?'

'And why should I issue such a singular order?' asked Eloise curtly, convinced that this time he must surely have overstepped the mark and that she should not permit this presumptuous conversation to continue.

'So that I may listen to you play without interruption,' he responded with a disarming smile, leaving Eloise with the impression that his answer was very far from the truth.

'Then I must beg to disappoint you, my lord, since I am even now on my way to Boscombe Hall, where I am expected by my friend Jane and her mother to discuss her fothcoming wedding plans.'

'Then I am desolate.'

He rode with her to Boscombe Hall, left her at the gates, expressed his expectation of having the privilege of seeing her again in the near future and cantered away.

Unsettled by his growing audacity, Eloise repented the fact that she had no one to discuss his behaviour with: no yardstick by which to measure his conduct. She was unable to decide whether or not she was being excessively gullible in receiving his attentions with such composure. Did the fact that she had not given him the set-downs which such forwardness surely deserved encourage him, portraying the misguided impression that she was nothing better than a Cyprian? Her father clearly did not consider her manners to be in any way wanting; in fact, he encouraged her intimacies with Richard at every opportunity, smiling enigmatically whenever the two of them were engaged together in lively conversation. But then, when had Mr Hamilton ever taken exception to anything she chose to do, however misguided?

There could be no denying that she was flattered by Richard's obvious interest in her. When he subjected her person to minute scrutiny through eyes that promised so much, when he spoke to her in that alluringly hypnotic cadence of his, his smile in turn both raffish and strangely captivating, his whole attention focused exclusively upon her as if no other girl existed on the entire planet, it was hardly to be wondered at that her heart did a strange little flip and her head spun giddily in the most alarming manner imaginable.

But what did it all mean? Richard Craven, most likely the next Duke of Esher, could not possibly have a serious interest in her. Eloise had warned Charlotte to be on her guard, and scorned her for her naivety when she had dared to hope that she had secured his attention, and Eloise did not intend to follow that same route. If it was impossible in Charlotte's case, then the situation was ten times worse in her own, and she simply would not spend the rest of her life regretting what might have been.

If Richard wishes to flirt with me, she thought to herself, as the left Molly in the care of the head groom at Boscombe hall and headed for the house, then I shall enjoy his attentions whilst they last, treat them with an air of detachment and the gentleman himself with insouciance. But, I will not, simply *will not* lose either my head or my heart to such a hopeless philanderer.

Easier said than done, Eloise conceded the following evening when her father arrived home in company with both Thomas and Richard. The latter naturally sat down to table with the family and spent the entire meal alternately bidding the hovering foot-man to refill his glass and flirting quite openly with Eloise. She had never before seen him partaking of wine quite so freely — Thomas either for that matter — and wondered what could have occurred to account for such behaviour.

Richard kept up a stream of light conversation throughout the meal, bringing Eloise out of herself by quizzing her on Molly's progress; he discussed a party he had attended in London, at which Charlotte had been present and had shone, already being the object of many gentlemen's attentions; talked of his sister and saying how anxious she was to renew her acquaintanceship with Eloise.

The meal came to an eventual end and, more confused than ever, Eloise left the gentlemen to their port. Richard was on his feet in an instant, pulling back her chair and beating Farthingay to the door, which he held open for her, smiling down at her as she thanked him and passed through it.

Eloise idly ran her fingers over the keyboard of her magnificent pianoforte, wondering what could be keeping the gentlemen: they had been sitting over the port for an inordinate amount of time. When the door eventually opened to admit them, Eloise's father offered her a vague smile, appeared more preoccupied than ever, and took his usual chair on one side of the fire. Thomas, plainly agitated, claimed its twin, appeared gratified that Richard had wandered in Eloise's direction and disappeared behind a newspaper.

Richard stood directly beside Eloise as she continued to play, his eyes trained disarmingly upon her face.

'What is it?' she asked, smiling, but not looking at him.

'I was just wondering,' he responded, his laconic drawl slightly slurred, illustrating to Eloise that he was more than slightly foxed, 'how much longer I can bear to look at you without taking you in my arms and kissing you.'

'My lord?'

'M'dear.' His smile was twisted and his features openly displayed the cynicism she had fleetingly observed on previous occasions. 'It is what I want and, I suspect, what you dream of when you are alone.' Eloise let out a gasp of outrage, which he did not appear to notice and continued to speak. 'So why should we continue to deny ourselves such harmless pleasure?'

'Because, my lord, I do not care to be the object of your attention when you have nothing better to amuse yourself with,' she told him, her stormy eyes brimming with anger. 'I am persuaded that you would not venture to insult any of the young ladies of your acquaintance in London in such a vulgar manner and take exception to the fact that you feel no such restraint when addressing me.'

Containing her fury by the sheer force of her will, Eloise went up to her father's chair, kissed his forehead, pleaded a headache and begged to be excused. She left the room without taking her leave of Richard and without a backward glance and did not return for the rest of the evening.

* * *

Far too angry to sleep, Eloise tossed and turned for most of the night, trying to decide if she had done anything to deliberately encourage Richard's words which, to any single young lady of good character, could only be construed as the most abominable insult. How dare he treat her thus! She pounded her pillows, giving full vent to the righteous indignation that was in danger of consuming her. Waves of fresh anger swept over her as she recalled the seductive allure of his sparkling eyes, the feel of his breath on her neck as he whispered his outrageous words and, hardest of all for her to bear, her guilt. Yes guilt, because in spite of everything her heart had briefly lifted when he suggested that he wished to kiss her and she had felt an almost overwhelming desire to oblige him by flying into the protective circle of his arms.

Eloise acknowledged that she was out of her depth. The need for advice was compelling, but to whom could she apply? Her father and Thomas were, of course, out of the question, Sarah was in London and Jane must be considered to be as ignorant about such matters as she. She thought next of Harry. Had he not always righted her wrongs for her in the past? But no, that was not possible either since Harry had twice warned her against Richard and would likely consider that she had brought her troubles upon herself by ignoring his caution. She discovered, to her surprise, that she did not wish Harry to think badly of her. That left only one alternative.

As usual she would have to resolve her problems without recourse to anyone.

* * *

Eloise was in the morning room, a book she was not reading open on her lap. The weather continued to be unpredictable, thereby preventing Eloise from taking her morning ride, which did nothing to improve her humour and left her with nothing to do except brood upon Richard's abominable behaviour. The sound of a caller at the front door intruded upon her introspective thoughts and a short time later Farthingay informed her that Lord Craven had called and was desirous of an interview with her. Eloise could not have been more surprised, but that surprise swiftly turned into panic and she considered having Farthingay inform Richard that she was not at home. She was, after all, here alone and suppose he had called with the sole intention of pursuing their conversation of the previous evening?

No, she was being fanciful: a moment's reflection was all it took for Eloise to reach that conclusion. He had been foxed, probably more so than she had realized at the time, and it was that which must account for his moment of indiscretion. That in itself was quite shocking and could not excuse his subsequent actions, but at least it helped to explain this most appalling lapse of manners. She would receive him now and use the opportunity to make it plain to his lordship just what she thought of his despicable behaviour, bringing any further intimacies between them to a definitive end. Lifting her chin defiantly she bade Farthingay have him enter.

Cheered by the return of her courage, and

confident that she would be able to conduct the interview without revealing the extent of her inner turmoil, Eloise barely had a moment to smooth the creases from her gown before Richard entered the room and made her an elegant leg. As always he was superbly attired and was today sporting a green herringbone coat that brought out the colour of his eyes to perfection. Angry at herself for observing such an inconsequential detail, she bobbed the merest suggestion of a curtsy and did not return his smile.

'Good afternoon, Miss Hamilton, I trust I find you recovered from your indisposition?'

'Yes, I thank you.' Her tone was glacial.

'And good afternoon to you too, Jacob,' continued his lordship, undeterred by his frosty reception. 'How do you do today?'

Jacob had still not relented in his antipathy towards Richard and cowered behind his mistress's chair.

'If you have come in search of my father or brother, Lord Craven, I fear you have had a wasted journey for they are both in the City today.' The formality of her address could not have been more marked.

'Indeed, Miss Hamilton, it was you I called in the hope of seeing.'

'Indeed, I cannot for the life of me imagine why.' Her eyes, regarding him with such bitter contempt, would have deterred anyone less intent upon their purpose.

'I came to apologize for my appalling behaviour towards you yesterday. I was unable to sleep when I considered it, so full of remorse was I.'

'I see.' The words were almost spat at Richard through tightly pursed lips and Eloise had the satisfaction of seeing him blanch as he finally registered the full force of her hostility.

'I do most humbly apologize, Miss Hamilton. I did you a great wrong and cannot bear to think of it without feeling the greatest remorse imaginable. I cannot understand what came over me. Dare I hope that you can find it in your heart to forgive me?'

Richard's expression was so contrite, so appealingly sensual; his eyes so full of remorse, that in spite of her best resolve Eloise offered him a reluctant smile. Forcefully reminding herself that she had every reason in the world to be angry with him she swiftly rearranged her features into an expression of disdain and deliberately allowed the silence to stretch between them for what seemed like an age.

'I cannot make up my mind on the matter,' she eventually stated, struggling to regain some of her earlier justified hauteur, recalling what liberties he had tried to take and resolving afresh not to let him off so easily.

Seemingly encouraged by her hesitation Richard continued to plead his case. 'Please!' He offered her his most engaging smile and Eloise could feel her resolve deserting her at a quite alarming rate. 'I do have an excuse, paltry though it is, if only you will permit me to explain.'

'Oh yes, my lord, this I *must* hear!' she said, despising herself for her weakness as curiosity won out over caution.

'The rain has ceased at last,' he remarked, indicating the French doors and the weak sunshine that was struggling to penetrate the room. 'Can I prevail upon you to take a turn in the garden with me?'

Eloise agreed and ran to fetch her bonnet.

They strolled side by side across the elegant lawns and headed in the direction of the lake, at the far end of the garden. Jacob followed closely at Eloise's heels, pointedly avoiding Richard's proximity but fixing him with a watchful eye, a soft growl rumbling at the back of his throat.

Eloise maintained a dignified silence. She was not given to idle chatter at the best of times and was certainly not of a mind, as matters stood, to make any effort to entertain Richard.

As the reached the lake the sun gave up its unequal battle against the clouds and a few heavy raindrops gave notice of the shower to come. Richard took Eloise's arm and guided her in the direction of the boathouse, but by the time they reached it both of them were drenched. Richard opened the door and shepherded his companion inside. Jacob refused the invitation, growled a warning at Richard and disappeared into the bushes.

'Here, take my coat, Miss Hamilton,' insisted Richard, divesting himself of the garment and draping it around her shoulders, 'before you take a chill.'

'Thank you.'

She settled herself on a bench and regarded him expectantly. Richard did not sit beside her, as she had half expected him to do. Instead he paced the width of the boathouse, clearly gathering his thoughts.

'You are, perhaps, aware of my family's circumstances?' he said, breaking the silence between them.

Of all the things she had anticipated he might say, any mention of his family had not been amongst them and she looked at him in blank surprise. Richard smiled captivatingly at her, with devastating consequences for her shaky equilibrium.

'My brother is seriously ill: he is afflicted

with a disease of the lungs and is not expected to see out the year. His marriage is childless and I, therefore, am likely to be the next Duke of Esher.'

'I am truly sorry for your bother,' said Eloise with sincerity.

'Thank you.' He offered her a slight bow. 'No more so than I. We have expended a small fortune, consulting the best physicians both here and abroad, but they are all of the same opinion: there is not the least hope for his recovery. Because of that unfortunate circumstance I already feel the responsibility for my family's future resting on my shoulders. It is a responsibility that I would happily be absolved from, if only it were possible since the future is, at best, uncertain. The degree of hedonistic extravagance indulged in by my forebears has brought my family to the very brink of ruin, Miss Hamilton. Bad investments, a propensity for games of chance that appears to run in the family's blood and substantial loans to the monarchy that have never been repaid have combined over the centuries to reduce us to our current impoverished state.'

Eloise listened in rapt fascination: at the same time astonished that Richard should choose to be so candid with her. On a visceral level she knew that it was not good form for him to be speaking of his family's intimate concerns with her and that, in any event, it was considered vulgar in good society to discuss pecuniary matters at all. Curious in spite of herself to hear more, she nevertheless made a valiant effort to bring his discourse to an end.

'My lord, I am persuaded that it is not proper for you — '

He ignored her interruption. 'I am determined to restore my family's fortune!' said Richard, his chin jutting with a combination of pride and resolve.

'An admirable ambition: and an entirely understandable one,' said Eloise gently, 'but I am still at a loss to understand how this concerns me.'

'I was getting to that. You are aware, of course, that I am engaged upon matters of business with your father?'

'Yes.' Another *faux pas* since persons of quality never discussed their business concerns openly; certainly not in front of young ladies. The fact that he felt he could do so with her indicated all too clearly that he considered her as nothing more than the inconsequential daughter of a Cit. This knowledge did not sit well with Eloise and she felt quite out of character with him. 'I gather,' she said in a diffident tone, 'that my father took on a client with interests in Southern Africa who has purchased a diamond-mining venture, and requires your assistance to attract gentlemen to the scheme.'

This demonstration of the artlessness which had so attracted Richard to her at Sir Graham's ball now caused his lips to twist in a noxious smile. 'Not precisely. A man by the name of Charles Granger was the manager of the mine in question. The owner, a Dutchman with Afrikaan roots, was in the right place at the right time to stake his claim and with the help of Granger and other experts he set up the business and made huge profits. But it went to his head; he gambled and drank to excess, and the mine was left in deep financial trouble. All his previous wealth was put into starting the business, which was his making but, ironically, also his undoing. His debts became pressing and Granger was despatched to England to look for a purchaser for the venture at a bargain price.'

'And that is where my father came in, I would imagine.'

'Not quite. Granger had connections amongst the plutocracy and, whilst many of them could see the opportunity the mine presented, none had the considerable blunt necessary to take it up. I was approached, but from what I have just disclosed about my own circumstances, you can readily imagine that I was in no position to assist. I examined Granger's books however and became very animated for I realized that I could perhaps have found the means I had been seeking to restore my family's fortunes. I thought of Thomas, presented the idea to him and your father, and we struck a bargain.'

'I see.'

'No, Miss Hamilton, you do not see. Your father supplied the money to purchase the mine, but it was *my* introduction and my connections amongst the aristocracy that has made it feasible. Without that even your father would not have had sufficient where-withal to undertake it.'

'But I do not understand you, my lord. If your aristocratic friends are, between them, supplying the funds, why did you need my father?'

Richard's responding smile was completely lacking in humour and came across more as a derisive sneer. 'You are right to say you do not understand. I, as an aristocrat and gentleman of the first order, have insuperable reasons for feeling aggrieved. I cannot openly involve myself in matters of business, any more than my friends can be seen to consort with your father.' Richard's pacing had

139

become frantic and he appeared unaware of quite how offensive his language was as he ruthlessly underlined the differences in their situations. 'Acting quietly as an intermediary, and bringing the two sides together, is another matter entirely and that is precisely what I have done.'

'Could my father not have done that?'

Richard almost snarled in response. 'They would have had nothing to do with him.'

'Then it seems to me, my lord,' suggested Eloise archly, opening her eyes very wide and adopting her haughtiest demeanour as she attempted to quell the quite ungovernable rage welling within her, 'that you require one another and I cannot see that you have any cause for complaint.'

'This is *my* venture,' said Richard brutally, 'but I did not realize until a few weeks ago the extent of the profits that your father is extracting.'

'Presumably in accordance with the agreement you made with him, which must surely be to your benefit as well.'

'Not to the extent that it should be, or to the extent that I had foreseen.'

'You are surely not suggesting that my father is being deceitful and withholding what is rightfully yours?' asked Eloise, anger causing her voice to sound unusually shrill.

'No, but I believe he knew when we made our bargain just what returns he could expect from it.'

'I do not doubt it;' said Eloise stiffly, 'he is, as you have just done me the honour of reminding me, a businessman as opposed to a gentleman.'

'I beg your pardon, Miss Hamilton, I intended no offence.'

'In that case I would recommend, my lord, that you select your words with greater care.' She lifted her shoulders and chin simultaneously, disdain for the insulting language directed against her beloved father apparent in the gesture. 'Anyway, presumably you took the precaution of satisfying yourself that your side of the bargain met your needs before you entered into it.'

'Again you are quite correct, but I did not realize that the mine would increase production to quite the extent that it has. My contract allows for a fixed remuneration, provided I find and retain sufficient backers for the scheme. I consider this to be unfair in the light of the upturn in profits and asked your father last night to review our agreement.' Richard looked her directly in the eye. 'He refused.'

'I see.'

And this time she did see. Richard had

been drinking in order to gain the courage to approach her father and, when that approach had failed, had permitted his guard to slip and took his disappointment out on Eloise.

'Yes, I believe you do,' he said quietly.

'I am sorry for you, my lord, but you must appreciate that you have, with these candid revelations, placed me in an impossible position. I really do not see that there is anything I can do to promote your cause, even if I felt the inclination to do so. My father never discusses his business affairs with me and would not listen to my advice even if he did.'

'Quite right too!' said Richard, a shadow of his more usual self emerging from behind the injured expression he had adopted whilst speaking of the mine. 'But you must understand that I have been working relentlessly, earning my parents' disapproval into the bargain, by lowering myself to such a degree, to bring this thing about. Were it not for me it would never have proved to be the success for your father that it now is and I feel very strongly that I have been wronged.'

Overwhelmed, Eloise twisted her hands in her lap but felt unequal to replying. But that didn't prevent her mind from racing frantically as she assimilated all she had heard. Her easy-going father had a reputation for being a hard-headed businessman, of that she was well aware, so could it be true that he was being unfair to Richard? Would he intentionally set out to swindle a man he appeared to hold in the highest regard? She did not for a moment believe that he would but here was Richard, sincerity replacing the conceit and arrogance that had momentarily disgraced his features, passionately pouring out the whole to her. Would he really do so, knowing how close she was to her father, if there was not some element of truth in what he said?

She stood and crossed the small room to join him. 'My lord, I know not what to say.' She smiled enigmatically, heartily wishing that their recent conversation had not taken place. The value of ignorance, she belatedly understood, had much to recommend it.

'You need say nothing, m'dear. I simply wished for you to know why I behaved so crassly last evening.'

Quite without warning he pulled her towards him and took her in his arms. It had been the very last thing she had been expecting and took her quite by surprise. Too startled to object Eloise simply looked up at him in confusion.

'Good God, Eloise,' he said, appearing to take heart from her passivity, 'have you any idea how much I have wanted to hold you thus? From that very first moment at Sir Graham's ball, where I first saw you — '

★ ★ ★

Harry, returning home a day earlier than expected, resolved to call at Staverley to satisfy himself that Eloise had not disobeyed his instructions. Looking forward to seeing her again and resuming their customary battle of wits he frowned upon learning that she was in the grounds with Lord Craven. What in the name of Hades had possessed her to stroll with the man unaccompanied? She could, at the very least, have taken an abigail with her. And what had become of them during the recent brief, but heavy, rainstorm?

He strode across the lawns and encountered a soggy Jacob in the vicinity of the lake. The dog trotted up to him, tail dripping all over Harry's pristine Hessians, as he wagged his greeting.

'Hello, old boy,' said Harry, scratching his floppy ears, 'where is your mistress then?'

Jacob galloped up to the veranda of the boathouse, tail still spiralling in watery circles. Something cautioned Harry not to enter immediately and instead he peered through the grimy window, wondering why Eloise and her visitor should choose to remain in such an uncomfortable location now that the rain had ceased. He soon discovered the answer to his own question and cursed softly under his breath.

Craven had Eloise in his arms and was comprehensively kissing her. Furthermore, from what Harry was able to discern, Eloise was making not the slightest attempt to escape from his embrace.

7

Spitting expletives beneath his breath, anger blazing from contemptuous eyes, Harry looked away in disgust. Had he taken a moment longer to observe the scene in the boathouse he would have been gratified to witness Eloise extracting herself from his lordship's embrace and turning wrathfully upon her aggressor. He might then have better understood the lady's disinclination for a situation brought about by her own carelessness and rescued her from it.

But Harry was not so fortunate as to observe any of this. Instead, his mouth compressed in a thin, hard line of disapproval, he endeavoured to assess his options. A moment's contemplation was all he required to acknowledge that he could scarce intrude himself upon their notice: a course of action he would not hesitate to take were it not for the fact that it could only result in humiliation for Eloise. Harry, as a gentleman of principle, and acting in his guise as Eloise's self-appointed protector, would either have to call Craven to account for his unseemly conduct or, at the very least, appraise Mr

Hamilton of the incident.

Either course was likely to compromise Eloise's reputation beyond recall, since Harry was well aware that it would be almost impossible to prevent such a juicy item of gossip falling into the public domain. Eloise would become the focus of the latest *on dits* and speculation as to the true nature of her relationship with Craven — particularly in view of his attachment to Mr Hamilton — would become rife, ruining what was left of her reputation and, by association, her sister Charlotte's season. As it was, the odds were stacked against Eloise's making a good marriage and the slightest whiff of scandal attaching to her would extinguish even the small glimmer that existed.

Harry was so angry with Eloise that he wondered at his ability to think straight. He silently inveighed against her stupidity in placing herself in such a vulnerable position as the various consequences pursuant to her folly tumbled haphazardly through his mind. Reluctantly reaching the only decision available to him he retraced his steps and approached the boathouse for a second time, calling loudly to Jacob as he did so.

The door opened almost immediately and Eloise emerged, looking shaken and disorientated.

'Harry, I was unaware that you had returned.'

'I was fortunate enough to conclude my business more quickly than I had anticipated,' he told her, somehow managing to keep his voice even.

Richard appeared behind Eloise. 'We were sheltering from the storm,' he explained to Harry, his demeanour as relaxed and unconcerned as Eloise's was agitated.

'So I apprehend,' responded Harry, casting a glower of disapproval over Eloise's damp gown, which clung to her form in a disconcertingly graphic manner.

'We were about to return to the house, Harry. Do join us.'

Harry nodded his agreement and fell in beside Eloise, still too angry to trust himself to converse with her.

When they reached Staverley Richard excused himself, bowed to Eloise and took himself off in the direction of the stables. Harry, unrestrained now that they were alone, grasped Eloise by the wrist and literally dragged her into the house, ignoring the startled Farthingay whom they passed in the hall. He pushed her ahead of him into the morning-room and slammed the door behind them.

'Just what the hell do you think you are

playing at?' he demanded of her, the anger he no longer felt the need to check seething from his every pore.

'Whatever can you mean?' countered Eloise, taken aback by the violence of his question; alarmed by the ferocity of his expression and minatory look in his eye.

'I saw you, Eloise.' He continued to glare at her, cold eyes glistening with displeasure. 'I saw you in that man's arms, kissing him and behaving no better than a common slut. What in God's name got into you?'

Eloise, angry and startled by Richard's behaviour, had been relieved beyond words to have Harry arrive just when he did. As they crossed the lawn together, returning to Staverley, she came to the conclusion that Harry was the very person — the only person, in fact — whom she could talk to about all that had happened to her if she hoped to understand it all. She would, in spite of previously deciding against it, relate the whole of Richard's behaviour to her, including his astonishing revelations about both his family and his business enterprise with her father.

Eloise hardly knew what to make of it: about Richard's apparent remorse at having insulted her — which she had gone a good way to believing — until he ruined it all by doing exactly what he had been attempting to apologize about in the first place and imprudently kissing her. At first too stunned to offer him any sort of reprimand she had given in to his kiss, just for a second or two, more than a little curious to discover how it would be. Then common sense and anger at his arbitrary attitude came belatedly to her aid and she fought him off; giving him a fair trimming as she did so for presuming to treat her in such a disrespectful manner.

But now here was Harry, standing before her, fuming with rage at what he considered to be *her* want of propriety! All right, she was sensible enough to concede that perhaps she had been unwise to walk with Richard unattended, but she could hardly be blamed for not wanting an abigail to overhear the particulars of what she had anticipated would be a sensitive conversation and, anyway, she had considered that she would be safe enough within the confines of the Staverley grounds. It was hardly her fault if Richard turned out to be not quite the gentleman she had supposed him to be.

Eloise herself was now starting to become irate. Harry not only had no business accusing her of behaviour that fell short of the mark, without first offering her the opportunity to explain herself, but he also had no business involving himself in her affairs and passing high-handed judgements upon her. She was not his responsibility and it was high time he recollected that fact.

Eloise's irritation slowly gave way to devilish impulses. Why should she explain her motives to him when it was obvious that he intended to think the worst of her? If he considered that she was behaving no better than a muslin then she would gratify him by reinforcing that opinion. Offering her would-be protector a transfiguring smile she waved his objections carelessly aside.

'His lordship finds me adorable!' she told Harry flippantly. 'And who am I, a mere helpless female, to argue with such an encomium, for you must be aware that none of my species is capable of resisting such flummery? He was unable to suppress his desires and felt the inexorable need to kiss me,' she added blithely, her deliberately provocative chatter stalling slightly beneath the intense hostility of Harry's gaze. 'I was curious to know what it would be like, since I have never been kissed before, and so I permitted him to have his way.'

She executed what she hoped would pass for a nonchalant shrug and fell silent, throwing a defiant glance at Harry before shame overcame her and she averted her eyes lest he detect the humiliation within them. She sat down abruptly: her knees were quaking uncontrollably all of a sudden and appeared reluctant to support her weight. She had never seen Harry half so angry before and she realized that she was not equal to the task of standing up to him in his current mood. But that did not mean she intended to answer his impertinent questions or apologize to him for her behaviour: she would simply have to defy him from a seated position instead.

'You little fool!' he said, pulling her back to her feet, clasping her shoulder and shaking her hard enough to make her teeth rattle. 'Have you any idea what you have done?'

'Nothing of consequence,' she responded capriciously, 'but I must own that it was a most instructive experiment. I should inform you, however, that I did not feel any occasion to swoon, which was a disappointment, for I was of the opinion that all young ladies are reduced to that weakened state when kissed for the first time.' She glanced up at him from beneath lowered lashes, her expression at once saucy yet projecting an air of polite enquiry, and refused to be intimidated into looking away first.

'Eloise, do you know what this could mean for your reputation?' said Harry, holding on to his temper by the merest thread as jealousy, occasioned not just by her casual dismissal of her unbecoming behaviour, coursed through every vestige of his person. 'You could be ruined beyond recall.'

'It is a matter of complete indifference to me,' she responded, so casually that Harry had to suppress the urge to strike her. 'I have already told you that I do not intend to marry and so it can be of no consequence.'

'Then, if you have no thought for yourself, consider Charlotte. Any shame heaped upon you must be shared by her.'

Eloise looked contrite for the first time. 'I had not considered the matter from that aspect,' she conceded. 'Still, it is of no import, Harry, since it was only you who discovered me and I know I can rely upon your discretion.'

'So help me, Eloise,' he said through gritted teeth. 'If I were to put you across my knee and thrash some sense into you it would be no more than your just deserts.'

'You would not dare!'

'Upon my honour, Eloise, your conduct is enough to try the patience of a saint and, believe me, I have never laid claim to the possession of saintly qualities.'

Eloise sniffed and straightened her shoulders. 'With good reason, I dare say! Harry, you are making far too much of a simple kiss: it amounts to nothing.'

'If you can look upon it in that casual light then you are even more at fault than I at first supposed. Had you been able to persuade me that you have feelings for the cad then I would at least have thought better of you than I do at this moment.'

'But, Harry,' reasoned Eloise, distressed to have earned Harry's disapproval but more determined than ever not to show it, 'I have already been made well aware that I am not in a position to harbour expectations in respect of any gentleman of consequence: especially one of Lord Craven's superior standing. You yourself have as good as told me as much on more than one occasion. So why would I make myself miserable by pretending otherwise?'

'Eloise, I did not mean to imply — '

'Anyway, I know now how it feels to be kissed,' she said, grasping at the first sign that Harry's anger was abating and taking the opportunity to become deliberately provocative, 'and it was very pleasant.'

Harry, still struggling with his temper, was pushed beyond endurance by this latest remark. Just as Richard had half an hour earlier he pulled Eloise roughly into his arms.

'If you felt the need for instruction in

respect of amatory matters,' he told her in a voice suddenly rendered thick with passion, 'then you should have applied to me. Have I not spent my life satisfying your curiosity on any number of subjects?'

'But, Harry,' she said sweetly, looking up into eyes that were now smoulderingly luminescent with a very different emotion to that which had afflicted them a few minutes earlier, 'you already do so much for me. How could I put you to such inconvenience?'

'An inconvenience you call it!'

With something resembling a growl of frustration Harry's lips closed over hers. Eloise's eyes fluttered to a close and she inexpertly pursed her own lips, not in the least bit reluctant to receive his caress. She intended to treat it in just the way he had implied she should: as a lesson to be learnt in the arms of a master of seduction. She would compare his kiss to Richard's and no doubt find it wanting. He might be considered by society at large as a rake of the first order but to her he was just Harry: her friend and protector; someone who had been a part of her life for as long as she could remember.

It was with some surprise that she experienced very different emotions engulfing her as Harry's arms tightened around her and the pressure of his lips upon hers ruthlessly increased. She felt an agreeable warmth pulsating through her veins as his tongue foraged her mouth, forcing her lips apart and darting with a tantalizing expertise that left her head reeling. She forgot all about being angry with him as her arms closed around his neck and her body responded to his with a reckless enthusiasm she was too inexperienced to conceal.

'Oh!' she remarked in a dazed tone, as Harry finally released her and she gulped air into her oxygen-starved lungs.

Harry smiled with satisfaction at her confused expression, being too experienced to misinterpret its meaning. He guided her to a chair and assisted her into it; correctly surmising that in her current condition she was incapable of standing.

'I think that was more than equal to anything that Craven might have been able to teach you,' he said, a note of smug satisfaction in his tone, 'since you do, indeed, now appear to be in danger of swooning.'

Infuriated by his assumption that he had reduced her to a witless conquest with one efficient kiss, even if it was true, Eloise was momentarily unable to respond with her customary vitality. She was still struggling to come to terms with what had happened to her; the way Harry's embrace had affected her to the core. The turbulence of her emotions; the heady passion that had enveloped her; the tingling she could still detect where Harry's experienced hands had gently explored every contour of her back: all of these new feelings combined within her, causing her to feel ashamed. But her shame lacked teeth and was replaced very quickly with a singular excitement, impossible to deny, leaving her desperate to repeat the experience.

She had never felt the need for solitude more. She craved the opportunity to reflect upon all that had happened to her in one extraordinary afternoon. Harry, she well knew, was as forbidden to her as Richard — a circumstance which until today she would have considered with complete equanimity. But what she had felt during their brief embrace was, she now realized, an exquisite passion of dizzying proportions which had been conspicuous by its absence from her sojourn in the boathouse with Richard.

Harry, alive to her needs, recognized in her confusion her desire to be alone. He picked up his hat and moved towards the door.

'We will talk tomorrow evening at Jane's party,' he said to her in a voice devoid of his previous fulminating anger. 'In the meantime, sweetheart, I must insist that you keep away from Craven. He means you no good and I cannot always be on hand to rescue you.' She opened her mouth to argue with him but he stayed her with a gesture. 'I am in earnest, Eloise, and will not tolerate any more of your disobedience. You fall under my aegis, whether you wish to admit to the fact or not, and I am determined that you will have nothing more to do with the man. And' — he paused to frown at her in a grave manner — 'if I discover that you have gone against my wishes for a second time I can assure you that the consequences will not be at all pleasant for you. And you will only have yourself to blame.' He blew her a kiss, his mood seeming to lighten with the conclusion of his stern oration. 'Behave yourself, if you can possibly manage it,' he adjured. 'And,' he added, with irritatingly becoming languor, 'should you feel any further curiosity about the matter we were just now discussing, you know where to come for your next lesson. You have my assurance that I will be happy to oblige you.' He winked at her, his air one of unruffled calm and complete confidence in his ability to control her.

Eloise, roused to anger by his attitude, belatedly recovered her wits and found the energy to protest. She sprang to her feet, grasped the nearest object and hurled it in the direction of his departing person with a gratifyingly accurate aim.

★ ★ ★

Taking a steadying breath, Eloise viewed her appearance critically in her pier glass. She was dressed for Jane's engagement party in a new gown of pale-blue dimity, adorned with few flounces, a bodice that was worn off the shoulder and a neckline cut daringly low: the height of fashion. It became her well, of that much she was unconsciously aware, even if it was perhaps not entirely suitable attire for a young girl who was not out.

Since the previous day her mind had, not unnaturally, been plagued by images of both Richard and Harry. How had she landed herself in such an impossible imbroglio and what could she now do to extricate herself with dignity? Richard, she supposed, she could simply avoid, since surely he would not actively seek admittance at Staverley after the infamous way in which he had conducted himself. But what of Harry: her friend and protector, who had so effortlessly succeeded in reducing her to a state of exquisite sensibility with just one expertly executed kiss? How could she face him again without recalling the feel of his lips upon hers; the

159

pressure of his hands as they slowly explored; the passion reflected in his dark eyes as his penetrating, gaze devoured her features? Things could never be as uncomplicated between them again as they had once been, she now accepted, and she felt that loss more acutely even than the embarrassment which engulfed her whenever she recalled their heated embrace.

Why in the world had Harry felt the need to kiss her like that and complicate everything? She would give anything to be able to turn back the clock and relive those fateful moments, secure in the knowledge that she would behave very differently a second time around. She dwelt upon his motives as her abigail continued to dress her hair and suddenly sat up very straight, causing Mary to drop her comb in astonishment. A truth so impossible that it made her head spin had just occurred to Eloise. Harry had kissed her so harshly, so possessively, and warned her so adamantly against Richard because he was jealous of her relationship with him! It did not seem credible but the thought refused to be dislodged from her brain and, try as she might, Eloise was unable to find a more plausible explanation.

When Eloise entered the carriage, in company with her father and brother, to make the short journey to Boscombe Hall, she felt strangely empowered by this new discovery. A hitherto unknown feeling of confidence infused her being and she no longer feared facing Harry.

Upon arrival the Staverley party were received with the customary casual affection that existed between the two households. Eloise, head held high, offered her hand to Harry and clearly surprised him by making no effort to avoid his eye. She could see that he was impressed by her gown: the fact that his smile slowly broadened as he took in her appearance, lighting up his handsome face and producing the inevitable predatory look in his eye, confirmed at least that much. As he kissed her hand with lingering exactitude he told her that she looked ravishing and made her promise to save him a dance.

'Quite a turnout,' remarked Thomas, as he stood beside his sister and glanced casually around the room.

About thirty guests were assembled for dinner and many more were expected for dancing afterwards. Eloise noticed that Lady Hannah was present with her aunt and uncle. Surreptitiously she studied the lady whom she suspected as being destined for Harry. She had a pretty rather than beautiful face, which boasted a pair of cornflower-blue eyes and was surrounded by a profusion of yellow ringlets. Her gown perfectly matched the hue of her eyes and, in spite of its fussiness, became her well. She was a tiny creature, her body devoid of any discernible curves, and she spoke in a high-pitched, breathless manner which lacked expression. Eloise could easily imagine her voice turning into an unpleasant whine if she did not get her way.

Eloise was surprised to discover that she did not much care for Lady Hannah and could not imagine why that should be. She hardly knew the girl and, having long since accepted that she could not rival her more acceptably born contemporaries, could think of no particular reason why she should bear her a grudge. The girl appeared to be a magnet for half the unattached gentlemen in the room and Eloise watched her as she leaned first towards one, exchanging a confidential word or two, which appeared to require a lavish fluttering of lashes and adroit deployment of her fan, before turning to her next admirer.

Eloise turned away: she had seen enough.

'Where can Jane be?' asked Thomas, his voice bringing her back to the present.

'There!' Eloise pointed with her fan towards Harry, who was slowly descending the stairs, his sister on his arm.

'Lord, who would have thought it!'

Thomas's lazy drawl concealed genuine astonishment and, looking at her friend, Eloise could understand why. Her gown was a deep green, the bodice cut so low and her breasts pushed up so high that they spilled alarmingly over the top. Harry's work, naturally! The skirts, also at Harry's insistence, Eloise later learned, had been cut to skim over Jane's hips and artfully conceal their size. Her hair was piled high and fell in a profusion of ringlets around her smiling face. Eloise had never seen her look better.

As she reached the hall, the earl stepped forward, his eyes trained upon her décolletage in evident fascination. Jane curtsied low, just as Harry had instructed her to, affording her intended an even better view of the wares on offer.

'I say!' Bingham raised her from her curtsy and kissed her fingers. 'You look enchanting, m'dear.'

'Thank you, my lord.'

The dowager chose that moment to interpose herself and Jane curtsied once again.

'Welcome to the family, Jane, I trust you will be very happy with my son,' said her ladyship graciously, sounding as though she did not trust anything of the kind. 'But, my

163

dear,' she continued, looking askance at Jane's neckline, 'your gown is, er — '

'Quite delightful?' suggested Harry smoothly, treating her ladyship to his most engaging smile. 'Exactly so! I am so gratified that you approve.'

'Indeed we do!' cried the earl, making no effort to hide his enthusiasm and studiously ignoring his mother's affronted expression.

Harry stole another look at Bingham's besotted face and knew that his plan would succeed: Jane had been made aware of the power she possessed to keep her future husband in her thrall and would have nothing to fear now from her mother-in-law.

'If I may have the honour, Lady Bingham,' he said, holding out his arm. 'I believe champagne is being served in the drawing-room.'

Harry winked cheerfully at his sister as he led the defeated dowager away. As always he looked devastatingly handsome in his evening clothes and even Lady Bingham, smiling in gracious acquiescence, did not appear completely immune to his charms. He installed her in a chair beside the fire, procured for her a glass of champagne and left her to hold court regally over the other matrons.

Dinner was over, the rest of the guests were arriving and the dancing had commenced.

Standing at the side of the ballroom, deep in conversation with Jane and her earl, the opening stanza of the first waltz of the evening went unnoticed by Eloise, until that is, she discovered Harry standing before her and requesting the pleasure. She considered refusing him, just to put him in his place, but the look of anticipated pleasure on Jane's face — for she adored seeing Harry paying attention to her friend — prohibited such action.

'Your ploy to outmanoeuvre the dowager worked splendidly,' said Eloise, laughing up at him in admiration, having generously decided to treat Harry as though the scene in the morning-room at Staverley the previous day had not occurred.

'It was simply a matter of convincing Jane that she has weapons to deploy that the dowager cannot counter,' said Harry with a dismissive shrug of his broad shoulders.

'Well, I am glad for Jane's sake because she appears genuinely fond of Bingham.'

'I have no doubt that they will get along together splendidly.'

'Why are you dancing with me, Harry?' asked Eloise suddenly, conscious of Lady Hannah's vengeful glare as she glided past them in the arms of an unknown gentleman. 'Should you not be bestowing your attentions upon your intended? In fact, now that I think about it, I do not recollect seeing you pay her very much heed at all this evening.'

Harry feigned indifference. 'You may be an obnoxious brat, but I feel it incumbent upon me to keep a weather eye on you, since how else can I assure myself that you are not getting into further scrapes?'

'Oh, Harry, do be serious! Now, tell me, what next do we do to move forward with our investigation?'

'What did you discover in respect of your maid and her amatory dalliances?'

'Nothing,' conceded Eloise with a pout. 'The only person whom I could usefully quiz on the matter without arousing suspicion was my abigail, and she was unable to shed any light on the matter at all.'

'It is of no consequence.'

'I am minded to visit the village again tomorrow and call upon Mary's family. They may have received some intelligence of their daughter.'

'My father would have heard about it had that been the case. Better to let it be, Eloise.'

★ ★ ★

As Harry waltzed with Eloise, privately admiring the lightness of her step and the

166

innate elegance which underscored her every movement, the incident at Staverley the previous day reclaimed the position at the forefront of his mind; a position which it had vacated for short periods only in the interim, and he found himself longing to repeat the experience. Her spontaneous reaction to his embrace, and unmistakable enthusiasm for it, was in direct variance to anything Craven's inelegant efforts could have produced from her, Harry felt assured. The mere thought of that unprincipled knave having the temerity to lay so much as one finger on Eloise, simply because her solitary occupation of Staverley left her in a vulnerable position he obviously didn't have the morals to resist, caused Harry's face to be invaded by an angry frown. He held on to his partner in a more proprietary manner, compelling reasons for protecting her from her own curiosity spilling through his brain as he did so.

Harry regretted that his dislike of Craven, and jealousy-fuelled reaction to seeing him with Eloise, had combined to make him incautious and give in to the temptation to kiss her himself. It had been, he now conceded, nothing more than a conceited attempt to prove to her just how little Craven had to offer. Had he not given way to such a hedonistic impulse he might not only feel better disposed now to remember his duty and embark upon the courtship of Lady Hannah but, conceivably, he might also manage to display a modicum of enthusiasm for the scheme.

As it was he could scarce bring himself to think about it without abhorrence, and it was all the fault of the little minx currently in his arms, who was gazing mischievously up at him, eyes sparkling with pleasure. She was an unconscionable temptation and he knew that, somehow, he must devise a way to banish all thoughts of her from his mind.

Had he not awakened passions in her that she was unaware she possessed, passions he was now desperate to sample one more time, it would have been so much easier to tolerate the vacuous Lady Hannah. Instead, all he had managed to confirm by his actions was that the only lady he had any interest in marrying was the one with whom he was currently dancing.

He also accepted, with a sinking heart, the fateful inevitability that it could never be. The waltz ended and wordlessly Harry ushered Eloise in the direction of the open doors to the terrace, determined to have her to himself for just a few minutes longer. He placed her hand on his arm and they joined other strolling couples, Harry unaware that Sir

Henry had been watching him critically as he laughed his way through a waltz with Eloise, or that his father was now hard put to suppress a frown as he observed them leaving the ballroom together.

'Why have we come out here, Harry?'

'To enjoy the fresh air.'

'No other reason?' she asked him suspiciously, narrowing her eyes in dire warning.

'Of course not!' he lied smoothly. 'Really, Eloise, whatever do you take me for?'

'Harry,' she said, her voice losing all its former gaiety, 'there is something I wish to discuss with you and now would appear to be as good a time as any.'

'What trouble have you got yourself into this time, little minx?'

'Not trouble exactly, Harry,' she responded with a winning smile, so gently persuasive as to send his mind reeling in the very direction he was valiantly attempting to resist, 'it is just that I have no one else with whom I can easily discuss such matters.'

Eloise, having decided that she would, after all, relate to Harry the whole of her history with Richard, paused, wondering where to begin. Before she could decide, they were interrupted by Sir Henry, who joined them and bestowed upon his son a steely expression of displeasure.

'Your presence is required in the ballroom, Harry,' he said curtly.

'I shall be there directly, Father,' he responded, annoyance at being interrupted and summoned in a manner better suited to a recalcitrant schoolboy clearly apparent.

'Oh, come along, Harry, we have had enough air anyway,' said Eloise flippantly, unconsciously repairing the rift that had threatened to develop between father and son as they smiled their amusement at one another over her head. It was now very obvious to Sir Henry that Eloise certainly had not been harbouring romantic notions when she agreed to stroll the terrace with Harry, whatever his son might have intended.

'And you, young lady,' said Sir Henry, restored to good humour once again, 'must promise to make an old man happy by dancing with him.'

Eloise stood on her toes and reached up to kiss Sir Henry affectionately on the cheek. Harry watched her, his impassive expression concealing the unnaturally heavy feeling which was weighing down his heart as he contemplated the course of action he could no longer avoid.

8

Harry was not surprised when his father sent word that he wished to see him the following afternoon, nor did he doubt the reason for the summons. He entered the library, still clad in his muddy riding clothes, and occupied the chair on the opposite side of his father's desk.

'You are to be congratulated upon your manipulation of Lady Bingham,' remarked Sir Henry, smiling at the memory. 'So formidable is she that I would wager few people have managed to outmanoeuvre her so adroitly in the past. I would venture to suggest that Jane's path into matrimony has been considerably smoothed by your actions.'

Harry shrugged. 'I could not have rested easy, thinking of Jane under that woman's predatory control. Knowing as I did of Bingham's particular appetites it was not difficult to devise a method of besting his mother.'

'Quite so.' Sir Henry leaned back in his chair, his smile slowly fading from his lips as he considered the next subject for discourse. 'Now, what progress have you made with your investigations?'

Harry had already told his father of the outcome of Eloise's visit to Meg's family.

'Eloise has a notion to visit Mary's family today.'

'She will learn nothing new there and can only attract unnecessary attention to herself by asking questions that are no concern of hers and which will be painful to the family.'

'That is what I informed her but I doubt that anything I say is likely to deter her from her purpose. She is frustrated because she can discover nothing more about the Staverley maid's habits and whether she favoured any one of her suitors in particular.'

'I thought George had thoroughly investigated that aspect,' said Sir Henry.

'So too did I, but I took the opportunity to have a word with him on the matter when I discovered him in the card-room last night. I had supposed that he spoke to all of his senior staff about the unfortunate incident in person but it appears that he merely instructed Farthingay to make the enquiries in his stead.'

Father and son exchanged an exasperated glance. Mr Hamilton, fastidious to a fault when it came to matters of business, was well known to be equally lax in respect of his domestic arrangements, leaving the running of the house entirely to Charlotte and, latterly, Eloise. Harry's irritation turned into something more tangible as he considered the way Hamilton blithely left Eloise to her own devices unchaperoned, and paid scant regard to her activities assuming, without enquiring too closely into the matter, that she was obeying his dictate and not leaving the house unattended. What could be regarded as his callous disregard for his daughter's safety, Harry now had good reason to be aware, only made her appear as an irresistible target to opportunist dastards such as Craven. Eloise herself had no notion of just how vulnerable her position was and could, he now accepted — having had sufficient time to consider the matter in a more rational light — hardly be held to account for falling prey to his questionable charm.

'We must, I suppose, assume that Farthingay is conversant with any intimacies or particular friendships between staff members at Staverley,' commented Sir Henry.

'I am assured that he is. However, my valet is on friendly terms with one of the senior footmen at Staverley,' responded Harry, 'and I have asked him to broach the subject with Smith when they next share a jug of porter together.'

'Hm, there is no disadvantage in being

thorough, I suppose,' agreed Sir Henry. 'I will be interested to learn if Jenkins discovers anything new. But in the meantime at least no other girls have gone missing.'

'Which leads one to suppose that if persons unknown to us are bent upon disreputable purposes then they are either lying low for the time being or have taken their activities to another area.'

'Quite, but only time will tell. Now, Harry, tell me about Lady Hannah: how do you progress on that front?'

Harry had been prepared for the question and met his father's penetrating gaze passively; his expression impossible to interpret. 'She receives my attentions with apparent pleasure, almost as though she has been primed to expect them,' he said with heavy emphasis.

'Her uncle and I speculated upon the likelihood of a match between the two of you some time ago,' responded Sir Henry, impervious to the angry frown which invaded his son's face, 'and given her uncle's enthusiasm for the scheme, not to mention Lady Hannah's obvious partiality for you, I would have been surprised had she been anything other than flattered by your interest in her.'

'I wish you had not discussed the matter

with Lord West without first consulting me.'

'And have you find further excuses for procrastination? Harry, I must urge you not to dally: there are several others with pockets to let sniffing round her petticoats and I would not have any of them roust you simply because you are disinclined to put yourself to the trouble of paying court to the girl.'

A glimmer of hope shone in Harry's eyes. 'Is it likely, do you suppose, that I might be usurped?'

'If you do not look to your purpose, then in all probability she will be stolen from you. And,' continued Sir Henry resolutely, 'if that were to happen, simply because you are unwilling to exert yourself, then you can expect to incur my extreme displeasure.'

'Then let us hope that she prefers me to any of her other beaux.'

'I think there can be little dispute upon that point. But you are hardly giving her the opportunity to make up her mind since I could not discover that you devoted much of your time to her entertainment last night.'

'Which only served to render her more receptive when I did single her out,' drawled Harry, attempting to make his indifference appear more a deliberate ploy.

'Maybe so,' conceded Sir Henry, who was not taken in by Harry's strategy, 'but even so,

I must advise you to — '

'Father,' said Harry in such a considering tone as to make Sir Henry regard him with suspicion, 'would I disappoint you if I chose someone other than Lady Hannah?'

'That would depend entirely upon your choice, Harry. Whom do you have in mind, given you know what is expected of you?'

Harry did not reply immediately. Instead, too agitated to keep still he got up, walked distractedly about the room, picking up objects at random and examining them as though he had never seen them before and found himself unequal to meeting his father's eye.

'Sit down, Harry,' said Sir Henry. He waited for his son to comply before saying, 'Eloise?'

Harry looked at his father in complete astonishment. 'How did you know?'

'Harry, I am not blind! I have seen the way you have been regarding her since you returned home from Shropshire and found her suddenly grown up; the way you have attention for no one else the moment she enters a room. I have seen the look in your eye when you dance with her and the way you try not to scowl when she is dancing with other gentlemen. Oh, don't worry, it is only because I know you so well that I have observed these things and the only other person who has any inkling as to your feelings is, perhaps, Lady Hannah herself.'

'Would it be so terrible if I were to offer for Eloise?' asked Harry bleakly, already knowing what his father's answer would be but desperate enough to ask anyway.

'Yes, Harry; we discussed Eloise and her likely prospects, or lack of them, just the other day and nothing has changed in that time. You know better than anyone what we are trying to achieve within the family and an alliance with Eloise, much as I admire her and share your affection for her, would reduce our efforts to naught. Think of the steps we took with your sisters to marry them well and raise the status of the family: we were quite ruthless in their cases and spared no thought for their own wishes.'

'But, Father, I — '

'Good God, Harry!' exclaimed Sir Henry, losing his temper. 'Do you imagine you are the only person who has ever fallen in love?'

Harry was momentarily too stunned to speak and an incredulous expression passed across his face. 'Is that what it is, Father? Do you suppose me to be in love with Eloise?' He shrugged his shoulders in a self-deprecating manner. He knew his feelings for Eloise were different to those he had harboured for any other female, but not for one minute had he supposed himself to be in love. 'I have never been in love,' he admitted, struggling to voice his thoughts in a coherent manner, 'and am unsure how to recognize the signs.'

'Then let me enlighten you,' said Sir Henry, his temper in check once again. 'You make any excuse you can to see her; you have eyes for no one else when she is in a room full of people; you feel protective in a manner previously unknown to you; you experience an agonizing jealousy when another gentleman so much as addresses her; if she were in trouble you would give your life to save her. In short, you would slay dragons for her.' Sir Henry ticked off the points on his fingers and smiled at the distracted expression on his son's face. 'Have I missed anything out?'

'Yes, Father. Just the thought of any other man placing his hands upon her body makes me want to commit murder.' Harry stood and took to striding about the room again. 'Father, I want her so much that I am unable to think of anything else and am in a permanent state of frustration as a consequence.' Lapsing into momentary silence, Harry's head abruptly snapped up. 'But how did you know, Father? About the signs of love, I mean.'

'I told you, Harry,' responded his father

equably, 'you are not the first person to be so fortunate as to fall in love.'

'Tell me about it, Father, if you have a mind to.'

Sir Henry hesitated and when he commenced speaking his tone was reflective, his voice distant and almost unrecognizable.

'When I was a little younger than you are now, before I married your mother, I fell as hopelessly in love as you appear to have done with Eloise. My father had an even greater sense of familial responsibility than I do and he told me then what I am going to tell you now.' Sir Henry leaned forward and looked earnestly into his son's tormented eyes. 'Love does not last, Harry, not in the way that you might imagine. You want Eloise, I suspect, partly because she is the first lady you have ever desired but cannot have. Am I right?'

'Possibly, but I could have her, I just know I could; she would not reject me. But for the first time in my life I have done the noble thing and not pushed my suit. But tell me, Father, if I have behaved so damned honourably in denying myself, why do I feel so wretched about it?'

Harry, in his agitated state, had talked himself into a frenzy of self-righteousness, forgetting in the process to apply to himself the yardstick he had already employed to measure Craven's behaviour. Eloise was not a servant, or a married lady, whom he could take up at will and then drop. Despite her lack of breeding she was still a lady of some quality and could not be subjected to his intimate attentions unless he then married her. He wondered now if perhaps that would be the simple answer to his problem: the decision would then be out of his hands and his father would just have to recover from his disappointment.

'Of course a man of your stamp could win an inexperienced girl like Eloise, if you put your mind to it: you could talk an innocent who is just discovering her own passionate nature into just about anything. That is not the point.' Sir Henry spoke emphatically and without any apparent sympathy for his son's plight. 'Just suppose for a moment that I approved of a union between yourself and Eloise; always supposing she would accept you that is, which is far from certain — what then? Would you be happy to spend the rest of your life with her and eschew all other intimacies? No more dalliances with the type of woman you amuse yourself with at the moment; no more wild evenings on the town or visits to some of the less-salubrious establishments you are wont to patronize.

'Harry, I know you better than you know

yourself and it is not in your nature to be true to just one lady. It would never be enough for you and after a while, much as you might love Eloise, you would become accustomed to her presence in your life and gradually slip back into your old ways, seeking diversions elsewhere. Eloise would not countenance that type of behaviour. There are some ladies who are content to run their own households, enjoy the society of their friends, concern themselves with their children's welfare and turn a blind eye to their husbands' indiscretions. Eloise is not one such. She would require total fidelity in her partner and, if she found you out, as doubtless she eventually would, she would lose all respect for you and, believe me, to have the lady whom you idolize no longer able to look up to you with respect would make you even more unhappy than you are at present.'

'How can you be so sure?' asked Harry bleakly. 'Perhaps I have sown my wild oats and am ready to settle down.'

'Is that what you really believe, Harry?'

Harry avoided answering the question, since if he were to do so honestly he was not entirely sure what that answer would be, and instead asked one of his own. 'What happened to the lady that you were in love with, Father?'

'She fell in love with a very suitable gentleman, married him, bore his children and is one of our most intimate friends. She was in attendance here last night.'

'Good heavens, Father, I had no idea! You are certainly full of surprises today. Do you love her still?'

'Yes, Harry, I do,' responded Sir Henry, without hesitation. 'Not the same overwhelming, exciting and all-encompassing love that you currently entertain for Eloise; that changes over time and becomes something more akin to exclusive affection. It is enough for me now to see her occasionally, to value her friendship and to know that she is well and content with her lot. But I still look out for her interests and would give my life for her, if it was asked of me, without hesitation. And to answer your unasked question: no, I never was intimate with her. She is as Eloise would be: totally faithful to her husband and not prepared to make compromises.'

Silence reigned as Harry considered the implications of his father's advice.

'I wonder what life would be like for me with Hannah?' he mused after a time.

'Extremely pleasant, I would imagine,' replied his father briskly. 'She, like your mother before her, would busy herself with her home, children and social agenda. Do you suppose that your mother has been in any way unhappy with her lot?'

Harry had never considered the matter before. 'No, Father,' he conceded slowly, 'I cannot persuade myself that she had ever shown any signs of being so.'

'Precisely! She knew well enough why I chose to offer for her and has been entirely content with her situation. She never questions how I occupy my time when I am not with her and we have grown quite fond of one another over the years.'

Harry observed his elegant father as he calmly made his startling revelations and felt a renewed respect for his wisdom and candour which, in spite of his currently tormented state, resulted in a determination to reward him by earning his approval and respect. Everything he had just said to him, Harry conceded, was founded on a wisdom that only years can bring about. Harry despondently accepted that if he wished to please his father there was only one course of action he could take, and it was thus that he reconciled himself to the final, fateful, commitment he was so loath to make.

'Harry,' said Sir Henry passionately, 'when it comes down to it, all that matters in this world is family and social position. My family is my life and I count myself fortunate to have you as my heir. You are everything a man could possibly wish for in a son and I could not be more proud of you. But do the right thing now, Harry: please, please don't disappoint me. I promise you that you will see things my way in the fullness of time. Eloise will still occupy a special place in your heart, your friendship with her will endure and in the end that will be enough for you.'

Sir Henry, knowing there was nothing more he could say on the matter, quietly stood and left the room. As he did so his parting words vibrated in Harry's head, ruthlessly cleaving their way through his brain more painfully than the sharpest of rapiers.

You are everything a man could wish for in a son: I could not be more proud of you. But do the right thing now, Harry: please, please don't disappoint me.

With a feeling of impending doom threatening to suffocate him Harry moved behind his father's desk, took up a sheet of paper and wrote a note to Lady Hannah's uncle, requesting a private interview with him on the following day.

9

Eloise remained in blissful ignorance of the fact that her progress into adulthood, and all the attendant difficulties that lay in wait for a girl in her invidious position, were the subject of such intense discussion between Sir Henry and Harry. Had she been privy to that information she would have surprised Sir Henry by revealing just how well she understood the restrictions placed upon her by a society that preferred to categorize everything neatly; expecting the populace to know its place and individuals not to get ideas above their station. Eloise's difficulty was that her situation defied all attempts at categorization. She fell into a bottomless abyss, lurking somewhere between lady of quality and the wealthy daughter of a Cit: a nebulous position somewhere below the salt but above stairs.

But Eloise had problems of another nature to wrestle with and having come to the conclusion that it was Mary's older sister, Beth, whom she most especially wished to interrogate, she decided to postpone her visit to the village forge until the following morning. If Mary had secrets to share prior to her disappearance — secrets that might offer some explanation for her subsequent actions — Eloise reasoned that her sister would have been her mostly likely confidant and that Beth would be more inclined to open up to Eloise if her distressed mother was not present.

Thursday was market-day in Epsom and Eloise knew that Mrs Dawson habitually journeyed to the town in order to sell her homemade honey, cured ham and fruit from the family's few apple trees.

Eloise set off on Molly the following morning, intent upon asking Mr Dawkins to look at her mare's shoes. She could not be *absolutely* certain, of course, but she was of the decided opinion that her near fore could well be loose.

Arriving at her destination she received confirmation that Mr Dawkins was indeed away from home, which must surely make it easier for her to gain access to Beth. Since the disappearance of Mary, Eloise understood that Mr Dawkins made a point of accompanying his spouse to the market, it being a magnet that attracted a wide spectrum of people from all localities. The Dawkinses, refusing to believe that they would never see their beloved child again, asked everyone they encountered during their weekly sojourn in the town if they had any intelligence of her.

It was Rob, Mary's older brother, who emerged from the forge in response to Eloise's summons.

'Miss Hamilton,' he said, acknowledging her presence with a lazy nod of his head. 'What can I do for you?'

Eloise regarded him in silence for a moment, shocked to find that the sight of his muscular body, glistening with sweat and honed to perfection from hours of physical work in the smithy, was having a most unsettling effect upon her. She was unsure when she had started to take such an exacting interest in the opposite sex but felt assured that the current salacious nature of her thoughts was not entirely proper. There could be no question that Rob, like his sister Mary, was blessed with extreme good looks, but that was hardly a justifiable excuse for Eloise to gape at him like some love-lorn doxy.

Perhaps because it was a reaction he was accustomed to engendering in susceptible females, a slow smile of understanding spread across Rob's features. It appeared to amuse him that he had the advantage of Eloise and he waited her out in contemplative silence.

'Oh, er, good morning, Rob. I expected to find your father here.'

'He's gone to the market with me ma.'

'Oh, I see. Well, never mind, I'm sure you will do just as well. I think Molly's near-fore is loose. Would you be good enough to take a look at it for me please?'

'If you don't mind waiting until I've finished this gentleman's hack,' he said, apparently satisfied that his request would not inconvenience her since he was already turning back to the showy bay that was hitched beside the forge.

'Not at all, Rob,' said Eloise, pleased for an excuse to dally.

'Why don't you step through into the kitchen and wait there? I'm sure Beth would be happy for your company.'

'Thank you, Rob,' she responded, smiling in triumph. 'I believe I will do just that.'

Half an hour later, Eloise left the village, well pleased with all she had learned, and headed straight for Boscombe Hall, intent upon reporting her findings to Harry.

Being admitted to the house, the first person she encountered was Sir Henry.

'Eloise,' he said, kissing her fondly, 'to what do we owe the pleasure?'

'I come with news from the forge for Harry,' she told him, bristling with excitement.

'I see. Well, in that case, my dear, perhaps I

should hear your intelligences too, for unless I mistake the matter, I would venture to suggest that you have made discoveries of some import.'

'Indeed I have, Sir Henry.'

'Harry has just come home and is in the drawing-room. Shall we join him?'

'With pleasure, Sir Henry, for I can scarce wait to receive Harry's apology. He was quite put out when I offered to assist him, but when he learns of my discoveries he will be compelled to concede that I am not quite the goose he had supposed.'

Sir Henry smiled as she linked her arm through his, perfectly at her ease, a sunny smile gracing her features as she chatted away to him. More than a little curious himself now to discover what she had learned he led her into the drawing-room, opened the door and propelled Eloise through it. She was not to know that Harry had just returned from offering for Lady Hannah: an offer that had been accepted with alacrity and that as a result he was enduring a bout of the most severe megrims, already regretting his hasty action.

As they entered the room Eloise let out a tiny gasp of alarm. She had never seen Harry looking so drawn, so completely defeated. He was resting his head in his two hands, shaking it slowly from side to side and muttering to himself in the strangest manner imaginable.

'Harry!' Her cry caused him to jerk his head up and look at her in surprise. 'Are you feeling quite the thing? You do not look at all well, you know.' She rushed up to him and placed her hand on his sleeve. 'Perhaps I should ring for Mrs Farmer?'

Harry somehow dredged up a smile of welcome, shook off his moribund thoughts and stood to greet her. 'No, no, there is no need, I am in perfectly good health.'

'Well,' she said, smiling impishly and taking a seat next to the one he had just vacated, 'if you are sure then I shall lose no time in acquainting you with all I have just learnt from my visit to the forge.' Her smile broadened into one of triumph: a gesture which lit up her dancing eyes, reminding Harry of the vivacious, reckless side to her character that so attracted him, causing his heart to miss a beat and his regrets to multiply ten-fold.

'What have you learned, my dear?' asked Sir Henry, stepping smoothly into a silence that was in danger of becoming uncomfortable.

'Well, you see, I decided to postpone my visit until this morning since I was aware that Mrs Dawkins is accustomed to attending the market on a Thursday. That being the case I thought it most likely that I would be able to converse with Beth without interference?'

'And what could you hope to gain from an interview with Mary's sister?'

'I have had the opportunity to think much about these disappearances, Sir Henry, and I cannot be entirely certain that they are in any way connected with one another.' Eloise frowned as she endeavoured to put her random thoughts into some sort of order. 'I cannot account for anyone wishing to abduct three such innocents, from such unexceptional backgrounds. What purpose could they possibly hope to achieve from such wickedness?'

Harry and his father exchanged a sardonic glance. The answer to that question was immediately obvious to them, but it was hardly a fitting matter to discuss with Eloise.

'Anyway,' continued Eloise, who fortunately did not expect an explanation to be forthcoming, 'things are seldom as they seem and I thought that if Mary had secrets, or perhaps difficulties of some sort that were causing her concern, then she might wish to share them with someone close to her. That being the case her sister would most likely be her confidant.'

The two gentlemen looked at her with new

191

respect and nodded in unison.

'And?' prompted Harry, when Eloise continued to sit beside him, grinning smugly as she prolonged her moment of triumph and fed her information to him in snippets.

'Well, I rode over this morning and was fortunate enough to discover that Mr Dawkins had accompanied his wife to the market, leaving Rob in charge of the forge. I could not be absolutely certain that Molly's near-fore was loose, of course, but Rob was kind enough to check it out for me.' Her eyes, sparkling with renewed mischief, had a mesmerizing effect upon Harry. 'I was even more fortuitous in that he already had a customer and asked me to step into the house and wait with Beth until he had the opportunity to look at Molly.'

'Very accommodating of him,' remarked Harry drily.

'Indeed it was most civil. Rob is fortunate enough to share Mary's handsome appearance and is also blessed with a very pleasant manner,' she continued warmly, blushing prettily at the memory and failing to notice the ominous scowl which took possession of Harry's features. 'I mention this because poor Beth is not so fortunate and I have long suspected that it might be a cause of resentment: her brother and sister constantly being heralded for their appearance, I mean, whilst she receives few such accolades.' Eloise hesitated. 'Well, let us just say that I am not entirely out of sympathy with her feelings in that respect and perhaps that is why I was so easily able to identify with them.'

'Go on, brat,' encouraged Harry, very anxious now to know what she had discovered and not prepared to tolerate too many more delaying tactics.

'Harry, Sir Henry,' she said, delivering her *coup de foudre* in a breathless whisper. 'The entire truth about Mary's circumstances is not known: not even to her parents. She was, prior to her disappearance, being assiduously courted by the squire's youngest son and her parents were very keen for an alliance between them to take place: it would have been a huge cachet for the daughter of the village blacksmith to be married to anyone in the squire's family, after all.'

'Yes,' said Sir Henry with asperity, 'I can quite see that.'

'Even though Gerald Penfold is a humourless, idle cove, with neither looks nor intellect to recommend him,' remarked Harry.

'Quite,' agreed Eloise, with feeling. 'He always makes me anxious, creeping up on one and listening to other people's conversations in the way that he does. He attempted to insinuate himself with Charlotte only last year but fortunately he was discouraged by my father from pursuing her. Anyway, Beth informs me that Mary was quite disgusted by his attentions and wanted nothing to do with him: especially since she had another beau.'

Sir Henry and Harry both sat forward in their seats. 'Did Beth know who this other admirer was?'

'Yes. He is the second son of the keeper on the Broughton estate. And,' said Eloise, eyes glittering with excitement, 'just a week or two before Mary disappeared he abruptly left home and took the King's shilling.'

'So he has gone for a soldier,' remarked Sir Henry. 'Well done, Eloise! Does Beth suppose that Mary is now following the drum then?'

'Indeed yes, Sir Henry. She confided in her sister that she would not abide being forced into a match with Gerald; nothing would compel her to do so and she was intent instead upon following the love of her life.'

'But not in the army, I think,' remarked Harry, who had been lost in contemplation for some minutes.

'Why not?' asked Eloise and Sir Henry together.

'Only consider, which regiments are recruiting since the end of the conflict in France? Do we not encounter officers on half-pay everywhere, desperate to sell commissions that are now virtually worthless?'

'Yes,' said Sir Henry, 'you have a point, but if that is the case where can Mary have gone to? Do you think it likely that she deliberately misled her sister, having used her as a confidant for just that purpose?'

'It's possible that she did not know her beau's true intentions. I do think that she is with this man however and that she is safe and well. Perhaps he has taken a position as a keeper somewhere else and is passing Mary off as his wife.'

'Would they have not made for Scotland?'

'Gretna Green, you mean?' responded Harry. 'I doubt they would have the blunt for such an expensive journey.'

'Very likely. But, Eloise, why did Beth not confess her sister's intentions to her parents?' asked Sir Henry. 'They must be desperate to know that, at the very least, she is alive and unharmed and Beth must be well aware of the agonies they are suffering.'

'I asked Beth just that question and she simply shrugged and said that no one had thought to ask her: in fact, I am the only person who has taken the trouble to discuss the matter directly with her. Besides, her sister swore her to secrecy. I was right to consider that Beth might feel resentment towards her siblings, having lived in their shadow for as long as she can remember. Ever since Mary's disappearance Beth tells me there has been no other subject of conversation within the family.' Eloise paused, her expression reflective. 'Beth is not so very unattractive in her own right but appears unfavourably so when set against her brother and sister. Without Mary there she is starting to come out of herself and enjoy her share of diversions. I cannot altogether blame her for keeping her parents in ignorance: although she claims that if applied to for information she will tell them all she knows, in spite of her vow of secrecy. Anyway, Mary assured her that as soon as she was settled she would contact her parents and let them know that she was safe and well. Beth expects her to do so any day now.'

'Well done, brat!' said Harry, picking up her hand and kissing it. 'You never cease to amaze me.'

'Yes, I do believe I have done rather well. And,' she continued playfully, 'as it turns out, I was wrong about Molly's shoe: it was perfectly safe after all. So silly of me to make such a mistake, but I could have sworn that I heard it clanking as I rode though the woods. It must have just been the sound of her foot making contact with stones that misled me.

But still, Rob was obliging enough to file down her clenches and trim her toes for me.'

'Very good of him, I'm sure,' commented Harry drolly. 'However, be that as it may, I congratulate you, Eloise, since I have reason myself to now believe you may be in the right to suggest the disappearances are not linked.'

'What reason, Harry?'

'Jenkins encountered Smithers last evening and discovered, during the course of their conversation, that your maid had a *tendre* for Carter.'

'What, our under-butler?' cried Eloise in astonishment. 'If that were the case then how could their attachment not be known about?'

'Because your father asked Farthingay to look into the matter and took no further part in the interrogations himself. Is my memory playing tricks on me or was it Farthingay himself who recommended Carter for the position of under-butler?'

'Yes,' agreed Eloise slowly, 'he did; less than a year ago.'

'Well, there you are then,' put in Sir Henry. 'Farthingay would naturally not wish his judgement to be found wanting. I dare say he blames the girl for getting herself into trouble, probably thinks she brought it upon herself and so made do with reprimanding Carter, letting the matter rest there.'

'But surely you are not suggesting that Carter is responsible for poor Becky's plight?' asked Eloise, scandalized.

'Who can say, but it is interesting that we have been kept in ignorance as to the connection. If it was innocent what harm could there have been in Carter making it known?'

'Yes, indeed, but I still wonder at the rest of the staff not knowing about it.'

'Perhaps they did but were warned by Farthingay against talking of it. He does, after all, have responsibility for their welfare and they would not dare to question his dictate.'

'Well, that settles matters,' said Eloise, in a determined tone. 'I shall go to London, stay with Sarah for a few days and visit Becky in the mission where she is housed. I don't doubt she will tell me the whole, if I assure her that no matter what she has done her position will still be kept open for her. It sounds to me as though she has been used most shockingly and I am determined to have the truth.'

'Eloise,' said Harry, rising elegantly to his feet and glowering his displeasure, swamping her with a wave of menacing disapproval, 'you will not, under any circumstances, go gallivanting around London unescorted.'

'Oh fustian, Harry, how else am I supposed

to visit her?' countered Eloise, demonstrating her perfect disregard for his protectiveness by offering him the sweetest of smiles. 'I can hardly take Sarah or Charlotte with me, not if you wish our investigations to remain confidential. Besides, they are far too easily shocked, both of them. And, if I went in company with you, not only would Becky not say a word in your presence, but I would also come in for even greater censure, being seen alone in your disreputable company.'

'Then take a footman,' snapped Harry irascibly.

'Yes, Harry,' she responded, so meekly as to cause his temper to abate and a bark of laughter to escape his lips.

'Anyway, I cannot possibly be in danger of abduction now: not if we agree that the disappearances are not linked.'

'We have not yet reached that conclusion,' Sir Henry reminded her. 'There is still the question of Meg, do not forget. And even though we now know your maid had a connection with Carter it does not follow that her account of her abduction by persons unknown, which so closely resembles Meg's, is a fiction.'

'I begin to wonder if I was not right about Meg in the first place,' remarked Harry speculatively. 'She is simple-minded, remember, and the only word she would say to Eloise was 'Jem'.'

'Her tormentor?'

'Yes,' said Eloise fiercely. 'And it vexes me beyond endurance to think of the way he will constantly bully that poor girl.'

'That is what we all thought she was referring to: his previous attempts to make her miserable. But supposing she was answering your questions honestly, Eloise, and it was Jem who was responsible for taking her?'

'Oh no, surely he would not go to such lengths?' Eloise looked aghast.

'Why do we not pursue our enquires regarding Becky and Carter before we dwell upon the more complex issue of Meg?' suggested Sir Henry. 'Will you speak to Carter on the matter, Harry?'

'I think not. After all, he is hardly likely to admit culpability to me, having kept his own counsel for so long and knowing he is likely to lose his position if he is found to have forced Becky into lying about her abduction. Let Eloise visit Becky first and see what she has to say.'

'Very well, Harry. I will write to Sarah and ask her when it would be convenient for me to pay her a visit.'

'Ride with me in the morning, brat,' invited Harry on an impulse, rising with her and escorting her to the door.

'With pleasure!'

It was only as he saw her to the stables and assisted her into her saddle by the simple expedient of placing his hands on her waist and lifting her into it that he remembered he had not yet told her of his good fortune in becoming engaged to Lady Hannah.

No matter, tomorrow would be soon enough to impart his glad tidings.

10

When Harry arrived on the heath the following morning he was surprised to find that Eloise was not already there: punctuality being one of her virtues, at least when it came to matters equestrian. He waited ten minutes, walking Sampson in circles to prevent him from getting cold, but when there was still no sign of Eloise he began to feel distinctly uneasy. He was still not convinced that the abductions were not linked in some way, or that she was not endangering herself with characteristic disregard for her own safety.

Making up his mind, Harry turned Sampson in the direction of Staverley. Riding into the stable yard he felt the first stirrings of alarm when he saw the curricle of the local veterinarian leaving it. All was commotion within the yard and Harry's heart missed a beat when he realized that the frenzied activity centred around Molly's box. He leapt from Sampson's back, threw his reins to a groom and strode across to see for himself what all the fuss was about.

The scene that greeted him stopped him in his tracks. Thomas, Eloise and Jacobs were gathered about a very distressed looking Molly. She was on her feet but barely; head hung low; eyes glazed and breathing laboured: her body was bathed in sweat. Thomas saw Harry and went to join him.

'I intended to ride early this morning before leaving for the bank,' he explained. 'Needed to clear my head and prepare my defences since I had a feeling I was in for another trimming from Father. Jacobs had just found Molly in this state and summoned Jones at once. He has just left but cannot identify the malady and can recommend no treatment other than 'wait and hope'. Eloise, as you can imagine, is beside herself and I know not what to do for her, or for Molly.'

Harry had never seen Thomas so agitated. 'It is not colic then?' he asked, knowing it was the first explanation they would have all hit upon, but feeling the question needed to be asked anyway.

'No, at least she is not displaying any of the usual signs if it is. She cannot seem to get any breath into her lungs. I own I have never seen anything like it.'

'Let me have a look at her.'

Harry entered Molly's box, laid a sympathetic hand on Eloise's trembling shoulder and turned his attention to her mare. He ran a hand gently along her sweating neck and observed for himself how her sides laboured with the effort it was taking her to snatch each breath. Her eyes were even duller than Harry had at first realized.

'It's all right, old girl,' he murmured quietly to Molly. 'We will make you well again, never fear.'

'Oh, Harry!' cried Eloise, appearing to register his presence for the first time through eyes brimming with tears and latching on to his words with all the hope of a person in danger of drowning. 'Do you think you can, for Mr Jones does not know what ails her?'

'It will be all right,' Harry assured her with a confidence he did not entirely feel. 'I have seen something like this once before and I have a notion what must be done. Thomas, take Sampson, he is faster than anything in your yard, and ride flat out to Somerton village. Go to the last cottage on the left and ask for Spiller.' Harry offered up a silent prayer to all he held most dear that Spiller would not be out on a call. 'Tell him I have need of his immediate services and that there is not a moment to lose.

'Jacobs,' he continued, turning in the direction of Staverley's head groom, 'keep Molly calm, sponge her with cool water but do not excite her in any way. If she wishes to lie down, allow it. She does not have colic so it can do her no harm. But on no account must you let her get excited or try to eat anything; unlikely though it is that she will attempt it. Miss Hamilton is exhausted. I will take her into the tack room in order for her to regain her strength and warm herself in front of the brazier. Call me immediately if there is any change.'

'Yes, sir,' responded Jacobs with alacrity, despatching a lad to fetch water and sponges, seemingly relieved that someone in authority had taken charge of the situation.

Eloise had been asleep when Thomas knocked at her door at a little after 6.30 that morning. Her brother had told her as gently as he could that Molly appeared to be ailing and that he knew she would want to be with her. It had taken Eloise just five minutes to pull on a thick plaid skirt and white blouse. She had tied her hair back with a ribbon and threw a shawl about her shoulders. She was with Thomas only a minute or so after he returned to Molly. Panic overwhelmed her when she saw the condition of her beloved mare: panic which was exacerbated when Mr Jones had eventually arrived but had been unable to make a definite diagnosis, or recommend any particular course of treatment. Four hours had passed since Eloise had arrived in the yard and since then no one had been able to persuade her to leave Molly's side.

Harry held out his hand to her and attempted to do so now. 'Come on, sweetheart,' he exhorted gently, 'you need to rest. Jacobs can look after Molly until Spiller arrives and he will call us at once if we are needed. Come with me and get warm. Jacobs,' he called over his shoulder, 'send a lad to the house for coffee and brandy. Miss Hamilton is in shock.'

Eloise had lost her shawl somewhere in the loose box and she was shaking now with a combination of cold and delayed reaction to Molly's predicament. Harry removed his coat and placed it about her shoulders. As soon as he closed the door to the tack-room behind them she threw herself into his arms, weeping inconsolably.

'Oh, Harry, she is going to die: I just know it! What will I do? I cannot bear to think about it. Is it my fault? Have I done something wrong: ridden her too hard, perhaps? Tell me what to do, Harry, please tell me!'

Eloise, who had been holding the tears at bay all morning, gave them leave at last to flow freely, feeling safe for the first time in the circle of Harry's arms. He stroked her hair and to his credit lent no credence to the fact that the ribbon had fallen from it; the silky mass now at the mercy of his caressing fingers. His shirt was soon soaked with her tears yet still she did not seem able to stop. Harry just held her tightly against him and let her cry. There was little he could say, in any event, that was likely to be of comfort to her and he contented himself with praying once more that Spiller would arrive in time to save Molly.

Slowly Eloise regained a modicum of composure. Harry explained to her, as he encouraged her to sip coffee, liberally laced with brandy, that Spiller had worked with his horses in the past. He was young and practised new and unorthodox methods that did not meet with everyone's approval. Although he would not say what he thought was wrong with Molly he did say he had seen something like it once before and was confident that Spiller would be able to relieve her suffering.

As he continued to soothe Eloise, racking his brains to think of further ways in which to diminish her distress, Harry understood exactly what his father had meant about putting your life on the line for the lady you love. One look at Eloise's distraught features when he entered Molly's box that morning and he would gladly have done anything,

anything at all to save the life of the horse she loved so much, regardless of the cost to himself.

After what seemed like an eternity but was, in fact, little more than an hour, Harry was advised that Spiller had arrived. Eloise jumped to her feet. She had recovered from her initial shock and distress and was ready to return to the fray.

'No, sweetheart,' said Harry firmly, restraining her with his hand. 'You stay here. This is not something for you to see.'

'But, Harry, I want to be with her.'

'No, Eloise. Do you not trust me to know what is best?'

'Yes, of course, but — '

'Stay here. It will not take long and I will come and get you as soon as it is done.'

★ ★ ★

Eloise had no strength left to oppose Harry and obediently resumed her seat, Jacob curled mournfully at her feet. She closed her eyes in exhaustion, pinning all her hopes on Harry's judgement, in which she had touching faith. She concentrated all her thoughts on her beloved mare, vainly hoping that the sheer force of her considerable will would enable her horse to pull through. She struck a bargain with God. If He would save Molly then she, Eloise, would in future contrive to behave with more decorum. It was a measure of her desperation that she promised Him she would even endeavour to look with a more sympathetic attitude upon the vile Miss Standish, if only He would save her mare's life.

Twenty minutes later the tack-room door swung open and Harry stood there. He was in his shirt-sleeves and was covered in dirt, sweat and, alarmingly, traces of blood. But he was also smiling.

'Come on, brat,' he said, holding out his hand. 'Molly is asking for you.'

With a disbelieving gasp Eloise was on her feet, taking Harry's outstretched hand and all but pulling him across the yard. Could it really be that her prayers had been answered and her horse was still alive? It must surely be so for Harry would never lie to her.

Reaching their destination Eloise discovered Molly still on her feet. Her coat and eyes were dull and she was caked with dried sweat but her breathing had eased considerably and she appeared calm. There was a small incision on the side of her neck; presumably accounting for the traces of blood she had observed on Harry's shirt.

'This is Miss Hamilton, Spiller,' said Harry.

'She owns the mare and would doubtless appreciate an explanation as to what ails her.'

'Well, ma'am,' responded the young veterinarian in a strong West-Country accent. 'She had something stuck in her throat that prevented her from breathing right, that's all. Most likely a piece of carrot too thickly sliced, or perhaps a piece of apple or a small twig picked up with the grass in her paddock. Anyway, we made an incision in her neck and managed to manipulate the blockage so that her wind passage is clear. She should recover soon enough now.'

Eloise was stroking Molly, whispering words of encouragement to her and plastering her soft pink muzzle with kisses. 'Mr Spiller,' she said quietly, 'I do not know how I will ever be able to thank you.'

'Thank Mr Benson-Smythe, ma'am,' he replied gruffly, clearly moved by the sincerity of Eloise's words, 'he was the one 'as sent for me.'

'Now,' said Harry briskly, after Spiller had departed amidst a further profusion of thanks from Eloise, 'you must make sure she eats nothing today except a couple of small bran mashes. We must avoid giving her anything that might grate upon her sore throat. Give her plenty of clean water since it would be beneficial for her to drink as much as possible but ensure the buckets are thoroughly scrubbed, Jacobs, for we cannot risk infection of any sort. Tomorrow she can have a little hay but make sure it is sweet and soft and in no way abrasive.'

As Jacobs and his lad rushed off to put these instructions into practice so Harry turned his attention to Eloise. 'I fear I must leave you now,' he said, genuine regret in his voice. 'I have business in London that I cannot avoid and I shall be gone for two days. I shall return in time for my mother's birthday party on Thursday, which you will still attend, I hope?' Eloise nodded abstractedly, hardly taking in his words, her eyes not once leaving Molly. 'I shall send daily for word of Molly and Spiller will also call every day. If you need him at any other time then Jacobs has his direction. And if you need me for anything, anything at all, just send word to Boscombe Hall: they will know where to find me and I will come to you at once. Do you promise me you will do that? I shall not go unless you can do so.'

'Yes, Harry, of course I will, and thank you so much!' She reached up and delicately placed a kiss on his lips.

Harry smiled into eyes that held him helplessly captive in their shimmering depths, in spite of the fact that they were still afflicted

211

with tears, and told her that she was entirely welcome. And then, summoning up every last molecule of his willpower, forced himself to walk away.

As Harry left the woman whom he now knew, beyond a shadow of doubt, that he loved more than life itself, he recalled that he had still not told her of his engagement, as he had intended to do during the course of their ride; before the events of the morning pushed all thoughts of his own concerns out of his mind. Eloise was equally unaware of the fact that he was going to London to do his duty by his future wife; to stand at her side and accept the congratulations of the *ton*.

★ ★ ★

Mr Hamilton and Thomas had planned to spend the day at their office and the following two nights under Sarah's roof, where Mr Hamilton would have the pleasure seeing Charlotte the centre of attention at a small soirée which Sarah was arranging to bring her sister to the attention of some of her acquaintance ahead of the season proper. Only Eloise's assurance that she would be quite content at home now that Molly was recovering could persuade Mr Hamilton to leave his youngest daughter and adhere to this commitment. Eloise reminded him that she would have Miss Gregson to bear her company and that anyway he could hardly disappoint Charlotte by not attending her party: especially for such a specious reason as Molly's illness, which Eloise knew Charlotte would neither understand nor forgive.

Easily able to slip the leash with which Miss Gregson half-heartedly attempted to keep her charge within doors, Eloise spent every second of her time with her beloved mare. She did not trust anyone else to care for her: not even Jacobs. She spent hours grooming her until her golden coat began to shine with health once again; combed her silky blonde mane; talking to her all the while and loving her the more for having almost lost her.

Jacob came and went, keeping a weather eye on his mistress; when he was not chasing rabbits and squirrels or terrorizing the stable-yard cat, that is. He would return to Molly's box after protracted absences with tongue hanging out, coat dirty and tail wagging in enthusiastic spirals. Only when Eloise had lavished sufficient attention upon him would he drink noisily from Molly's bucket, turn in several tight circles and flop untidily in the corner of the box, head resting on huge paws, eyes rapidly closing.

On the day following Molly's illness Eloise was, unsurprisingly, with her mare when she heard the sound of hoofs on the stable-yard cobbles, heralding the arrival of a visitor. Wondering who it could be, Eloise glanced over the half-door and was astonished — not to say a trifle alarmed — to observe Lord Craven astride a handsome chestnut hunter and, in spite of everything, felt a reluctant admiration for his mettle. After the infamous way he had behaved towards her; the lack of respect he had demonstrated towards her position, she had certainly not expected to see him at Staverley again — especially when her father was not there — and wondered how she could avoid speaking with him. Could she manage to send word to the house and have Miss Gregson join her before he found her out, perhaps?

Before she was able to put this plan into effect she saw Richard throw his reins to a groom and, in response to an enquiry made of that servant, turn in her direction. She attempted to draw back into Molly's box but it was too late: he had seen her. Raising a hand in greeting, he crossed the yard to join her.

'Miss Hamilton, how fortunate, I called especially in the hope of finding you at home.'

He spoke quite as though their sojourn in

the boathouse had never taken place; as though his behaviour at that time had been everything that was proper. His breathtaking arrogance brought home to her, as doubtless it was intended to, the difference between their respective situations since Eloise could not imagine Richard treating the daughters of his social equals in such a dishonourable fashion. A flare of contempt flashed in her eyes, concentrated fury accentuated her every word as she offered him the briefest greeting that politeness would allow, informing him in a significant manner that both her father and brother were not at home.

'I did not call in the anticipation of seeing them,' he responded, with barely an effort at civility.

'Then you must excuse me, my lord, for I am not at liberty at present to receive visitors.'

'Molly is looking remarkably well groomed,' he said, treating the frostiness of her dismissal with amusement rather than as a discouragement. 'Are you about to ride out?'

'No,' she responded with icy calm, 'Molly has been very ill indeed; in fact, she almost died and I am too anxious about her to leave her unattended for even a second.'

Richard expressed concern and asked for the particulars of her ailment, which Eloise supplied as concisely as possible.

'Well,' said Richard, appearing neither alarmed nor especially interested by her disclosure, 'she appears none the worse now for the unfortunate incident. It is as well though that Benson-Smythe was able to recognize what ailed her and knew how to address the malady.'

'Indeed yes,' agreed Eloise, showing the first signs of genuine animation since Richard's arrival, 'I shall always be in Harry's debt for saving her.'

'I am surprised that he was here at all,' remarked Richard casually, 'what with all the other commitments he now has.'

'Harry? Why should he not be here? We often ride together in the mornings.'

'Why, surely you are aware, intimate as you are with the family, that Benson-Smythe has recently become engaged to Lady Hannah West?'

A small gasp of surprise escaped Eloise's lips and she took a moment to recover from this revelation. 'Harry, engaged to Lady Hannah! Are you sure? He made no mention of it to me.'

'Quite sure; the announcement is in this morning's newspaper.'

'Oh, well, I daresay he intended to inform me of it but Molly's illness must have driven it from his mind. Yes, that would explain it.'

Richard appeared diverted by her confusion but made no comment on it. Instead he dwelt upon the virtues inherent in Harry's choice of bride. 'Your friend is to be envied; engaging the affections of such an eligible heiress. I dare say there are several gentleman rueing the fact that they did not push their respective suits earlier.'

'Yes, I daresay,' agreed Eloise absently, wondering why news of Harry's engagement should have such an unsettling effect upon her. After all, she had known well enough that it was likely to take place. Perhaps it was because Harry had not thought to impart the intelligence of his forthcoming nuptials to her himself. But then again, why should he trouble to do so? They were good friends, but it was not to be supposed that he would consider it necessary to acquaint her of his good fortune in person, for it really was none of her concern. But she was hurt nonetheless: hurt but determined not to show it and equally determined to befriend Harry's future wife — even if she could not entirely approve of his choice.

Richard was observing her closely, a derisive half-smile playing about his lips.

'Shall we take a turn in the grounds

together?' he suggested with exaggerated politeness.

His insolent self-confidence was such that Eloise could scarce contain her ire. Sensing that it would be a miscalculation to lose her temper with him though, she dismissed the suggestion with a haughty toss of her head.

'I wonder at your making such a suggestion, my lord, when it is obvious to you just how ill Molly has been and how I cannot know a moment's peace if I leave her.'

'Come, Eloise,' he said, his tone a mocking challenge, 'I am persuaded that she is restored to perfect health and that your presence here is superfluous.'

'If that is your opinion then you have gravely misconstrued the matter,' she told him with a brittle smile, 'and I can see no reason to prolong this conversation.' She turned her back on him and concentrated her efforts upon strapping Molly's quarters.

Richard took hold of her shoulder, compelling her to turn and face him. 'Do not imagine that this little display of coquettish behaviour is likely to cut any ice with me,' he said, his eyes boring into hers with an intensity that caused her to shiver with apprehension. 'It is a little late, I think, after our time together in the boathouse, for you to pretend indifference towards me.'

Eloise's anger was rapidly giving way to panic. The yard, she could see at a glance, was devoid of any human presence: Jacobs and his underlings were occupied in the lower paddock, schooling the youngsters. If she were to shout for assistance it was doubtful that they would hear her and, anyway, that would only draw attention to the unseemly nature of her situation. It was bad enough that Richard should single her out, making little if any attempt to disguise the fact that he was doing so simply because he could. Should it become known to her father that she had received him alone; or indeed that she had placed herself in a position where she was vulnerable to his advances, instead of sitting quietly with Miss Gregson as she was supposed to be doing, then he would be gravely disappointed in her. Richard, she suspected, was aware of that and was pursuing her for that reason: he wanted to revenge himself upon Mr Hamilton and was using her solely as a means to an end.

'What is it you require of me?' she asked him in an even voice, playing for time.

'An opportunity to finish the conversation we were having when Benson-Smythe inter-rupted us,' he responded smoothly.

'In the house, perhaps?'

'Certainly not! You *will* accompany me,

Eloise, and this time there is no one to interrupt us. I merely wish to speak to you, m'dear, and you may rest assured that no harm will come to you if you do as I ask. You have my word as a gentleman,' he added when she stared at him in frank disbelief.

'Why can we not speak here?'

'In a stable!' His disparaging expression told her precisely what he thought of that suggestion.

'Very well, if you insist upon it.'

She forced her shoulder from his grasp and turned towards the stable door, her heart beating wildly as her mind sought a means of escape from a situation which she knew to be slipping rapidly out of her control.

They left Molly's box together, a respectable amount of daylight separating them. Eloise turned in the direction of the rose garden and Richard followed her lead.

'What is it that you wish to say to me?' she asked him with smooth civility.

'I come to crave your intervention on my behalf with your father,' he said calmly. 'I believe he will listen to you. I need you to persuade him that he is being unjust and that he should reconsider the terms of our agreement.'

Eloise glared at him in frank astonishment. 'I am sorry, my lord,' she said, her palliative tone concealing her shocked reaction to the indelicate nature of his request, 'but as I informed you before, my father does not discuss his business affairs with me; neither would I expect him to. And even if he did, I doubt there is anything I could say to him that would alter his mind.'

'On the contrary, I think you have but to ask him passionately enough and he will give you anything your heart desires.'

'But to even discuss such a matter with him — and I would know not how to start anyway — would be to imply that you have spoken to me about it which, in turn, would alert my father to the fact that we have been alone in one another's society.'

Richard raised a brow, his expression one of droll diversion. 'And you suppose he is unaware of that fact? He leaves you here for days at a time, unattended, and knowing your character supposes you will turn visitors away for want of a chaperon?'

'Thank you, sir,' said Eloise, her icy diction concealing a fulminating anger, 'you have made it clear, both by your conduct in the boathouse and your insulting language today, precisely what you think of my situation. I must thank you to leave Staverley and not call again unless you have a specific appointment with my father.'

'Be careful, m'dear,' warned Richard, with a mirthful chuckle, impervious to her set-down, 'we are, if you recall, quite alone here. It is the most natural thing in the world for me to call, given my relationship with your father, and I wonder who would be believed if you were to suggest that a man in my situation would take any interest in someone of such social inconsequence as yourself; much less make improper advances.'

The last words were spoken with such arrogant disdain as to make Eloise want to strike him. But his tone also brought home to her the fact that Richard Craven was both resentful and unpredictable. He clearly bore her father a grudge of monumental proportions that was eating away at him like an incurable illness and was not above using her to exact revenge. They had stopped walking and were facing one another; battle lines drawn. Eloise forced herself to remain calm and think rationally about her next move. Should it be, in accordance with her natural instinct, confrontational and challenging or would she be better advised to make an attempt at conciliation?

Her turbulent thoughts were in direct variance to the stillness of the moment, the tranquillity and heady perfume of the rose garden that surrounded them. Richard was watching her face closely, leaving Eloise with the distinct impression that he understood the battle she was conducting with her own fiery temperament: the difficulty she was experiencing in coming to terms with his audacious demands.

'You have made your position crystal clear,' she eventually said in a glacial tone, 'but are misguided when you suggest we are here entirely alone.'

For the first time Eloise had the satisfaction of seeing Richard's eyes widen in surprise as she let out a soft whistle and a scruffy blond whirlwind erupted from the walk behind them and hurled itself in Richard's direction, growling with displeasure. Eloise had noticed the tell-tale signs of Jacob's presence just moments before: his soft panting and the noisy flapping of wings as he clumsily chased the pigeons from beneath a nearby tree. He had come looking for Eloise, and not a minute too soon.

Richard backed away until he encountered the garden wall, where he was held captive by a snarling Jacob.

'Call the damned beast off, Eloise!'

'I often wondered why Jacob did not care for you, my lord,' she responded in a pensive tone, almost enjoying herself at last, 'but I now understand just what a good judge of character he is.'

'You do not mean that! I apologize if I have upset you, m'dear, but you must understand matters from my point of view. I have been wrong — '

'Enough!' cried Eloise, with such passion as to cause Jacob to let out a threatening rumble of a growl. 'I wish to hear no more about *your* perceived wrongs. That you can be so arrogant as to even contemplate using me in order to gain revenge upon my father is beneath contempt and so, sir, are you. Now, have the goodness to leave Staverley at once and oblige me by not returning.'

She called Jacob off and Richard, with a darkling glance in her direction, made good his escape.

'You have not heard the last of this,' he told her, as he headed back towards the stables. 'No one threatens me and gets away with it.'

11

Eloise did not see Harry again until the evening of his mother's birthday party. Entering the drawing-room at Boscombe Hall she found Lady Hannah standing beside him, her hand resting upon his arm in a proprietary manner, the huge sapphire glittering on her finger outshone only by the enigmatic smile of satisfaction which played about her lips.

Eloise said all that was proper to Lady Hannah, shaking her hand with genuine warmth. Then she turned to Harry.

'Congratulations, Harry!' she said, smiling up at him. 'I hope you will be very happy indeed.'

She reached up to kiss his cheek and Harry's arms caught her easily to him. 'If I had known this would be your reaction,' he said lightly, 'I would make a point of becoming engaged more frequently.'

Everyone laughed at the light banter between these two old friends: everyone except Lady Hannah, who frowned with distaste at such a vulgar public display of affection.

225

'And how is the patient?' Harry enquired of Eloise.

'I left her eating a manger full of hay,' responded Eloise, large eyes sparkling with the pleasure this thought afforded her. 'Harry, you saved her life and I did not even thank you properly.' She moved across the room and once again reached up to place a kiss upon his cheek. 'Thank you, with all my heart!' she whispered softly.

'You are very welcome, brat,' he said lightly, placing an arm around her waist and pulling her against him for a few precious seconds. 'In any case it has been worth the small effort on my part just to see you smiling again.'

Almost everyone in the room that evening was either a neighbour or friend of long standing: all intimately acquainted and on the friendliest of terms with one another. They knew of Eloise's dedication to Molly, of her illness and the part Harry had played in her recovery. They were accustomed to seeing Harry and Eloise, comfortable in their sparring with one another, and saw nothing strange in the continuance of that relationship this evening.

But anyone taking the trouble to observe Lady Hannah's countenance would have easily been able to detect that for her it was entirely another matter. She had been overjoyed to receive the very eligible Harry's proposal — especially after the humiliation of her treatment at Lord Craven's hands two seasons previously and the gossip that his behaviour had generated — and had lost no time in accepting it. She had particularly enjoyed the sophistication of their reception in London and took perverse satisfaction in the jealousy she had noted in other aspirants for Harry's hand. His behaviour towards her since then had been everything that it should be and Hannah, a hopeless romantic, was persuaded that he was daily falling more in love with her.

But there was something about his friendship with the socially questionable Eloise Hamilton that disquieted her. Even though it was Lady Benson-Smythe's birthday it was obvious to anyone who looked in Lady Hannah's direction that she felt the attention of the assembly should be directed towards her. And it had been — until Eloise arrived. Now the conversation revolved exclusively around her wretched horse; the subject appeared to be inexhaustible and Hannah not only felt ill-qualified to make a contribution but was unable to understand what all the fuss was about anyway.

'How did you come to know about this

man Spiller, Harry?' asked one of the guests.

'Yes, Harry,' added Eloise, 'I would like to know about that, too.'

'He had a practice near our estate in Shropshire,' replied Harry. 'Father and I had occasion to call upon his unorthodox methods on several occasions when the usual treatments did not work. An opportunity arose in this part of the country and I was able to recommend him for the position. It was fortunate for Molly that I did so.' This remark earned Harry another grateful smile from Eloise. He winked at her, seemingly oblivious to his audience; a gesture which earned a sharp gasp of disapproval from his intended and caused several heads to turn enquiringly in Lady Hannah's direction.

'And Molly is well on the way to recovery now?' asked one of their neighbours solicitously.

'Oh yes indeed, I thank you, sir. I left her not an hour ago, tucking into a manger of the softest hay we were able to find in our loft.'

'Surely you cannot mean an hour ago, Miss Hamilton?' intervened Lady Hannah disbelievingly. 'What about your toilette?'

'It most certainly was only an hour ago,' Thomas assured her, laughing affectionately at his sister. 'We literally had to drag her up to the house to make her preparations.'

'But, Miss Hamilton, I do not comprehend.' Lady Hannah looked genuinely perplexed.
'How could you ready yourself in less than an
hour? I do so hate being rushed myself. You
preferred to spend your time with your horse
instead of attending to your appearance?'

Eloise confirmed that it was so: refraining
from informing Lady Hannah that for the
past two nights, in spite of Miss Gregson's
objections, she had taken advantage of her
father's absence to miss dinner altogether,
staying with Molly instead until dusk.

'But I do not understand,' persisted
Hannah, truly perplexed. 'I realize that your
horse has been very ill and that my Harry
saved her for you, but she is, after all, just a
horse. Surely you could just buy another?'

A stunned silence greeted this spiteful
remark. Everyone was embarrassed on
Hannah's behalf but she appeared blithely
unaware that she had said anything amiss.
Eventually Harry's voice broke the silence.

'I think Molly is a lot more than just a
horse to Eloise.' It was obvious to all that he
was containing his temper with the greatest
difficulty. He looked at Hannah through
hooded eyes, his jaw set in a rigid line of
disapproval, his expression one almost of
dislike. Then he turned to look at Eloise, his
eyes glowing, tone caressing and a smile

curling softly about his lips. 'Is that not so, minx?'

'Molly is my best friend,' said Eloise simply. 'Along with Jacob, naturally!'

This made everyone laugh and lightened the mood.

'And who pray is Jacob?' asked Hannah faintly.

Dinner was at that moment announced and, given the speculative look in Sir Henry's eye, it could be supposed that Hannah was not the only person in the room glad to have this conversation brought to a peremptory conclusion.

When the gentlemen rejoined the ladies at the end of the meal Sir Henry sought out Eloise. It was not long before Harry joined them.

'Why are you monopolizing this tiresome child?' he demanded lightly of his father.

'I was just singing your praises, Harry,' explained Eloise, smiling at him. 'I was telling Sir Henry, at his request mind, all the particulars of Molly's illness.'

'Were you indeed: I never would have guessed what subject was occupying your mind,' he teased.

'And, Harry,' added Eloise in high-spirits, 'I have just agreed, now that Molly is out of danger, to accompany Papa to London tomorrow. I shall stay with Sarah and, of course, take the earliest opportunity to call upon poor Becky.'

'Then I shall accompany you,' said Harry, in a tone that booked no argument. 'On Monday morning I shall call upon Sarah, ensuring that I time my arrival to coincide with her morning calls. I shall counter my disappointment at not finding your sisters at home by prevailing upon you to take a ride in my curricle with me. Nothing could be more natural.'

'Hm, I do not think that Lady Hannah will — '

'You are not going to that place alone!' said Harry, so emphatically as to warn Eloise of the futility of argument. 'Your father would never forgive me if I permitted it.'

'Miss Hamilton,' said one of the gentlemen present, surprising the group by soundlessly joining them, 'I believe there is talk of the instrument being opened. Can we prevail upon you to play for us?'

The neighbour offered Eloise his arm, she accepted it and they traversed the room together. Father and son watched them go, their gazes following the elegant sight of Eloise's gently swaying hips. Her escort leaned closer and said something to her that caused her to laugh up at him in delight.

'When does it start to get easier, Father?' asked Harry in an undertone. 'I am unsure how much more of this agony I can bear.'

Sir Henry patted his son's shoulder but was unable to make him any answer.

'Harry,' said Lady Hannah, walking up to join him. 'If Miss Hamilton is to play then perhaps I should sing. Is that not a good notion?'

Hannah had a sweet voice, which she seldom needed much persuasion to display. Harry suspected that her anxiety to do so on this occasion had much to do with his preference for Eloise: a preference he had made little attempt to disguise this evening, he realized with a pang of conscience, even if Hannah had earned his displeasure through her thoughtless remarks earlier.

'As you wish,' he said, concurring with her suggestion, dutifully making to escort her to the instrument.

But his brother James was there before him. Both Harry and his father had noticed that he had a marked preference for Lady Hannah, which had the happy affect of drawing him out of the deep *ennui* that had been settled upon him for so long.

★ ★ ★

Eloise sat in a small courtyard at the mission inhabited by Becky. As she waited for their former maid to be brought to her she went over in her mind the reason she would invent for her visit; the questions she would pose. A weak sunshine struggled to penetrate the narrow space, bathing the bench upon which Eloise sat with its ineffectual rays. A few small birds settled on the wall, chirping shrilly and causing a pigeon to take off from the opposite corner with a noisy clatter of wings.

When Becky emerged, Eloise was unable to conceal her astonishment. The girl looked terrible. Her swollen eyes indicated that she occupied much of her time crying, rendering her finely etched features ugly. Her hair was lank and unwashed, her garb grimy and she was unrecognizable from the lively beauty who had swept floors and cleaned grates at Staverley with such spontaneous gaiety. She was also far heavier with child than Eloise, who admittedly knew little about such matters, would have thought possible.

'Hello, Becky,' said Eloise brightly, ineffectually attempting to hide her surprise.

'Miss Hamilton.' Becky's voice was deferential but sullen and full of suspicion.

'I came to see how you fare. Please do sit with me.' Eloise patted the bench beside her and the girl lowered her bulk into the space with obvious reluctance. 'Now tell me how you get on. Are they good to you here?'

'I can't complain, miss.'

Eloise suppressed a sigh. This was obviously not going to be as easy as she had supposed. 'Everyone at home is thinking of you,' she said, trying another tack. 'I promised them a full account when I return to Staverley.'

A sound escaped Becky's lips; something between a sneer and a snort of disdain. 'Tell 'em, thank you, and that I do just fine,' she said morosely.

'Becky,' said Eloise, frustrated that several further attempts to engage the girl in light conversation had got her nowhere, 'tell me more about your abduction, if you will, I have never heard the particulars from your own lips.'

'There's nothing more to tell, miss,' said Becky sullenly, her eyes darting furtively about as if looking for a means of escape and resting everywhere expect upon Eloise.

'I ask only because we are attempting to discover if the people who took you did the same thing to others. You must know about poor Meg and Mary.'

'Yes.'

'Becky, look at me.' Becky lifted her eyes to Eloise's face with obvious reluctance. 'Were you really abducted?' she asked quietly.

Becky let out a short gasp, but whether in astonishment or fright Eloise was unable to decide and so, instead of trying further persuasion, she waited Becky out in silence.

'It happened just like I said.'

'Really? It had nothing to do with Carter then?'

Becky's mouth fell open. 'How did you know about him?'

'I made it my business to know,' responded Eloise nebulously.

Quite without warning Becky dissolved into a bout of heart-wrenching sobs. 'It's no good,' she choked. 'I've gotta tell someone.'

'Then tell me, Becky. Whatever you say, whatever you have done, your job will still be there for you at the end of all this: upon that I give you my word.'

'Thank you, miss, you're too good to me: I don't deserve it after what I've done.'

'What have you done, Becky?'

Becky blew her nose on the handkerchief Eloise handed her and took a moment to compose herself. 'Having come from the workhouse I was determined to make the most of the opportunity I had at Staverley, since I knew what life would be like for me otherwise; I'd had ample time to see that firsthand. Everyone was kind to me in your house and I knew that if I worked hard and kept out of trouble I would be able to improve myself.'

Eloise nodded her encouragement when Becky's words trailed off. 'Did you enjoy working at Staverley?'

'Oh yes! But, as I got older the men, well, they started to go after me. I knew enough by then to understand what would happen if I let them anywhere near me, so I didn't.' She paused. 'Well, not at first. But Carter, he seemed different. He didn't keep trying to persuade me to walk out with him on my afternoon off. Instead, he knew I wanted to improve my reading and writing and he helped me. Lent me books and a slate and encouraged me. It all seemed so natural.' Becky paused, her expression reflective. 'I'm not sure quite how things changed between us, but the next thing I knew we were sweethearts. He kept telling me how beautiful I was and he had such plans for our future as made my head spin. We would be married, but we had to keep our relationship a secret until the time was right because he wasn't sure if your father would be willing to employ an under-butler that was married.'

Eloise's gasp of astonishment was not lost on Becky and she smiled ruefully, suddenly looking a lot older than she was. 'Oh ay, I can see now that I was taken in,' she said bitterly, gesturing towards her bulging stomach, 'in more ways than one.' She looked Eloise in the eye for the first time. 'I know now that your father would not have objected to our marriage. But at the time I really believed him, miss, really thought he knew about these things. I really believed him when he said that he loved me and that we would be wed. But when I told him I suspected I was with child, everything changed and it was as if he wanted nothing more to do with me; even going so far as to suggest that the child might not be his.

'Well, I was so angry that I threatened to go to Mr Farthingay and risk telling him everything. That's when Sam came up with the plan to say that I'd been abducted. He knew about Meg having been taken and thought everyone would easily be able to believe that what had happened to one could happen to another. He said he thought your father would keep me job open for me if I went along with the story. If I didn't he said he'd deny all knowledge of my situation and I would be thrown out on me ear.' She looked at Eloise through tear-stained eyes. 'Given the circumstances what else could I do, other than to agree?'

'So you were already carrying your child

when Sam hatched this despicable plan?'

'Yes, miss,' confirmed Becky, dropping her head in shame.

Eloise, outraged by the callous way Samuel Carter had treated an innocent girl, offered her a smile full of determination and purpose. 'Cheer yourself, Becky, you could have done nothing else. But fear not, I will make things right.' She patted the girl's hand. 'Just concentrate on bringing your baby safely into the world and coming back to us at Staverley as soon as you are strong enough.'

Becky was reduced to tears again in the face of Eloise's compassion. 'I am so sorry, miss. I have brought shame upon your house and deceived you all most dreadfully, when all the time you have been so kind to me.'

Eloise smiled at Becky and waited until she had regained some sort of composure before speaking again. 'You have done nothing to feel ashamed of, Becky. You were used monstrously by Carter and a man in his position should have known better. But,' she added with determination, 'I will ensure that Carter is made to account for his conduct.'

* * *

Eloise recounted the particulars of her discussion with Becky to Harry, anger flashing in her eyes, her tone one of disgust, as he drove her away from the mission.

'It is deplorable! How Carter could have treated the poor girl in such a base manner is beyond my understanding. What should I do about him, Harry?'

'Nothing, for the moment,' responded Harry emphatically. 'We cannot deal with the situation ourselves; it is your father's household and we cannot avoid involving him. He must be informed of the situation and will naturally wish to know how we gained our intelligence. If he becomes aware that you visited Becky, and that I condoned your decision to do so, he is likely to be exceedingly vexed.'

'Humph! You are right, I suppose. Oh, how I wish I was a man sometimes!' she cried, clenching her gloved hands in frustration.

'And how pleased I am that you are not,' countered Harry lightly.

'Will you think of a way then to bring the matter to my father's attention without mentioning my specific involvement?' asked Eloise, confused by the unusual note of sincerity in Harry's voice.

'You may depend upon it.'

'Thank you. I cannot tolerate the thought of Carter getting away with such despicable behaviour for a moment longer than necessary.'

'At least now we know that there has only been one abduction: that of Meg,' said Harry thoughtfully. 'Mary and Becky's circumstances are altogether different.'

'Can I now consider it safe to ride out at Staverley without fear for my person?' Eloise enquired sweetly, the anger in her eyes replaced with the more familiar mischievous light.

'Absolutely not, brat! Your father is to be congratulated upon his sterling attempts to moderate your behaviour, even if his chances of succeeding can hardly be looked upon with optimism.' Eloise grinned at him and made to argue. 'I mean it, Eloise,' said Harry, his tone uncharacteristically grave, 'it is unseemly, now that you have reached maturity, to venture out on horseback unescorted.'

'Yes, Harry,' she responded, so meekly that Harry, with a sigh of resignation, accepted there was little chance of her paying the slightest heed to his stricture.

'When do you plan to return to Staverley?' he asked her, knowing he had said all he could on the subject of her conduct and that, for all the good it was likely to do, he might just as well have saved his breath.

'Papa is to escort me home on Sunday.

Thomas plans to stay in town for a little longer.' Eloise's eyes took on a calculating shine. 'I believe the news that Lord Craven's sister is now in town with the rest of her family and likely to be at many of the events attended by Sarah and Charlotte might have some bearing upon his decision.'

Harry raised a brow in frank surprise: he had not realized that Thomas's interest in Lady Emily was in earnest. He happened to know that whilst an alliance between Eloise and Richard Craven was out of the question, for Lady Emily — a youngest daughter who was not held in any particular regard by her mother — a partner with Thomas's prospects could not be lightly disregarded, given the precarious state of the Craven fortune.

'I see,' said Harry. 'All right, I too am remaining in town for a few more days, but I will endeavour to speak with your father as soon as I return to Boscombe Hall.'

12

Even being on the fringe of events in the capital for a few days held little pleasure for Eloise and it was with a feeling of unmitigated relief that she returned to Staverley with her father. The brief glimpse she had managed of London on the brink of a new season, the strict code of conduct and suffocating restrictions placed upon Eloise, were sufficient to dispel any lingering regrets she might have harboured about not having her own turn at presentation to look forward to.

The familiarity of her surroundings at Staverley, the reassuring routine, the tranquillity of the countryside and comfortable opulence of the house itself combined to wrap themselves around Eloise like a favourite old shawl, offering her their own particular brand of solace. This assuagement was cheering for, much as she disparaged all ideas of presentation and wanted no part of society, being made so brutally aware over the past few days of just how unacceptable she was to the denizens of the *ton* had not been a pleasant experience. In high ropes at their grandiloquent form of expression and practised ways of making her feel unwelcome, Eloise had longed to scream at these people; to berate them for their outmoded ideas and make them aware that she represented no threat to them; that their respectability was not in danger of being tarnished by her presence since she had no wish to be embraced by them anyway. Such hubris, such double standards were antipathetic to her; especially since she was aware that some of her most violent critics were quietly benefiting from her father's diamond-mine venture. For Charlotte's sake, however, she schooled herself to hold her tongue on that score.

She put all thoughts of her disagreeable visit to London out of her mind now and instead revelled in the freedom of being once again at home: the more so because Molly greeted her with a whinny of welcome and abundance of energy, her eyes bright and alert, eyes in which her anxious mistress could detect no residue of her recent distress. It was clear that she had completely recovered, was restless for a very different reason and anxious to be ridden once again.

'Tomorrow,' Eloise promised her in a conspiratorial whisper, smoothing her sleek neck, 'when Papa is occupied with business and we can be ourselves again.'

The following morning Eloise went about her usual occupations at Staverley, impatiently waiting for her father to become immersed in his business affairs, as surely he must? Unaware, when he finally took his leave of her after luncheon, that he was bound only as far as Boscombe Hall in response to a request from Sir Henry and Harry for a private word, Eloise thought herself to be at leisure to do as she pleased.

Smiling with satisfaction she lost no time in replacing her gown with Thomas's old breeches and setting out astride Molly for the woods. A good fast canter was what she needed to clear her head of all the nonsense she had encountered in London and to feel truly herself again: something she needed to do alone.

★ ★ ★

Harry and his father related to Mr Hamilton the whole of their findings in respect of the three abductions. Fortunately he was too shocked about Carter's perfidious behaviour to enquire too closely as to the source of Harry's intelligence.

'I am relieved beyond words to discover that there is no sinister hand behind these incidents. You can have no notion how fearful

244

I have been for Eloise's safety. In spite of my best efforts I am not satisfied that she always heeds my dictate and rides out with a groom. But short of forbidding her to ride at all, which is a punishment I could not bring myself to inflict upon her, I did not see how I can make her comprehend the dangers without unnecessarily alarming her. However,' he continued, bestowing a benevolent smile upon his neighbours, 'it would appear that I can now rest easy, at least on that score.'

'Indeed!' said Harry, his expression amused as he imagined anyone, even her beloved father, managing to prevent Eloise from doing precisely as she pleased.

'I am furious with Carter for using that girl so contemptibly,' continued Mr Hamilton, anger radiating from his eyes as the enormity of his under-butler's crime registered with him. 'I have been most grievously deceived in respect of his character.'

'Quite so, George,' agreed Sir Henry in a placating tone, 'but what shall you do about it?'

'Speak to him myself and discover the truth,' said Mr Hamilton emphatically. 'He does, I suppose, deserve the opportunity to explain himself. But it is clear that he had no real intention of marrying the girl for his reasons in that respect simply do not ring true. It is well known that I have no objection to my staff marrying.'

'Perhaps you should insist that he does the right thing by the girl now?' suggested Harry laconically.

'I would not inflict such a callous brute on the child, not for any consideration. No,' said Mr Hamilton, standing and pulling himself up to his full height, the expression of grim determination on his face one that Harry had never seen there before but which, he suspected, his business associates must have learned to look upon with foreboding, 'if what you tell me is true, and believe me I shall discover for myself whether or not it is, then Carter will lose his position and will be turned out of my house within the hour with no character.'

'Quite right too!' agreed Sir Henry.

'And then I must speak with Farthingay. I shall be vexed if I discover that he knew of this relationship and covered it up for he at least I supposed to be entirely trustworthy.'

'It is possible that he remains in ignorance of it.'

'True,' conceded Mr Hamilton, 'but it is not likely. That is why I trusted him with the delicate task of investigating the matter and accepted his findings without question. I realize now that I should have taken more of an interest myself.'

'In your position I — '

A knock at the door prevented Sir Henry from completing his reflection. Rogers, the Benson-Smythe butler, entered the room, his attitude as stately as ever but his demeanour disconcertingly grave.

'Your pardon for the interruption, Sir Henry, but Jacobs is here from Staverley and desires an immediate audience with Mr Hamilton.'

The three gentlemen exchanged an expression of concern. 'What the devil? All right, Rogers, have him step in at once.'

Jacobs entered the room in a state of considerable agitation. He was clad in his workday attire and looked strangely out of place in such elegant surroundings. He held his cap in his hands and screwed it nervously into a tight ball as he faced the three expectant faces.

'Your pardon, gentlemen,' he said breathlessly, 'but I lost not a moment in coming to impart distressing tidings. Molly has just returned to the stable yard.' He eyed his audience, his agitation escalating. 'Alone.'

'What!'

'Miss Hamilton must have taken her out whilst I, and the others, were in the lower paddock schooling the youngsters, as we are wont to do at this time every day.'

'Dear God!' cried Mr Hamilton, sinking into a chair and clutching his head in his hands, his shocked countenance devoid of all colour. 'It is as I have feared all along; she has been abducted!'

Harry patted his shoulder, but felt scarcely more in control than Mr Hamilton himself and did not trust himself to speak.

'I suppose she was riding alone,' said Sir Henry, already anticipating the answer he would receive.

'Ay, sir, and she was riding bareback as well. Molly returned with no saddle on her and none is missing from the tack-room.'

The door opened to admit James Benson-Smythe, who had come to discover what all the commotion was about. Harry swiftly enlightened him.

'Are you sure there is no possibility that Eloise was riding with anyone else?' asked Harry, clutching at straws. 'Could a visitor, perhaps, have called and invited her to ride out?'

'It is hardly likely, Harry,' put in Sir Henry. 'Not if she was riding bareback for that would mean that she would be clad in Thomas's clothes. She might feel at leisure to ride dressed in such a manner alone but even she would hardly do so in company.'

'True.'

'Actually, sir,' put in Jacobs, 'I sent one of the lads back to the yard to fetch a schooling whip and he remarked that he did observe a visitor leaving, but he was alone.'

'Who was it?' asked three voices in unison.

'The lad could not be sure. He only saw the gentleman for a second and that was from behind. But it was a gentleman, apparently, and he was astride a fine-looking chestnut hunter.'

'Craven!' James's voice surprised them all; the more so since he spoke the one word with such menace.

'What is it, James? Why do you sound so fearful? If Craven was in the vicinity we must make contact with him at once. It is possible that he may have news of Eloise.' Harry spoke with renewed hope and unmistakable urgency.

'That will not be necessary,' said James, his voice more decisive than either his father or brother had known it to be for many a long day. 'I think I know who has Eloise and where she will be. Harry, come with me, if you will.' Mr Hamilton clambered to his feet, intent upon joining their party. 'No, sir,' continued James, staying him with his hand, 'I suggest you remain here, we shall not be gone for long and I feel confident that we will return with your daughter unharmed. I will explain it all to you then.'

'Very well, James, I trust you to know what you are about, but if anything happens to my beloved girl — if anyone dares to lay so much as one finger on her person then, by all I hold most dear, I shall expend every last guinea I possess in exacting revenge.' He thumped his fist on a nearby table, oversetting a vase of flowers but not seeming to notice. 'There is nothing, nothing I tell you, that means more to me than Eloise.' His voice broke and he took a moment to bring himself under control. 'I give you due warning — '

But Harry and James, having no time to listen to his warning, or the likely consequences for the perpetrators of this outrage, were already gone.

'Where are we bound for?' asked Harry, striding towards the stables at his brother's side.

'Esher Castle,' said James, already mounting his horse. 'Come, we must make haste. I believe Craven has Eloise and I think I know where he has taken her. Whether we can keep my promise to George however, and return her unharmed is altogether another matter. Time is of the essence if we are to stand any chance of success.'

'I thought the whole of the Esher family were now in town,' shouted Harry, as he and James left the yard at a flat out canter, heading in the direction of the castle.

'They are and that is why Richard would be able to take Eloise there without fear of detection.'

'But the servants?'

'Will know nothing about it,' said James with grim authority.

'But what can he hope to gain by abducting Eloise?'

'I cannot explain now, Harry. Let's save our energy by not talking unnecessarily and concentrate on getting there as quickly as we can. It could make all the difference to Eloise's safety.' James turned in his saddle and briefly faced his brother, his features arranged in a rigid mask of determination. 'Richard has a depraved side to his nature which, for the most part, he manages to keep under control, but in his current state of desperation I would not put anything past him.'

'Dear God!' The grim authority beneath his brother's quietly spoken words made Harry wonder anew just what it was Craven and his brother were caught up in. 'Whatever else happens, James, we must save Eloise.'

'We are almost there now.'

Upon reaching the vicinity of Esher Castle James slowed his sweating horse to a walk and indicated to Harry that they should avoid the main driveway. Instead he led his brother on a circuitous route until they came to a large, unkempt building — the dowager house. Harry supposed — some distance from the castle itself. James dismounted and Harry followed suit. They tied their horses to a nearby tree, approached the building on silent feet and listened at the door for several tension-filled minutes but the only sound they could detect in an otherwise peaceful setting was that of birdsong.

'If he has got her then you can be assured that this is the place where he will have brought her,' said James, his tone still full of authority.

'How do we discover if he has?'

'There are two of us; he will not have anyone else with him yet.' Harry's expression at his brother's exacting knowledge of the situation was incredulous. Observing it, James smiled briefly. 'Just trust me,' he said, gently turning the handle to the main door, 'and pray we are not too late.'

The door swung open on rusty hinges, making an inordinate amount of noise, which could only act as an early warning of their arrival to anyone who might be inside. So much for stealth, thought Harry wryly, following closely in his brother's footsteps. James moved with assured confidence through the house, which was clearly not in use. It was obvious that James was no stranger here; especially since he dismissed the downstairs rooms without going to the trouble of even peering into them. Only Harry's concern for Eloise exceeded his burning curiosity about his brother's activities, but explanations would have to wait.

Reaching the upper floor of the house James headed for the principal bedroom and without hesitation opened the door. He stopped dead in his tracks, causing Harry to cannon into his back, as he took in the scene that greeted him. Eloise was lying on the bed, bound hand and foot, a gag covering her mouth. Richard Craven sat in a chair beside her, a smile of such evil intent twisting his lips as to make Harry doubt his sanity and feel truly fearful, especially since he held a pistol in his hand which he was pointing directly at James.

'You have broken the code,' he said, his tone as dead as his expressionless eyes. 'Such treachery can have only one outcome and you are well aware what that must be.' He raised the gun a fraction higher and steadied his aim.

'You cannot imagine I would stand by and allow you to get away with this,' responded James, his voice gratifyingly even, displaying none of the terror that the combination of Richard's lethal expression and the sight of that pistol levelled at him in a hand that did not shake must surely have engendered. 'You have gone too far this time.'

'Why? She is but the daughter of a Cit,' he responded with dismissive contempt, his eyes never once leaving James and Harry. 'A Cit moreover, who has most monstrously cheated me and upon whom I intend to exact revenge. It will be our most glorious escapade yet.'

'No, Richard,' said James emphatically, taking a step forwards, 'there are boundaries which must not be crossed, no matter what the provocation. Let her go.'

'I think not,' responded Craven with infuriating calm, his finger tightening upon the trigger. 'It is you who has forgotten about boundaries, and loyalties, by betraying the organization.'

'I will not be a party to abduction: or worse.'

'Then you are a bigger fool than I took you for.'

Richard, his eyes unblinking and expression still devoid of all emotion, pulled the trigger. As he did so two things happened in quick succession. Eloise lifted her bound legs and barrelled them into Richard's side with all the strength she could muster, whilst Harry, sensing that Richard really did intend to fire the gun, pushed his brother roughly out of its path.

The bullet hit Harry on the upper left-hand side of his chest. He crumpled slowly to the floor, an expression of mild surprise on his face, as his form absorbed the full impact of the shot. A pool of blood was already forming beneath his inert form when consciousness left him.

13

For what seemed like an eternity no one moved, as horror and shock followed close on the heels of Richard's action. Then everything happened at once. With barely a glance at the prostrate Harry, and seeming not to care whether or not he had killed the heir to one of the foremost families in the vicinity, Richard pushed past James and fled the room. Eloise, squirming frantically on the bed, caught James's attention. He cut her bonds with a dagger he produced from about his person and immediately turned his attention to his unconscious brother.

'He lives!' he said to Eloise, his voice thick with emotion. 'I think the bullet has passed straight through his shoulder.'

'Thank God!'

Eloise's voice was as unsteady as James's due to a combination of the crude gag which she had only just managed to remove and delayed shock at seeing her dearest friend so brutally shot down. She was on her knees beside Harry in a trice, cradling his head as James cut away his coat, the better to examine his wound. There was a worrying amount of blood and Eloise could only pray that James was right in his assertion that the bullet had passed straight through without causing a fatal injury. Unused to dealing with such matters it seemed to Eloise that Harry's wound was worryingly close to the vicinity of his heart and anyway, surely no one could be expected to survive such a colossal loss of blood?

'It is as I supposed,' said James, his voice steadier now. 'If we can stop the bleeding I think he will survive.'

'Strip the sheets from the bed, James,' suggested Eloise, 'and perhaps we can use them to staunch the flow.'

James did as she asked with commendable speed and between them they packed the wound, binding it tightly to prevent unnecessary seepage.

'Ride for the apothecary,' said Eloise, stroking Harry's hair out of his eyes, gazing upon his familiar face, which was now unnaturally grey and set in a deathlike mask, simultaneously willing some of her own strength into him.

'I cannot leave you alone with him; Craven might come back.'

'I think not, but in any event it is a chance we must take if we are to save Harry. Leave your dagger with me. You may rest assured that if he does return I shall not hesitate to use it. Go now!' she ordered, when James still hesitated. 'Harry's life could depend upon your speed. And send word to your father too: he should be here.'

Alone with the unconscious Harry and willing herself to remain calm, Eloise had ample opportunity to ruminate upon her perilous situation. She was less sure than she had led James to believe about Richard's intentions but her own safety was a secondary consideration when compared to saving Harry's life. He had come here with the intention of saving her and she must now return that favour. She cursed her wilful independence in riding out alone and for the first time acknowledged that her father's anxieties for her welfare had been well-founded, even though he could never have imagined that the danger would emanate from Lord Craven.

So anxious had she been to shake off the crippling restrictions which had governed her every movement whilst in town that she had chosen to ride Molly bareback, the better to chase hell for leather across the heath and rid herself of their shackling influence.

'Had I been riding with a saddle,' she explained aloud to the motionless Harry, 'I would have been better able to remain mounted when Molly unexpectedly shied at what I at first supposed to be a squirrel. It was only when she deposited me on the ground and I attempted to sit up and assess the damage that I realized someone had been lying in wait for me behind a tree: someone must have called at the house and discovered that I was riding out and knew the route I was likely to take: someone had deliberately caused poor Molly to shy. I became conscious that someone was standing over me when my eyes were drawn to a pair of shiny Hessians. I knew at once that Richard Craven was the owner of those boots, but must confess to being terribly dense for it took a moment for me to appreciate that my fall had been deliberately contrived.

'I shook my head to clear my confusion and actually grinned at him, if you please,' Eloise said to Harry, full of indignation at her naivety, 'and told him that he had startled me, which of course, I realize now, was precisely his intention. And then he waved a crop at Molly in the most threatening manner imaginable and sent her prancing off a safe distance away. That was most unnecessary and I told him as much, in no uncertain terms. And then, well,' — Eloise paused, attempting to regain control of her emotions before continuing — 'well, then he had the temerity to strike me quite harshly and order me to be silent.

'I was not about to accept that, as you can imagine, but before I could do anything about it Jacob came to my rescue and threw himself at Richard,' she said with satisfaction. 'Jacob has never much cared for Richard and I must own now that he is a very good judge of character indeed! Anyway, he managed to clench his teeth around Richard's calf and keep them there. Richard cursed and kicked out at him most savagely. Jacob, the poor darling, was obviously hurt and was eventually obliged to let go. That gave Richard the opportunity to pick me up and carry me a short distance to where a closed carriage was waiting. He dumped me most roughly inside but by then Jacob had recovered and came at Richard again. The fiend aimed another harsh kick at his ribs. Howling with pain, poor Jacob still attempted to come to my rescue, growling at Richard and trying to attack him as he tied my hands and made to drive away. Jacob was disabled by his injuries and quite unequal to the task of jumping high enough to reach Richard. The last thing I observed, before my eyes were roughly covered with a blindfold, was my faithful Jacob limping behind the carriage, determined not to let me out of his sight.

'Well aware by now that I was in serious trouble, I at first felt anger at Richard's callous treatment of my dog rather than fear for my own safety. I had received a sharp knock on the head when I fell from Molly and I can only surmise that Richard's rough treatment of me exacerbated that injury, causing me to pass out. When I came round again I was bound hand and foot, lying on that cursed bed. Richard was sitting beside me, watching me quite calmly as he bathed and bound his injured calf. It was only then, as I observed the look of malignity and eerie determination in his eyes, that I fully appreciated the danger of my situation and became truly afraid.

'Not that I allowed my fear to show, of course: I was not prepared to offer him that satisfaction. Richard started to talk to me, gently and politely, wishing to be assured that I was as comfortable as the circumstances would permit, if you can credit it,' said Eloise indignantly, outrage causing her voice to rise. 'He sounded almost as though he was in a drawing-room conversing civilly about something as inconsequential as the weather. Anyway, Harry, as you can doubtless imagine, I was unsure quite how I was expected to react to him; given the fact that I was not only tightly bound but gagged as well and so

I made do with putting up my chin as haughtily as I could manage, attempting to disguise my fear and anger at his treatment of Jacob and me behind a defiant gesture, but it did me little good and as far as I could tell I only succeeded in amusing him.'

Eloise fell momentarily silent. She ran her hand across Harry's forehead, which was covered in perspiration and as cold as the grave. Panic caught in her throat and she racked her brains, trying to remember exactly what actions one was supposed to take in such circumstances. It was hardly a situation that occurred every day but common sense told her that she must, at the very least, attempt to keep Harry warm. She reached out towards the bed with one arm, conscious of the fact that she must not move Harry and risk his wound opening up again. At last her fingers connected with the edge of the counterpane and she dragged it towards her, draping it around Harry's inert form. Still he did not move but at least she could detect no signs of fresh blood seeping from his shoulder. Heartened by this small victory she continued to talk to him, not imagining that he could hear her but taking comfort from the sound of her own voice in what was otherwise a perilously surreal situation.

'You really did misunderstand the situation

in the boathouse, Harry,' she told him with mock severity, 'and if you had not reacted so pompously I would have told you the truth of it all. Richard was telling me of his involvement with my father's diamond mine, complaining that Papa has cheated him by not paying him as much as he considers to be his due. Of course, I told him that I was powerless to intervene and, anyway, privately I could not bring myself to believe that Papa would behave so shamefully. Richard kissed me, I think, because he assumed that such attentions would persuade me to see things from his point of view.' Eloise managed a small giggle. 'He must have considered that being kissed by a future duke would be all that was necessary to bring me about.

'Well, let me tell you, Harry, that had you continued to observe us through the window you would have seen that I pushed him away from me and gave him a good piece of my mind into the bargain. He was very shocked at my reaction but before he could respond to it you intervened.

'I did not much care for being kissed like that; I did not feel at all as I had always thought I would when kissed for the first time. I would never admit as much if you could hear me, Harry, but your kiss made me feel very different indeed. It was exceedingly pleasant and made me quite giddy. Lady Hannah is to be envied,' she added, on a wistful note. 'I must own that I do not much care for your choice of wife, Harry, she is a self-centred scatterbrain and not at all worthy of you, but I do understand why you offered for her and, for your sake, I will make a greater effort in future to look upon her kindly,' she promised generously. 'We will, after all, be neighbours once you are wed.

'Anyway, Harry,' she said, her tone businesslike once again, 'Richard is very resentful and feels he has been greatly wronged. I suspect that he intended to keep me here until my father paid him what he considers is due to him. How he imagines he will get away with it I cannot conceive, and that must have been apparent from the expression in my eyes, since he merely smirked, most offensively, and remarked that one abduction more or less was neither here nor there. He knew all about the poor girls who had gone missing, it would seem. Thomas told him about our maid, and about Mary, too, and he had already gained intelligence of Meg's plight from, of all people, Jem. You were right to suggest that Jem was responsible, Harry. Richard couldn't resist telling me that he found out about it by accident when he left his horse in the care of a friend of Jem's, a groom at the coaching inn in the village, and overheard Jem boasting of his exploits; about how he had given poor Meg the fright of her life, and what good sport it had been.' Eloise puffed out her cheeks in disgust. 'That is just the sort of depraved behaviour Richard would remember and exploit for his own ends.

'How anxious poor Papa must be about me now: I do so hope that James gets to him quickly and reassures him as to my safety. It is entirely thanks to you and James that I am safe, of course, and I shall never be able to repay you for your chivalrous behaviour. You are my hero, Harry, and I love you to distraction.'

She leaned over and placed a delicate kiss on his forehead which, she noticed, was now disproportionately warm. Was that a good sign? She was unsure. And how long had James been gone? It seemed like forever. Surely he should have returned by now? Eloise could only pray that Richard had not lain in wait for him: he had seemed so determined to punish James for some breach of faith but surely the shooting of Harry — the enormity of his crime — would have pushed everything out of Richard's head except escape?

Eloise gazed once more upon Harry's

chalk-white countenance and her spirits plummeted. This was all her fault. If only she had listened to her father — and to Harry too, for that matter — and taken her groom with her, none of this would have happened and she and Jacob would be safely back at Staverley now, free from injury; Harry would be as healthy and robust as ever, teasing her about something of inconsequence and, undoubtedly, upbraiding her for her want of propriety. How desirable and unattainable that situation now appeared, she thought with a regretful sigh.

'I am so sorry to have caused you all this trouble, Harry,' she said softly, stroking his hair and allowing the love she felt for this sophisticated rogue to course through her unchecked. 'If I had only known what danger I was getting you into I would never, for a moment, have gone out alone. You warned me, as well, did you not, Harry? You warned me to be wary when in Richard's presence and I just dismissed your concerns, assuming that you were being over-protective, as usual. I should have known better,' she graciously conceded.

Harry remained motionless, his head still resting in Eloise's lap, his breath rasping unevenly in his throat. Anxiety caused her to become incautious and suddenly, quite without understanding why she did it, she started to rail against him.

'Harry Benson-Smythe, don't do this to me! When I think of all the times we have had together, all the things we have been to one another, I am quite beside myself at the thought of losing you.' She paused in her ranting and brushed a tear impatiently from her cheek. 'Harry, if you dare to die on me I shall personally bring you back to life for the sole purpose of killing you all over again. Harry, I warn you — '

Eloise gasped. So swiftly she had no time to take in what was happening, Harry's good arm circled her waist and pulled her towards him.

'Tell me again that bit about loving me?' he requested in a weak voice.

'Harry, you're awake! How do you feel? Does it hurt terribly?'

'It was almost worth being shot just to hear you so full of remorse, little brat.'

'Harry, you brute! You mean you were awake all the while and allowed me to run on so. How could you?'

'It was irresistible; especially when you confessed that you enjoyed being kissed by me.'

'That was when I thought you were about to die,' she explained reasonably.

Harry managed a low chuckle, which turned into a hollow cough. 'I am still very frail,' he pointed out, 'and any shock is likely to set me back.'

'Humph! I should have known that a mere bullet would never be sufficient to do away with you. Harry, you are no gentleman!'

This time Harry's chuckle was decidedly wicked. 'So you have noticed at last.'

The arm about her waist tightened and in response her head lowered towards his, seemingly of its own volition. His eyes were alight with an emotion Eloise could not identify and, as his lips slowly covered hers, she soon gave up any attempt to do so. Instead she surrendered herself to new-found pleasures; to the meltingly passionate nature of his kiss; impossible to resist given the very impossibility of it ever occurring just minutes before. Desire overwhelmed reason and Eloise returned his kiss with fervour. Pleasure spangled through her entire body in response to the exotic cadence of his lips working upon hers. Fire lanced through her veins and an explosive amalgamation of desire and awakening passion drove her to the point of insanity, even as a dizzying sense of shock played havoc with turbulent emotions embroiled in the heady passion of first love.

First love for a man who was already engaged to another lady.

In an erotic daze Eloise reluctantly lifted her lips from Harry's, just as the door opened and a white-faced Sir Henry stepped through it. He had, Eloise realized with some embarrassment, observed their embrace, but in the light of recent events that hardly seemed important.

'Hello, Father,' said Harry, with a weak grin.

'He is conscious,' explained Eloise, unnecessarily.

'Thank the Lord!' said Sir Henry and James in unison.

Mr Hamilton walked into the room on the other gentlemen's heels and reached out to his daughter.

'Ella, my love, thank God you are safe!'

'I am unharmed, Papa,' she assured him with a smile, 'but I cannot move for fear of jolting Harry.'

As the apothecary arrived at that moment Eloise was gently relieved of her burden. The doctor congratulated James and Eloise on their quick-thinking which, he gravely assured them, had almost certainly saved Harry's life. Had they been slower in binding his wound he could well have bled to death. This prospect had a sobering effect upon the whole party.

With his wound now properly dressed Harry was supported to his father's carriage by James and Sir Henry himself.

'Let us make for Staverley, if you please, George,' suggested Sir Henry. 'We need to fully understand what has happened and, more to the point why, before we expose Harry's condition to his mother's scrutiny.'

'Absolutely,' agreed Mr Hamilton, lifting his daughter bodily into his own conveyance and insisting upon covering her legs with a rug, since he was sure she must be suffering from shock. 'Staverley is closer than Boscombe Hall and so Harry will not be exposed to quite so much jostling in the carriage. Besides, I myself require a few answers,' he said, his face set in an unusually grim line.

'Where is Jacob, Papa?' asked Eloise. 'Did he return home?'

Before Mr Hamilton could answer, a pathetic whining drew the attention of the party to the garden behind the dowager house. Jacob was lying there, trying desperately to get to his feet but falling down again with each attempt. Jacobs, who was driving Mr Hamilton's carriage, immediately jumped down and went to the dog's aid. Eloise was prevented by her father from doing likewise, and looked on instead with anxious concern.

'His ribs are damaged but nothing appears to be broken,' Jacobs assured her, as he ran his hand gently over Jacob's body, expertly assessing the damage. 'If I just lift him into the carriage we can attend to him at home.'

'Richard kicked him,' said Eloise, fury blazing from her eyes.

She then burst into a noisy bout of tears: tears prompted by anger, delayed shock and dismay at the condition of her dog.

14

Upon arrival at Staverley, Harry was assisted into the drawing-room and settled in the most commodious of chairs beside the fire: Jacob was taken to the stables to be thoroughly examined by his namesake and Eloise was despatched to her chamber by her father, with the solicitous request that she rest and restore her strength before bathing and changing her attire.

Upon being assured by Harry that he was quite comfortable and, although pale and light-headed, as anxious as his father was to hear James's explanation, Sir Henry turned to his younger son and spoke with surprising gentleness.

'I think it is time you informed us about whatever it is you have become entangled with, James.'

'Indeed, Father, I have wanted to for a long time now, but was prevented by an oath of secrecy from so doing.' He stood, back towards the blazing fire, hands clasped behind him, looking unconsciously grim yet more like his old self than he had done for weeks. 'When Richard and I were on our

Grand Tour we separated for a few weeks in order that he might make a call upon acquaintances in Seville. He needed to make that call alone, but I was able to meet up with a few people I knew who were already in the area and was happy to wait for him to rejoin me.

'Richard had informed me that he intended to call upon the Duque de Sanchez, with whom his family were on the most intimate of terms. The *duque* is from an established family of impeccable lineage quite equal to Richard's own. He has just one child: a daughter, Isabella, who is heir to his considerable fortune. Richard had persuaded himself that he was genuinely in love with the girl and that a union between the two families could only be looked upon with favour from both sides. Richard was sufficiently arrogant to never once suppose that the *duque* would raise any objections to the match.

'Richard's family, I should explain, was by this time in the most terrible straits financially and an alliance with Isabella would have put everything right at a stroke. Richard was trying very hard then to do the right thing and not give way to the weakness for games of chance that runs in his family and which can be held responsible in the greater part for many of their difficulties; the current duke, as you probably know, Father, is a frequent inhabitant of the gaming halls.'

Sir Henry nodded. 'His penchant for hazard is well enough known and his name is frequently to be seen in the book at Whites. It is said that the more obscure the wager being offered, the keener the duke is to take it on, regardless of the odds.'

'Exactly so, but Richard was anxious to put matters right. At the time family honour mattered to him more than anything and he was able to suppress the baser side of his own nature in favour of scheming to right their circumstances. He was very proud of his plan to restore the family's fortunes through marriage: and very taken with it too. He did not doubt for a moment that his suit would be looked upon favourably.'

James paused, took a generous sip from his glass of Madeira and kicked absently at a log that had fallen into the grate as he gathered his thoughts. 'When Richard returned to join me in Seville I knew at once that things had not gone as he had planned. He got thoroughly foxed that night and told me it all. Sure enough, not only had the *duque* turned him down but he had not even taken the trouble to do so politely. He was not prepared to sacrifice his beloved daughter on the altar of such an impecunious suitor; one moreover whom he did not consider to be her social equal. It was that more than anything else that enraged Richard, I think. He has always set great store by his social position and did not think to have a foreigner question it.

'He had confidently expected that his impeccable breeding would be more than enough to overcome any objections that the *duque* might harbour, especially since he was persuaded that Isabella herself had feelings for him. But the *duque* was not prepared to listen to Richard's arguments in favour of the match, his daughter would not be applied to for her opinion, would not dare to defy her father's wishes and Richard was left feeling slighted and humiliated.

'The whole experience changed him and it was then, I think, that he started to give way to the instincts he'd thus far fought so valiantly to suppress. We chanced, shortly after that, to meet Lord Naismith in Portugal — '

'That unconscionable rogue!' put in Harry.

'Yes but Richard in particular was in no mood to mind his sullied reputation. He introduced us to what we then thought was good living; got us some good games of cards and involved us with a rather disreputable set. Richard lost heavily and borrowed from Naismith; as did I.'

'James, why did you allow yourself to be beholden to that knave?' asked Sir Henry, not unkindly. 'You could have applied to me for more funds.'

James looked uncomfortable. 'I felt that I had already imposed enough, Father. Besides, I naturally thought my luck would soon change. And it did: Richard was not so fortunate. Anyway Naismith, in a fit of generosity I was unable to explain at the time, tore up our vowels but said that when we returned to England he would introduce us to some good sport. That,' said James, looking more distressed than ever, 'is when I should have insisted upon repaying him. Instead I unwittingly placed myself at his mercy.'

'Who is this Naismith?' asked Mr Hamilton. 'I know his name, of course, but not why it is looked upon with such dishonour.'

'He is of Irish descent,' said Sir Henry. 'A relation by marriage to the Whartons.'

'Ah, now I understand!' This from Harry. 'The Medmenham Monks,' he added quietly. When Mr Hamilton still looked confused, Harry elucidated. 'The Irish Hell Fire Clubs that so flourished a hundred years ago were started by them.'

'Good God!' cried Mr Hamilton in genuine surprise. 'Does that sort of thing still go on?'

'I was not to know it at the time,' said James defensively, 'but yes, sir, it does. At first nothing terrible happened. He introduced us to a set that were wild, it's true, but nothing too extreme. We met in private, gambled, drank to excess, dreamt up bizarre initiation ceremonies and enjoyed the society of muslins rather more brutally and publicly than sits comfortably with me. But still, they were well enough rewarded for their efforts and did not appear to take exception to the treatment meted out.'

'Which people were involved, James?' asked Sir Henry.

James named several notable persons from within the *ton*, causing Sir Henry and Harry to exchange a surprised glance. 'Things got more complicated when Naismith went abroad again and Richard became the self-appointed head of our set. He decreed that we would meet quarterly and no excuses for absenting ourselves would be accepted. We are also sworn to secrecy and the one person who attempted to abuse that vow recently met with an unfortunate accident.' James shuddered. 'Richard has never attempted to deny that he was responsible for the poor man's misfortune, implying that we had given our word as gentlemen to keep the activities of our society secret and that anyone base enough to renege on that vow deserved all he got.

'Richard researched the history of the whole Hell Fire organization and became obsessed with the society launched by François Rabelais. You know,' he continued, in response to the blank looks that greeted this statement, 'the wayward French priest, who in 1535 launched a mixed-sex community with the slogan, 'Do What You Will'. He has read everything that has been published about the man and has copied him more and more precisely as the months have progressed, growing bolder all the while and exhorting us to emulate his example.'

'So the Hell Fire Clubs really still exist,' breathed Sir Henry in a daze voice. 'Dear God, James, what have you got yourself into?'

James had the grace to look thoroughly ashamed. 'In my own defence I must own that I was in the thick of it before I realized what was happening. Richard, you must understand, was still nursing his grievances, which appeared to multiply daily, and was becoming more and more debauched. When he suggested wilder, increasingly depraved activities at our meetings, I wanted to call a halt to it and get out.'

'Then why did you not?' asked Harry.

'Because I had given my word as a

gentleman,' said James, in torment. 'It was tearing me apart but I did not know what else I could do. I know one or two of the others felt as I did, but when they saw what happened to Sutton when he tried to distance himself from the activities we all lost the heart to rebel.' He paused, his expression reflective. 'I suppose we thought it would run its course and we would eventually be able to escape honourably.'

'Oh, James!' sighed Sir Henry.

'I was wrong to assume that our rituals would lose their appeal for Richard: in fact it turned out to be quite the reverse. The modish occultism he dabbled in became wicked and overtly harmful: ill-informed black magic and devil worship, if you will. We indulged in wild orgies at secluded hunting lodges; fortified ourselves with hot scaltheen; toasted Satan; invented sinister names for one another and even, God help us, indulged in mock crucifixions.'

'How did you know that Craven had taken my Eloise to his dowager house?' asked Mr Hamilton, his disgust at James's behaviour hidden behind the anger which swirled through him still at the treatment meted out to his daughter.

'Because our quarterly meeting was due to take place there tomorrow,' responded James with transparent honesty. 'The rest of the family have gone up to town for the season and Richard said we would have been able to meet there without fear of detection.'

'How would that meeting have involved her?'

James hung his head. 'I do not know precisely what Richard had in mind, but I can guess. He boasted that this meeting would leave everything that had gone before it in the shade and raise our activities to a new level. I was wary of his burning passion for such extreme pleasures and argued with him about it, advising caution, but he paid not the slightest heed to me.'

'I observed you at Staverley engaged in a lively conversation with him,' remarked Harry.

'Yes.' James thumped his fist against the mantelpiece in frustration. 'I knew he was out of control, but just did not know what I ought to do about it. He told me we had never used a lady of quality against her will before and that, when we got away with it, it would be the ultimate testament to our power. I did not know at the time that he had Eloise in mind but, in any event, tried to dissuade him from his purpose. I was feeling more than uncomfortable about the whole thing, knowing that we were fast overstepping all bounds of human decency.'

'That is something of an understatement,' said Mr Hamilton, his lips clenched tight in anger.

'I can but apologize, sir, and assure you once again that I did not know it was Eloise he had in mind.' James paused and looked Mr Hamilton directly in the eye. 'You have my word on that. I can, in retrospect, see that if it was revenge against you that he was seeking then, to a mind warped by perceived injustices, it would be the ultimate way for him to go about it. Striking at Eloise would be a worse punishment than striking your own person.'

'Dear God! James, are you suggesting that his purpose was not merely to blackmail me?'

'It is the only explanation that makes any sense.'

'I thank you, James, for at least coming to your senses and rescuing her before any lasting harm was done,' said Mr Hamilton.

'You must understand, sir, that had I attended the meeting tomorrow and found Eloise being held captive there I would not have countenanced that. Somehow I would have found the strength to overcome Richard, and any of the others who would follow his lead.'

'Thank you,' grunted Mr Hamilton,

choked with emotion.

'You are out of it now,' said Sir Henry, placing a reassuring hand on his son's shoulder. 'Richard will not risk showing his face and you can assume yourselves released from your vow.'

'I thank God for it! I shall make a point of contacting the others and telling them that it is at an end.'

'But not why,' put in Harry. 'If we own what happened to Eloise, her reputation, even though she was not at fault, will be as nothing.'

'True,' agreed Mr Hamilton reflectively. 'But what of your wound, Harry, you cannot surely mean to allow it to pass without seeking vengeance?'

'I am hardly in a position to do anything about it at present,' said Harry ruefully, indicating the sling that held his left arm in place. 'But I shall certainly devise a way to get even with Craven in the fullness of time, without revealing Eloise's part in the matter. In the meantime I think it would be prudent to attribute my injury to an accident on horseback.' Harry laughed briefly: a sound that conveyed little humour. 'Sampson spends half of his life trying to dislodge me from his back so it will come as no surprise to anyone to learn that he has at last succeeded in his endeavours.'

The three gentlemen listening to Harry nodded their agreement.

'What do you suppose Craven will do now?' asked Sir Henry.

'I would not like to begin to guess at that one,' said Harry, his face pale and drawn, his strength clearly spent. 'But when he has had time to consider the matter he will doubtless reach the same conclusion as us in that we can hardly call him to account without compromising Eloise.'

'Well, we may not be able to do anything about his ill-treatment of my daughter, but I can most certainly bring his involvement in my business affairs to an end,' said Mr Hamilton with determination. 'And that is precisely what I intend to do.'

'I feel assured that you did not deal in any way dishonourably with him,' said Harry, 'but, if you have no objection, I should like to satisfy my curiosity by hearing just what happened between you and why he should suppose himself to be ill-used.'

'And you shall hear my explanation,' responded Mr Hamilton. 'When Thomas first suggested to me that Lord Craven might be just the person I sought to introduce the backers I required for my scheme I could see at once the sense of it, but before we came to an agreement I told him in detail what my intentions were.

'The mine, you see, was being sloppily run: there was widespread theft of loose stones as they were being extracted from the ground. That in itself was difficult to control because the stones come from deposits that are to be found at the confluence of the Orange and Vaal Rivers in earth found wide distances away from the river source: a practice known as dry digging. My first resolve was to tighten up procedures to avoid unnecessary pilfering. I have made some progress in that respect but intend, in the fullness of time, to send my own man to the mine to take personal control of security. The answer possibly lies in improving the living conditions of the workers, which are just about as basic as you can imagine: make conditions in my mine better than in any other, encouraging workers' loyalty and negating their requirement to steal from me.'

'Negate human greed?' queried Harry. 'Call me a cynic, George, but — '

'I am not entirely without wits,' responded Mr Hamilton, with a smile that softened his sharp retort, 'and whoever I choose for the position will have his work cut out. Be that as it may, Granger, the manager of the mine, is convinced it represents the opportunity of a lifetime, and I tend to agree with him — but only if we can put the operation back on a firm footing. Granger is articulate and personable and has a firm knowledge of the business, having lived in Africa for all his adult life. Gold and diamond fever is currently sweeping the African continent; greed is causing men to lose their heads and I understand the Prime Minister is considering sending troops to the region to maintain order and protect British interests. It is, without doubt, a decidedly risky venture but I've had a good feeling about this one from the outset.'

'Granger approached you direct?' asked Harry in surprise. Initially lapsing in and out of consciousness whilst Eloise chattered recklessly away to him, he had entirely recovered his wits by the time she embarked upon an explanation of Craven's conduct, but had chosen to conceal the fact from her; anxious to hear her justification for her behaviour in the boathouse. 'Craven has put the word about that the scheme was his and that *he* involved *you*.'

Mr Hamilton gave a small laugh. 'I will leave you to decide for yourselves whose account to believe,' he said acerbically. 'Mine or that of a man who is completely deranged. It is true that some initial overtures were made to one or two of Craven's peers, but Granger had the good sense to appreciate that no one in that sphere was likely to have the funds or the expertise necessary to rescue the project and so he made his way to the City, and eventually to me.

'However, as I was explaining, at present the diamonds are being mined and sold on to the many agents who are flooding the area, but I plan to do better than that. Granger knows of a diamond cutter in Amsterdam to whom we could ship the stones direct. I have a jewellery designer in mind here in London who is prepared to offer individual designs according to the wishes of his customers. The designer is well known in good society, which is why I have him in mind. I want only the best customers: those wishing to make purchases for wives and daughters — and mistresses as well for that matter: we must not forget how lucrative that line of business can be.' A polite ripple of laughter eased the tension in the room.

'We could create a reputation for exclusivity and discretion,' continued Mr Hamilton, warming to his theme, 'and soon have some of the most eminent people in the country clamouring for our designs. We could make a fortune and, at the same time, save one as well by shipping our stones direct to the cutter and having our own designer on hand, thereby keeping control of the entire operation from mining to the finished product.'

As Mr Hamilton paused to catch his breath so Harry and his father exchanged a glance that implied respect for Mr Hamilton's business acumen. He had long ago, Harry had reason to suppose, learned to suppress his resentment at the tight-knit rules governing the class system, using them instead to his advantage.

'Craven could be even more use to me in that respect, don't you see? He could not only involve the type of people I needed to make the venture a success — and you must understand that it was one of the riskiest I have yet undertaken — but could also persuade the gentlemen in his set to commission select pieces of jewellery for their ladies.'

'It sounds like a masterful scheme,' remarked Sir Henry, much impressed.

'Indeed, but you see I knew, like all things, that it would take time for the profits to start coming in. I offered Craven two alternatives: he could take a fixed stipend from the outset, or wait until the scheme was into profit and then take a percentage. There was a risk involved with the latter, since it was always possible that it could fail and, even if it did not, there would be a delay before he saw a return on his efforts since it would take time for the coffers to fill. However, I was strongly of the opinion that he should bide his time and have faith in our combined abilities to pull the scheme off and was convinced that if he exercised a little patience he would eventually reap far higher rewards. I told him as much, quite forcefully, on several occasions, for I was keen for him to make full use of the opportunity I was offering him. He ignored my advice however, and opted for a fixed stipend. Perhaps now, in view of what you've told us about his dire circumstances, James, I can understand why he did so. I did, however, warn him that he could not at a later date change his mind. When the profits started to mount I was less than surprised though, being well used by now to the ways of human nature, when he attempted to do just that.'

'But can you now break your agreement with him altogether?' asked Harry. 'Presumably you have a written contract.'

'We do indeed, but do not imagine that these things are cast in stone!' said Mr Hamilton emphatically. 'I shall have my attorney draw up the termination papers first thing tomorrow. To try and trick me out of

my own funds is foolhardy enough.' Mr
Hamilton's scowl twisted his features into a
mask of determination. 'If he took me for a
simpleton and thought me so blinded by his
title and elevated position that I could not see
what he was about then he will not be the
first young man arrogant enough to suppose
that he could manipulate me.' Mr Hamilton's
jaw tightened. 'But to attempt to involve my
beloved Eloise in his twisted attempts at
revenge is quite simply beyond the pale and I
will not rest until I have wrested all the
revenge that is within my power.'

He stood to pace the room, his expression
reflective. 'The withdrawal of the finance
which he is undoubtedly relying upon to keep
his creditors at bay should be a good enough
start: then we'll see what more is to be done.'

'Why did he suddenly become such a
frequent visitor to Staverley?' asked Harry.
'Were you not accustomed to having your
meetings with him in the City?'

Mr Hamilton's expression of determination
gave way to one of discomfort. 'I blame
myself for that: for that and for the
subsequent danger that Eloise become
embroiled in. You see, at Sir Graham's ball I
observed that he danced with her twice, took
her into supper, appeared to enjoy her society
and seemed much enamoured of her.'

'Surely you did not imagine — '

'That he would offer for Eloise, Harry, is that what you find so hard to conceive?' countered Mr Hamilton haughtily. 'Well, no, I own I did not think it likely, but I did, as I have already said, observe that he was much taken with her. It would be difficult, I think, to feign the pleasure he clearly derived from her company.

'Eloise, as you know, is unlikely to enjoy the diversions and corresponding attention from young men that a season would bring her way. We all know why that must be and I take full responsibility for the unfortunate circumstance of her birth.'

'Of course, George,' interposed Sir Henry, embarrassed by this public display of emotion from a pragmatic man who rarely permitted his true feelings to show. 'We did not mean to imply — '

'I love her so much,' continued Mr Hamilton, a break in his voice, 'that I foolishly encouraged Richard to frequent Staverley, making it clear that he did not need to restrict those visits to times when I was likely to be at home. You see, I thought that if he continued to pay court to my Ella she would, at least, enjoy a brief period of being admired by someone whom I then considered to be a gentleman of consequence. I also intimated to Richard, in the vaguest of manner only, of course, that if he wished to pay his addresses to her then he had my approval.'

Harry had difficulty in believing what he was hearing and suspected that his incredulity showed in his expression. That Mr Hamilton, a sharp-witted businessman who could evaluate every opportunity in the blink of an eye and exploit it to its limit, a man who did not suffer fools gladly moreover, could show such want of sense as to encourage someone of Richard's ilk to hang round Eloise's petticoats for such nebulous reasons was quite beyond his comprehension.

'Oh, Harry, I can see what you are thinking, but only consider for a moment. Eloise has a very substantial portion: far greater even than anything I felt the need to settle upon Sarah or Charlotte. You might think of it as a small effort to assuage my guilt at her illegitimacy, I suppose. Besides, it is not completely unheard of for alliances between such unlikely parties to be negotiated. And if they really liked one another and Richard was, as it appeared to me at the time, prepared to overlook her circumstances, well . . . .'

'You did what you considered to be for the best then,' said Sir Henry, unable to resist a final sidelong glance of incredulity in Harry's direction.

'And I shall continue to do so by destroying the man,' said Mr Hamilton, with quiet determination. 'His family property is mortgaged up to the hilt and I happen to know which house holds those mortgages.' In response to yet another expression of surprise on Sir Henry's face Mr Hamilton permitted himself the ghost of a smile. 'I am not quite the trusting fool that some people consider; not when it comes to matters of business in any event. I couldn't help but ask myself why someone of Craven's ilk would wish to dirty his hands by becoming so heavily involved in my scheme. Financial expediency appeared to be the only answer. I made enquires and discovered that I was in the right.'

'I see,' said Sir Henry with a slight bow in acknowledgment of his neighbour's astuteness.

'No one,' said Mr Hamilton emphatically, 'dallies with my beloved girl's affections and gets away with it.'

'Have a care, George,' cautioned Sir Henry. 'Do not act in anger. Richard's father still wields considerable power.'

'So, Henry,' countered Mr Hamilton, pulling himself up to his full height and bestowing an expression of brittle determination upon his neighbour as he considered Richard's infamous conduct, 'do I. What is more I have the means to discover who holds Craven's current vowels; his father's too. A few carefully chosen words in the right ear to the effect that the family are more than usually stretched could well find their creditors becoming less patient than has previously been their wont.'

'Richard lost a vast amount on the prize fight last month,' put in James. 'It was a last-ditch attempt to recoup his recent losses. He bet not only on the champion prevailing but also took several substantial side-wagers on his own account in respect of the length of the fight, and so forth.'

'And the champion was beaten,' said Harry.

'Yes, he was planted a facer early on,' said James, lapsing so naturally into pugilistic cant as to cause his father to smile involuntarily, 'and never recovered his ground.'

'And it was at about that time that he both started to pester me for additional funds and to pay court to Eloise,' remarked Mr Hamilton thoughtfully.

As Eloise chose that moment to enter the room, demurely clad in sprigged muslin, looking as fresh as summer and outwardly none the worse for her ordeal, the discussion of necessity came to an end.

15

The fact that Harry was powerless to do anything to redress the balance with Craven did not sit easily with him; especially when he learned that his nemesis had calmly returned to London and was participating in all the diversions society had to offer as though he had not a care in the world, apparently oblivious to the fact that he had fired a pistol at Harry with murderous intent. He must, Harry supposed, be aware that he had not been successful — nothing so momentous as the death of one of Harry's standing could be kept secret for long — but the arrogant manner in which Craven ignored his actions, confident that he could not be exposed without implicating want of propriety on Eloise's part reduced Harry to impotent anger.

James, having just left him to return to London, did not help matters by informing his brother that Craven had been at the same ball as Charlotte Hamilton only two nights previously. He had sought her out and deliberately flirted with her, much to that young lady's apparent delight. Sarah, knowing nothing of Eloise's abduction, had seemingly viewed his attentions towards Charlotte with detached interest, wise enough to appreciate that they could come to naught and preferring instead, she had confided in James, to encourage Mr Meyers' obvious interest in her sister.

Thomas, also in attendance, was ignorant as to Eloise's plight also, since Mr Hamilton had not yet been persuaded to leave his daughter's side and return to the City. Thomas, in his turn, had been in temporary residence with Sarah and nowhere near Staverley for over a sennight. Harry understood that Richard's sister, Lady Emily, had also attended the ball in question and Thomas, making no attempt to hide his growing admiration for that lady, had eyes for no one else.

Had Craven lain low for a while it was possible that Harry might have been able to overlook his behaviour, if only for Eloise's sake, but in the face of such deliberate provocation he knew now that he would gain no peace until he could devise some means of redressing the balance. He might be physically disabled but there was nothing wrong with his cognitive powers and thinking up fiendish methods of revenge was as good a method as any of passing the time. Even so he viewed his injured arm, still tightly bound in a sling, with impatience. It was a week now since the incident and although he was fast regaining his strength, thanks in no small part to his age and previously robust health, the requirement to sit idly about and wait for nature to complete the healing process was rapidly reducing Harry to a bad-tempered devil, impossible to reason with. The servants did their best to avoid him whilst his mother and Jane, unaware of the true nature of his injuries, had hastily removed themselves to London to attend to Jane's trousseau. Only Eloise refused to be browbeaten by his bad temper. She sat through his tirades during her daily visits with perfect equanimity, giving as good as she got if she decided Harry was getting above himself.

The only good thing to have come out of it all was the fact that his fiancée had been away for several days, engaged upon social activities with her aunt, and knew nothing of Harry's injury. She was, however, returning to the capital on the morrow and Harry was engaged to escort her to a ball two days later. He was unsure whether he was up to the ordeal: not the ball itself that is, where he could always take refuge in the card-room, but Lady Hannah and her gushing ways. She would be appalled when she learned of his disability and would require more details of the fictional riding accident that Harry had thus far troubled to invent.

Eloise's visits had saved Harry's sanity. Unknowingly she diverted him from plotting fiendish and ever more outlandish schemes to revenge himself upon Craven. Her guileless chatter about her daily activities engaged his complete attention. She rode decorously to Boscombe Hall, always escorted by her father, who could not be persuaded to quit her side and return to his office — a previously unthinkable state of affairs — and treated him in much the same way that she always had, sparing little sympathy for his injured condition.

The comments she had made to the supposedly unconscious Harry, her admittance to being charmed by his kiss and Harry's delirious attempt to repeat the action could not be mentioned in Mr Hamilton's presence, but hung instead in the air between them, creating a palpable tension and permanent state of heightened perception in their dealings with one another.

Eloise professed to be perfectly recovered from her ordeal and made little comment about it, other than to express the occasional regret that Richard could not be publicly exposed for the scoundrel that he was. But

Harry was not deceived. There was a pallor about her countenance, shadows beneath compelling eyes lacking in their customary sparkle, lending proof to the fact that she must be sleeping badly. Her chatter was interspersed with long stretches of silence, about which she appeared unaware, as she stared off vacantly into the distance. God forbid that she should ever discover the true nature of Craven's intent! Harry longed to protect her — from that possibility and so much more: longed to pull her against him and soothe away her concerns; inform her that he had dealt permanently with Craven and that she need never fear him again.

But he could do none of those things and his enforced inactivity, his impotent inability to redress the balance, was doing little for his peace of mind; even less for his mercurial temper.

Wondering still how best to acquaint his fiancée with the particulars of his injury and excuse himself from escorting her to the promised ball, without causing her to descend upon Boscombe Hall in a flurry of anxiety, Harry was diverted by the sound of wheels on gravel. Looking through the morning-room window his heart lightened at the unexpected sight of Eloise, demurely seated in a gig, a bundle of something he couldn't quite identify in her lap, Jacobs with the reins in his hands and, for the first time in a week, no sign of her father.

'Good morning, Harry!' she exclaimed brightly a short time later, as she entered the room and joined him. 'I can already see you are feeling much better today,' she added, as she stood on tiptoe to kiss his cheek. 'Your colour is returned to normal and you are looking quite yourself again.'

'Good morning to you, brat,' he returned, smiling softly as she ushered him back to his seat, bustling about him with perfect disregard for his grumpiness as she struggled to keep the squirming puppy in her arms in check. 'And what, pray, do we have here?' he asked dubiously, peering at the puppy which, at closer quarters, distinctly resembled Jacob.

'Ah well, that is precisely what I called to discuss with you. I have just been to call upon Squire Penfold,' she said, amusement winning out over contriteness.

'For what purpose?' asked Harry, smiling as the puppy fought against Eloise, a wriggling ball of good-natured energy desperate to carry out a closer inspection of Harry's person.

'Well, you will recall the squire's prize hunting bitch, of course.'

'Indeed,' agreed Harry, with a broad grin.

'The squire took great pains in her breeding and is justifiably proud of her lineage.'

'Yes, and she whelped a few weeks ago. The squire was anticipating a first-rate litter but unfortunately, well — '

'Jacob got there first, I assume,' said Harry, chuckling, as he observed the misfit in Eloise's arms.

'Yes, I fear so.'

Harry threw his head back and roared with laughter. 'Well done, Jacob: a dog after my own heart! But what pray did the squire have to say on the matter?'

'Well, as you can imagine, he was not best pleased, but it was pointed out to him that he was partly to blame for not taking the trouble to confine his bitch more securely. Anyway, I have calmed matters down by agreeing to find suitable homes for the litter.'

'And this is the best of them?' asked Harry dubiously, eyeing the misfit with renewed amusement and scratching his floppy ears.

'No-o, not exactly.' She swung round to face him, her eyes dancing with a merriment that caused Harry to abandon his smile and hastily avert his gaze. He needed to be on his guard with her at all times now if the growing desire, the heartfelt longing to have so much more of her than just her friendship, was to remain his own secret. 'Oh but, Harry, this one was the smallest and his brothers and sisters did not seem to care for him one jot. Whenever I observed him he was always curled up alone and I just could not bear it! I think I have found homes for the others, but this one I shall keep for myself.'

This latest example of Eloise's soft-hearted nature did little to quell the inexorable need Harry felt for her, but he disciplined himself to concentrate his mind on the less frustrating matter of misfit puppies and hid the salacious nature of his true feelings beneath an avuncular smile.

'And how do you suppose Jacob will react to sharing you? How is he, by the way?'

'So much better,' beamed Eloise. 'Jacobs thinks he will soon be quite as good as new. And as to sharing with little Patches here, well — you know how amiable Jacob is: I feel sure there will be no difficulty on that score. The only problem is — '

Giving up the unequal struggle Eloise placed the puppy on the floor and watched rather helplessly as he initiated a fight to the death with an exquisite rug, growling and wagging at the same time, whilst digging needle-sharp teeth into its fringe.

'Oh do stop it!' she cried, more in hope than expectation.

The puppy did not even look up, much less

pause in his endeavours.

'Cease!' commanded Harry in a lazy drawl, that conveyed a wealth of authority. Immediately the puppy's bottom hit the floor and he glared up at Harry through devoted eyes that were just visible beneath his disorderly fringe.

'How did you do that?' demanded Eloise, impressed as much as she was annoyed.

'You're too soft with him, sweetheart. He clearly only chooses to respond to commands that are voiced with determination.'

'Obviously,' agreed Eloise, rolling her eyes in exasperation. 'But, Harry, an idea occurs to me. Since he clearly adores you perhaps I should make a gift of him to you? He could bear you company during your convalescence.'

'Thank you, but no! The house would be wrecked in a matter of days,' remarked Harry, watching dispassionately as the small puppy deposited a disproportionately large puddle in the corner of the room.

'Oh dear, yes, I do see what you mean. Perhaps we had better leave you in peace,' she said, gathering the offending creature under one arm and turning to take her leave. 'I will call again tomorrow, Harry, but is there anything you require in the meantime?'

'Just your company for a little longer, if you have a mind to stay. You will easily be able to ascertain from that request the degree of tedium which I am forced to endure. If you do not do something to put me in better humour within a very short space of time I fear that half the staff will give notice.'

'Oh, of course I will stay, Harry, if you are sure you can tolerate Patches.' The puppy, deposited on the floor once again, was now vigorously attacking a table leg, advancing and retreating with all the enthusiasm of a campaign veteran, causing Harry and Eloise to laugh at his bemused expression when the table made no effort to repel his advances.

'Where is your father today?'

'I have at last persuaded him to return to the City. There was not the slightest need for him to remain beside me for so long, but he would not have it otherwise. However, I sensed that his mind had become concerned with matters of business this last day or so and in the end it was the work of a moment to convince him that I would be perfectly safe without his protection.'

'Hm, no doubt a week without relief from your constant society would be enough to reduce the strongest of men to instant compliance,' quipped Harry, surmising that Mr Hamilton's real purpose in returning to town was to acquaint his son with the particulars of Eloise's abduction and to put into action his plans for financial retribution against Craven.

'I cannot imagine why you are being so disagreeable, Harry; especially since I have taken the particular trouble to call upon you every day, when everyone else is scared to come anywhere near you in case you growl at them like a disgruntled bear.'

'I am not in the habit of growling,' protested Harry, in a futile attempt to deny the truth.

'Is that so? Then why, pray, did your mother and Jane, both of whom love you to distraction for some reason that is quite beyond my comprehension, feel the overwhelming desire to remove themselves to London in such a tearing hurry?' Eloise's eyes were alight with mischief, was in no mind to tolerate his restless mood.

'In my experience even love for an injured son and favoured brother is insufficient to withstand the call of the modiste.'

'Hm, that I doubt. Still, I suppose you did save me from an awkward situation and so it is only fair that it falls to my lot to tolerate your ill-humour. Besides, I have not thus far had the opportunity to thank you properly for your timely intervention.' She stood over his chair and dropped a delicate kiss on his brow. 'Thank you, Harry!'

'I believe,' he said softly, the first serious note since the commencement of their conversation entering his voice, 'that it is I who should thank you. You precipitate action doubtless saved *my* life.'

'Nonsense!' Eloise turned away, colouring slightly. 'Anyway, we were talking of Papa,' she continued hastily. 'You know, he was supposed to be in town last night. He had been most particularly invited to attend a soirée hosted by Lord and Lady Meyers. Their son has developed quite a *tendre* for Charlotte apparently, which is all to the good of course, what with him being the son of a viscount. I believe I made his acquaintance during my short sojourn in town and recall forming the opinion that he was an engaging, quite agreeable young man. Doubtless he requires Charlotte's money, but still that does not signify so much if she likes him.'

'No doubt your father will avail himself of the earliest opportunity to meet Meyers.'

'Oh yes, I should think he most likely will. I dare say Charlotte is quite put out because Papa had to make his apologies, but Charlotte being put out about something or another is not the slightest bit unusual. Anyway, both Thomas and Sarah were in attendance so Charlotte can hardly claim that we all abandoned her.'

Eloise chatted along in similar vein for some minutes but Harry scarcely heard her. There was an indefinable air of something hovering between them on this, the first occasion upon which they had been completely alone together since Eloise's abduction. The fact that she, too, was aware of it was hardly in question. There was so much Harry wished to say to her; so many things he would have her hear, that she *would* hear, but for the existence of Lady Hannah. Frustrated beyond endurance, when Eloise again talked of taking her leave Harry made no effort to prevent her.

Alone again he penned a dutiful note to his fiancée, making light of his accident and begging to be excused, on the strength of his injuries, from the ball he was committed to attend with her.

The following afternoon, he was sitting in company with his father when Eloise rode up to the house, escorted by a groom but thankfully without the recalcitrant puppy. Instead a fully restored Jacob bounded into the room ahead of her and made straight for his friend Harry, wagging an excited greeting.

When order was eventually restored, Harry expressed his pleasure in seeing the dog in such robust health. Eloise, seemingly grateful for Sir Henry's presence, displayed none of the unease that had prevailed during their interview the previous day and was able to answer Harry as saucily as ever.

Not ten minutes into Eloise's visit the sound of a carriage halting at the front steps alerted Harry to the unappealing prospect of visitors. Lady Hannah and her aunt were announced very soon thereafter and immediately shown in, Lady Hannah bustling through the door ahead of her aunt, unnaturally pale and full of concern for Harry's situation. With the briefest possible curtsy for Sir Henry and an impatient scowl in Eloise's direction, she launched herself upon Harry.

'Oh, sir, I confess your note put me quite in a spin and knew I would not gain a moment's peace until I could ascertain for myself that you were not mortally wounded.'

'It was not my intention to overset you,' said Harry blandly, taking her gloved hand and dutifully brushing his lips across her knuckles, 'but merely to express my regrets. As you will observe, I am hardly in a position to take you dancing.'

'That does not matter in the least. My only concern is that you did not advise me of your misfortune before now. I wish I had known of it.'

'I thank you, but there was not the slightest

need for me to curtail your pleasures by calling upon your generous nature. I have everything here for my convenience and Eloise has been obliged to be on her best behaviour this whole week together,' he added on a whim, pretending not to notice his father's frown of warning, 'making herself unnaturally agreeable and pandering to my every need. It has almost been worth the injury just to see her struggling with her usual instinct to argue with everything I say and being obliged to do as she is told for once.'

'Well,' said Lady Hannah with a distracted glance at her aunt and a superior, glassy smile for Eloise, 'I am sure we are all much obliged to Miss Hamilton but really, sir, I do not altogether see the need for your neighbour to put herself out now that I am on hand.'

'Oh, I have not been in the slightest bit put out,' said Eloise brightly, picking up Harry's capricious mood and sharing a complicit smile with him. Harry had no difficulty in believing that she still harboured grudges towards his fiancée for her indelicate remarks when Molly had been unwell and that she was incapable of wasting this opportunity to retaliate. Harry knew he should disapprove and attempt to rein her in: instead he smiled his encouragement.

'Well, be that as it may, I cannot possibly

go to the ball without you,' said Lady Hannah, warming to her role as the caring fiancée and dangling her hand casually over the arm of her chair. 'After all, I . . . arghh!' Lady Hannah let out a blood-curdling scream and leapt to her feet. 'What is *that*?'

Jacob, still a little wobbly after his accident and tired after loping beside Molly to reach Boscombe Hall, had taken the opportunity to curl up for a quiet snooze beside Hannah's chair. Her dangling hand had disturbed him, causing him to lift his head to investigate the intrusion with his wet nose.

'That is Jacob,' said Harry, also on his feet in response to Hannah's distress, but now valiantly attempting to contain his laughter.

'*That* is Miss Hamilton's dog,' she said, infusing the words with a wealth of distaste, making it clear precisely what she thought of poor Jacob. 'Whatever is he doing here?'

'Doing me the honour of paying a visit,' responded Harry succinctly.

'How very singular,' said Lady Hannah, walking as far away from Jacob as possible, taking another chair and casting a look of pure vitriol in Eloise's direction.

'I trust you are not too overset, my love?' said Lady West, her tone both solicitous and weary. Harry got the distinct impression that Hannah's aunt would not rue the day when she saw her niece safely married and her guardianship came to an end.

'Not at all, Aunt, I am simply concerned about Harry and really do not see how I can attend the ball whilst he is an invalid.' Lady Hannah was nothing if not single-minded.

'I would not have you curtail your pleasures on my account,' remarked Harry, with rather more candour than correctness.

A brief frown creased Lady Hannah's forehead. 'Oh no, I would much rather not be seen at such a public forum without you, my dear.'

'I think you have forgotten, Hannah, in your justifiable concern for your fiancé's condition, that we are in fact obliged to attend,' put in Lady West. 'I have promised Lord and Lady Blaney that we will join them for dinner before the event: they are quite depending upon us to support their daughter's launch upon society. Mr Benson-Smythe's absence will be unfortunate and his regrets must be passed along immediately, of course, in order that Lady Blaney can adjust her seating arrangements whilst there is still time to do so, but other than that I do not see what else is to be done.'

Harry's good humour returned with the revelation of this irrefutable logic: Lady West could always be relied upon to place the dictates of society, and more especially her friend's seating plan, before anything else.

'I would not wish to cause any more difficulties than can be helped,' he said, dredging up a winsome smile for his fiancée's benefit: a smile which did much to mollify her disgruntled attitude.

'Well, that's settled then. Come along, Hannah, we have much that requires our attention. Make your adieus, my dear.'

And, as abruptly as they had arrived, they left again in a swirl of petticoats and protestations of returning again immediately after the ball on the morrow.

★ ★ ★

Before Lady Hannah could pay her visit to Harry on the day after the ball he received a summons of a very different nature that caused him to quit Boscombe Hall for the first time since his accident. It was a hastily scribbled note from Eloise asking him to attend her immediately at Staverley, if he felt equal to making the short journey. Knowing that she would never have asked such a thing of him unless it was a matter of extreme urgency, Harry was immediately concerned for her and lost no time in ordering his carriage, impatient to be with his love and to discover what it was that had so overset her.

Upon being announced at Staverley, Harry discovered Eloise angrily pacing the length of the morning-room looking pale and distraught; evidence of fresh tears on her face. Seating himself, Harry refused all offers of refreshment and set about discovering the reason for her distress.

Composing herself as best she could, Eloise advised Harry that her brother Thomas, full to brimming with excitement, had returned home late the previous evening, having attended the same ball as Lady Hannah, and deliberately stopped at her chamber to wake her and announce his spectacular news.

'And what news could that have been?' asked Harry, with a gentle smile. 'And more to the point, if it was such good news why has it overset you so?'

'Thomas declared himself to be the luckiest man alive since he had just become engaged to be married.'

'It is as I expected then; a cause for celebration. I assume you are simply feeling low at the prospect of sharing Thomas's devotion?'

'No, Harry, it is a matter of far greater concern.'

'Then what? Who is the fortunate lady?'

'Lady Emily Craven,' said Eloise, briefly meeting Harry's astonished gaze before dissolving into a bout of fresh tears.

16

In two strides Harry was beside Eloise, his good arm encircling her waist, her face buried in his lapel as she sobbed tears of bitter anguish. Helpless to know what to say in the face of such devastating grief, Harry played for time and simply allowed Eloise to cry out the worst of her pain, his mind whirling with a cacophony of explanations: none of which made the slightest sense.

The torrent of tears which afflicted Eloise appeared destined to last an eternity, but eventually they were spent. Even though the features revealed to him when she finally raised her head were blotched and reddened with distress, to Harry she had never appeared more captivating. Powerless to resist, he offered her not only his handkerchief but a smile of reassurance tinged with an inappropriate degree of rakishness. Despite the enormity of the situation Harry could not recall a time when he had desired Eloise more. Her current state of vulnerability; her devastated emotional condition and the fact that her first conscious thought when faced with an insolvable problem had been to send for him, all combined to heighten his instinctive protectiveness towards her.

Somehow there must be a way out of this impossible situation and, whatever the cost, Harry was already determined to find it out. The reward for his efforts he permitted himself to anticipate with something akin to erotic pleasure. It would be the return of the captivating, habitually challenging and monstrously disrespectful smile on the lips of the girl-woman whom he now privately acknowledged as the love of his life. He also knew that if getting even with Craven required him to sacrifice that life on the altar of his love for Eloise then it would be done without a moment's regret.

'Tell me all about it from the beginning,' requested Harry, sensing that Eloise had regained a modicum of composure.

'Well, as I said, Thomas woke me. He was in a state of great agitation and it was immediately obvious to me that it sprang from something of consequence: something that made him supremely happy for I have never seen him more animated. The sparkle in his eyes, the radiance in his countenance: he was like a stranger, a most desirable one, and it was impossible not to be caught up in his excitement.'

'And then he told you about Lady Emily?' suggested Harry, when Eloise fell silent.

'Not immediately. He was enjoying himself too much, you see, and wanted to prolong the moment. He insisted upon describing the ball in detail: who was there; who said what to whom; what the ladies of consequence wore. He supposed I would be interested in such nugatory matters,' she added with a flash of her old spirit. 'He informed me that Charlotte was there, receiving much attention from her Mr Myers and from Richard Craven too, by all accounts, as was your Lady Hannah.' This time outrage and disgust were clearly evident in her tone, giving Harry fresh heart.

'But how did Thomas's engagement to Lady Emily come about so quickly? Surely he would need to seek permission to address her from the duke which, and I'm sorry if you consider this to be a slight, Eloise, would be unlikely to be forthcoming. And then, of course, there is the matter of seeking your own father's approval before he went ahead with his plan.'

'Well, of course, I realize all of that, Harry,' she snapped irascibly, 'I am not a complete widgeon, you know. As soon as I recovered my wits I congratulated Thomas as heartily as I was able, for I could scarce think what else to do, and he was looking at me so expectantly, so keen for my approval, that I was powerless to disappoint him. But after that the questions you just raised were some of the first that I addressed to him.'

'And what responses did you receive?'

'Well, Thomas confided that he had been in love with Emily since first setting eyes on her.' Eloise rolled her own eyes; Harry was unsure why. 'Really, as if we were not all aware of his feelings!' she added, giving Harry the briefest flash of a smile and an unasked for explanation. 'But, like you, he considered that his suit would be hopeless. He fortified himself with the notion that Emily herself would not be averse to the match, but did not imagine that the duke would ever give him leave to address her.'

'I can understand his reasoning,' remarked Harry softly. 'The duke is very conscious of his position,' he added, uncomfortably reminded of his own father's strict stance in respect of such matters, 'and would have no wish to denigrate his family's standing by permitting his daughter to make what he would doubtless perceive as an unsuitable alliance.'

Eloise's expression was one of lofty scorn, her tone underlined with haughty disdain and a touch of anger too as she answered him.

'Exactly so, Harry: God forbid that the portals of Esher Castle should be thus polluted. But that is why Thomas had decided he would never be able honourably to take matters forward with Emily. But then one day, about a month ago, when he and Richard were out on the town together, Richard himself brought the subject up, quite without any encouragement from Thomas apparently. He said he had noticed Thomas's preference for his sister, and hers for him, and led Thomas to believe that he sympathized with his friend's plight.

'Thomas admitted to his *tendre* for Emily at once but said he understood he would never be considered suitable and would not presume to put himself forward. But Richard gave him cause to hope. He said that Emily was the youngest of his three sisters; the other two already being acceptably married: that Emily was his mother's least favourite child, with a dowry so small as to be insignificant. Richard went on, with what Thomas considered to be quite exceptional candour, to admit that his family were on a repairing lease and if a respectable gentleman of independent means were to show a preference for Emily then the duke might just be persuaded to encourage his interest.'

'Good God!' expostulated Harry, astonishment taking precedence over good manners.

'Exactly so! Thomas was both surprised and delighted and would have approached the duke then and there but Richard advised caution. He explained that his mother would require careful manipulation if her agreement to the match was to be forthcoming and he, Richard, being her favourite child, was best placed to talk her round.

'And so Thomas bided his time as patiently as he could, waiting for Richard to tip him the wink, but every time he asked if he had made any progress Richard found reasons to procrastinate, dashing Thomas's fledgling hopes in the process.'

'And in the meantime he discussed his plans with your father?'

'Well, no. He said he did not wish to tempt providence and would only do so when he had the duke's approval to proceed.'

'I see.'

'Yes, Harry,' agreed Eloise despondently, 'so do I, far more clearly than I could wish to be the case. Richard approached Thomas during the course of yesterday, informing him that he had obtained his parents' permission for Thomas to address Emily. Well, as you can imagine, he was euphoric and went immediately in search of Papa to acquaint him with his intentions.' Eloise paused, fresh tears brimming. 'But of course Papa was not in the City but here with me instead.'

'And Thomas was too impatient to delay?'

'Exactly! He admitted to me that he should have done Papa the courtesy of consulting him first, but he had waited so long that he could not bear to delay even one more day. Besides, he knew that Papa held Richard in high regard, what with the fact that he was working with him on the diamond-mining enterprise and that Papa was impressed with the results he had achieved. He also pointed out that Papa encouraged Richard to come to Staverley, even when he was not here to receive him himself, and so did not see that there could be any difficulty. And, apart from anything else, he is of age and independent means and can technically marry wherever he pleases, without the need for parental approval.'

'That is, of course, true.'

'Oh, Harry, what are we to do?' The tears won their battle against Eloise's feeble attempts to contain them and were once again cascading down her face. 'This is all my fault! If I had obeyed Papa and ridden out in company with a groom Richard could not have abducted me.' Harry shook his head, but she would not allow him to utter the words of reassurance that were on his lips. 'And then, if I had insisted that Papa return to his office before now then Thomas could have consulted him, he would have known about the abduction and the engagement could not have taken place.'

'And Thomas's heart would have been broken.'

'Better that than Papa's,' she countered with asperity. 'Just imagine, Richard will have free rein to call here whenever he wishes to do so now, and tap Thomas for loans to his heart's content. It would be the most natural thing in the world and short of revealing to Emily, whom I like very much indeed by the way, the true nature of her brother's character, then I do not see what else is to be done.'

'It is indeed a delicate situation but surely — '

'He has done this deliberately to get even with us,' said Eloise bitterly. 'I just know it! He is such a monster that he is even capable of manipulating his sister's feelings in order to get his way.' She paused and looked directly at Harry through eyes still blurred by tears. 'I hate him with a passion for being so vile, but he has comprehensively outwitted us and I do not see that there is anything we can do about it.'

320

Without hesitation Harry pulled her against him and gently kissed her: a gesture designed to reassure rather than excite, but Harry was unsure afterwards how true to his intentions he had managed to remain: when it came to Eloise he was wont to lose sight of his objectivity. 'You are forgetting one thing, sweetheart,' he murmured with determination into the top of her head. 'Richard Craven is not the only person on this earth capable of manipulation.'

★   ★   ★

Mr Hamilton entered the room, too distracted to notice anything untoward in Harry's behaviour towards Eloise. He greeted Harry absently and seemed not at all surprised to find him at Staverley at such an early hour.

'Leave us, Ella,' he said, patting his daughter's hand abstractedly, 'I would have a word or two with Harry.'

Eloise made no objection to being excluded from the discussion, knowing there was little she could hope to add to it that would be of much worth and reluctant to remind her father that the situation had only arisen in the first instance due to her rebellious character. She wandered into the music-room and ran her fingers slowly across the keys of her pianoforte, instinctively heading for the comfort to be derived from music.

As she played, Eloise permitted her mind to wander, wishing she could turn the clock back as easily as she could abandon a piece of poorly executed music and start it again. There were so many things that she would do differently, given the opportunity. For a start she would not have been foolish enough to entertain hopes in respect of Richard Craven: she was honest enough now to admit that she *had* briefly wondered about his feelings for her, even allowing herself to believe that something so impossible could actually be managed.

Eloise laughed aloud at the thought: a laugh that was devoid of humour and came out more as a sob. What a dim-wit she had been! If she had not been constantly reminded about the impossibility of her position time and again by a spiteful Charlotte, then she should have comprehended for herself by now just how slight her prospects for making a good match were. She certainly should not have allowed her resolve to remain a spinster wobble on the very first occasion when a handsome gentleman glanced in her direction and get carried away with fanciful ideas that had no place in the real world.

Her fingers slammed on the keys with an uncharacteristic lack of finesse as she considered the whole question of social etiquette. It was perfectly acceptable, apparently, for the son of a duke to repair his family's fiscal position by taking employment with her father: there was nothing dishonourable about his peers benefiting from her father's business acumen and boasting about their foresight to their friends; it was quite another thing for her father and his prodigy to expect to be accepted on an equal footing by the leaders of fashion. Such double standards made Eloise want to stamp her foot in frustration, but she made do instead with determining never to repeat her moment of weakness. Never again would she allow her heart to rule her head and be tempted to hanker for that which could never be hers.

Just look at Harry: her friend and protector for as long as she could remember. Even he was a victim of the class system. It must be obvious to anyone with eyes in their head that he was not the slightest bit in love with Lady Hannah and had offered for her only to raise his family's standing, in accordance with his father's wishes. For the aristocracy emotional attachment played little part in the decision process when it came to marriage; the question of compatibility was another aspect that had no place in the negotiations but, when it came to social suitability . . . well, that was clearly looked upon as another matter entirely.

Eloise, determined to further blacken a mood that was already as dark as pitch, dwelt upon it at length and found herself disgusted with Harry for not showing more backbone and standing up for what he really wanted. She wondered idly what that something would have been, had he been free to make his own choice and surprised herself by wishing it might have been her: knowing well enough it never could have been. He simply regarded her as another sister. Taking one hand from the keyboard she touched the lips he had so recently kissed and recalled the cataclysm of emotions that had beset her on the three occasions when he had treated her with passionate disregard for the rules: the bewildering paradox of pleasure and excitement she had experienced as a result of his expert caresses, the riot of sensations that ran amok within her, leaving her breathless and quite unable to think or act for herself.

Leaning on Harry was such a long established habit of hers that it hardly surprised Eloise to find herself doing so whenever her wits deserted her. That explained her behaviour, but not why Harry had suddenly started to show an amatory interest in her: she had spent many sleepless hours seeking an explanation for that inexplicable event. She felt hot with embarrassment when she recalled her candid confession to him: a confession made when she had considered Harry to be unconscious and incapable of hearing her. He had heard her though; every shaming word that she had spoken had been clearly understood by him and she had been incapable of properly meeting his eye ever since. Harry had at least had the decency not to refer to the incident again but even so, what could he think of her?

The answer was not difficult to anticipate. He undoubtedly considered her feelings to be the result of her immaturity and placed little stock in her infatuation. That was all to the good since Eloise could now admit to herself at least that, inexplicable though it might be, she was nevertheless in love with Harry.

She could admit it because he was engaged to the loathsome Lady Hannah.

Slamming down the lid to the pianoforte, Eloise called to Jacob and, more restless than ever, headed in the direction of the stables.

★ ★ ★

Mr Hamilton, much as his daughter had half an hour earlier, paced restlessly in front of the fireplace attempting to rein in his anger. Harry watched impassively, waiting for him to break the silence between them. It did not take long for him to do so.

'Eloise will have acquainted you with Thomas's disastrous news?'

'Yes,' said Harry, 'a very regrettable circumstance.'

'Regrettable, you call it!' said Mr Hamilton, his voice rising by several octaves. 'Hardly the description I would choose. It is completely devastating.'

'Where is Thomas now?'

Mr Hamilton's responding smile conveyed no humour. 'Unlike Eloise he spared me a night's sleep before coming to me first thing this morning for my approbation.'

'Which you gave?'

'In my surprised and shocked state I could think of no other course. Thomas, fortunately, was too preoccupied to notice my restraint. He then took himself off to town to advise his sisters of his good fortune and place an announcement in *The Chronicle*.' Harry raised a brow in frank surprise. 'He presumably does not wish to allow anyone sufficient time to think better of the arrangement. Also he was anxious to examine some of the finished products from the mine in order to place the most splendid example upon the finger of his betrothed and appear at the Duchess of Devonshire's ball tomorrow evening with Emily on his arm.'

'*The* social occasion of the season,' remarked Harry languidly. And yet another at which he would not put in an appearance with his fiancée. He was probably sufficiently recovered to do so and knew he ought to make the effort, but had already written a note of regret to Hannah, begging to be excused. Knowing she would be disappointed held no sway with him and he clung fast to his valid excuse to miss the crush with a sense of unmitigated relief. 'But surely something can be done to put the matter right?' he continued, bringing his mind back to Thomas's situation.

'What would you suggest?' countered Mr Hamilton acerbically. 'Craven has done this deliberately to get the better of me and he could not have devised a better means of revenge. I am helpless to retaliate!' George Hamilton raked his hands through his hair in a gesture of desperation and attacked his pacing with renewed vigour.

'You had acquainted him with your intention of releasing him from his contract, I presume?'

'No, I had not yet had the opportunity since I wished to remain here with Eloise and ensure that she was entirely safe and recovered from her ordeal. I did not feel comfortable trusting her protection to anyone else when I still felt her to be so vulnerable.' Mr Hamilton paused and looked directly at Harry. 'And that was my mistake, don't you see. I had assumed that he would regret his abduction of Eloise and attack upon you and have the sense to remain in seclusion until matters quieted down. I understimated the extent of his arrogance though, that much at least is now abundantly clear. Can you but credit it; he appeared in society quite as though he had not a care in the world, just one day after attempting to murder you? He could not, at that stage, possibly have known whether he had succeeded in doing away with you, but clearly did not think that sufficient reason to absent himself from Lady Northover's ball. How anyone could behave thus is quite beyond my understanding.'

Mr Hamilton threw himself into a chair, stood again and poured two glasses of Madeira, in spite of the early hour, handing one to Harry.

'Thank you,' said Harry, as Mr Hamilton seated himself again. 'George, rational thought is required here. There must be some way to resolve the situation. Can you not think up some reason to prohibit the marriage?'

'No, that is obviously out of the question. Firstly Thomas has reached his majority and does not actually require my permission; secondly, were I to attempt to interfere it would not only alienate me from my only son but would also put paid to what small steps we have made as a family within society; to say nothing of what it would do for Charlotte's expectations. After all, the duke's permission was sought before Thomas addressed Emily and everything was done just as it should be. If I attempted to persuade Thomas to change his mind then the duke could sue on his daughter's behalf for breach of promise which could, I suppose, be Richard's safety net. He must realize how abhorrent the union will be in my eyes, after what he attempted to do to my daughter, and it no doubt affords him great satisfaction to have boxed me in so neatly.

'I am well known to be a wealthy man and a settlement for breach of promise would even the score, as far as Craven is concerned, and go a good way to filling his family's depleted coffers into the bargain.' Mr Hamilton smacked one clenched fist into the palm of his other hand, his face stained an angry red as he faced up to the impossibility of the situation and struggled to contain his temper. 'We have been comprehensively outwitted by a conceited bastard who thinks nothing of manipulating the people closest to him when it serves his purpose.'

'He presumably must have realized that you would find a way to call him to account for abducting your daughter?'

'I trust he knows me well enough to comprehend that I would never allow anyone to abuse my beloved girl in such a way. God alone knows how he supposed he would get away with it: that is a subject which I prefer not to dwell upon since it has already caused me many wakeful hours. Perhaps that is why I did not deal with the scoundrel as quickly as I should have done.' Mr Hamilton paused to sip his drink, appeared to take some comfort from the infusion and when he recommenced speaking his tone was calmer. 'I did however send him a note yesterday asking him to wait upon me tomorrow.'

'And it was that note, we must assume, that caused him to execute his plan in respect of Thomas and Emily.'

'Undoubtedly.'

'Eloise told me that he first spoke with Thomas about the possibility of the match over a month ago. He must have decided even then that he intended to exploit you to the maximum and that a liaison between Thomas and Emily would be an assured way to achieve his objective.'

'Yes,' said Mr Hamilton despondently, 'and never was a man more neatly outmanoeuvred. I liked the boy from the start and trusted him completely. God forbid that I too was dazzled by his connections and considered him incapable of duplicity because of them, but I can think of no other explanation for being taken in by him. I pride myself on being able to judge a man's character pretty astutely: it has been a key factor in building a successful business. But,' continued Mr Hamilton, the temporary note of defeat in his voice replaced with one of steely determination, 'I care not how much it oversets Lady Emily and my son but Richard Craven will *never* be admitted to Staverley. I will acquaint Thomas with the particulars of Eloise's abduction as soon as I can and between us we will devise an explanation for his exclusion that will satisfy his sister and prevent Eloise being exposed to the man's venal company.'

'Do you have objections against the lady herself?' asked Harry.

'None whatsoever: she is everything that is charming. The ingrained arrogance and conceit for their elevated position within society that afflicts the rest of her family has left Emily entirely untouched; perhaps accounting for why the duchess has such little time for her. No, I can quite see why Thomas is so enamoured with her and if the circumstances were different would be honoured to welcome her into my house as its next mistress.'

'That is what I anticipated you would say.'

Harry lapsed into deep thought. He had always known, on a visceral level, that he was ill-qualified by nature to let the bad blood between himself and Craven remain unaddressed. It explained his recent foul temper since subjection did not sit easily with Harry, even if it was the best way to protect Eloise. He had spent hours considering how best to resolve the matter, concluding that he would bide his time and meet Craven sometime in the not too distant future: one-to-one, with no witnesses present and nothing to tie the acrimony between them to Eloise. Then they would discover who was the better man.

But perhaps this situation with Thomas could provide a more satisfactory and immediate solution.

'George,' said Harry in a musing tone, 'if Craven were not actually in England then it would be unnecessary for you to bar him from Staverley, or distress his blameless sister in any way.'

'Whatever do you mean, Harry?' asked Mr Hamilton, a glimmer of hope in his eyes.

'How did you propose to break your contract with Craven?'

'Well, his initial duty was to sell all of the shares in the mine to his connections.'

'And has he done so?'

'No.'

'Then how did you intend to dispense with his services? Would he not have had redress in law?'

'Not if I took up the remaining shares myself.'

Harry smiled. 'That is what I thought. How many remain?'

Mr Hamilton told him, outlining the amount required to secure them.

'It sounds like a very sensible investment for a man of means to make.'

'It is certainly proving to be so,' agreed Mr Hamilton absently, his mind for once clearly not focusing on his business concerns.

'Then would you accept my father and me as your remaining shareholders?'

Mr Hamilton gasped his surprise. 'With the greatest of pleasure, Harry, but it is a vast amount of money to invest. Are you quite sure?'

'Entirely certain: I am already anticipating a healthy return on our investment.'

'That I can virtually guarantee. I will arrange for the papers for your signature to be drawn up immediately.'

'Excellent.' The gentlemen shook upon the deal and sealed it with a further glass of Madeira. 'Does the sale of all the shares mean that you can dispense with Craven's services, or does the contract provide you with the right to use his services in other directions?'

'The terms of the contract are nebulous, deliberately so. I did not imagine that he would be completely successful in selling all the shares within the two-year period the contract spans, but I am a cautious man and like to cover all eventualities. In the event that he did manage to sell all the stock I have the choice to either dispense with his services — '

'Which is presumably what you planned to do tomorrow, before Thomas's announcement, that is?'

'Yes, absolutely!'

'And the other alternative?' asked Harry, alert with anticipation.

'I can redeploy his services in whatever area I feel would most benefit from them.'

'And he agreed to that clause?' asked Harry in surprise.

'I am not sure he fully comprehended its

meaning but he was so desperate to take the commission I do not imagine he dwelt much upon the likelihood of the clause being called upon.'

'All to the good,' said Harry with satisfaction. 'George, did I understand you correctly the other day when you described the workings of the mine to my father and me? Did you not say that you urgently require someone trustworthy to travel to the mine and reevaluate security?'

Mr Hamilton looked thunderstruck and was rendered temporarily speechless; then a broad, infectious grin suffused his features. 'My God, Harry, but that's brilliant! The perfect solution! Why did I not see it before? Oh, but no.' Mr Hamilton's grin gave way to a bleak expression. 'I require someone trustworthy to strengthen security, not to add to the myriad risks of deception that already exist.'

'Could the position not be an administrative one? I cannot, in any event, somehow picture the suave heir to the Esher dynasty being prepared to dirty his hands, or to befriend the miners responsible for extracting the stones and lowering himself to form an alliance with them in order to feather his own nest. We already know that everything he does is driven by his arrogance and sense of self-importance. He would never degrade himself to such an extent.'

'Yes, quite possibly.' Mr Hamilton's grin made a brief reappearance. 'I will devise something before tomorrow to place before him in any event.'

'But what if he refuses to go?'

'He cannot. If he does then he runs the risk of breaking the contract between us and no monies owing to him need then be paid by me.'

'But if he does decline the commission it will give you the perfect excuse to exclude him from Staverley: one that his sister cannot possibly take exception to.'

'Exactly! Harry I don't know how to thank you.'

'Thanks are quite unnecessary. I have a score to settle with the man, too. To that end there are two items of information that I would ask you to ensure he fully comprehends.'

'Anything, Harry; anything at all. What is it you would have me tell the rogue?'

17

George Hamilton promised to call at Boscombe Hall upon his return to Staverley to recount the full particulars of his interview with Craven. Harry filled the intervening hours by acquainting his father with all that occurred and enduring another visit from his fiancée, most of which she spent attempting to persuade Harry to change his mind and accompany her to the duchess's ball.

'I can see at once that you are much recovered, my dear,' she wheedled, 'and I so wished for you to admire my new ball gown.'

'I dare say there will be many opportunities in the future for me to express my admiration of your person,' said Harry smoothly, casting a *what have you got me into?* look in his father's direction as he did so.

Only the absense of Eloise appeared to mollify Lady Hannah and prevented her from descending into a bad-tempered sulk — a form of behaviour that had always got her what she wanted thus far in life. Instead, she settled in for a lengthy visit, prepared to flirt charmingly with her fiancée and coax him into good humour with her. Mercifully her aunt suddenly remembered that they had an appointment with their milliner. All thoughts of flirtation abruptly deserted Lady Hannah in favour of the more weighty considerations pursuant to aigrettes for the duchess's ball and the latest fashion in poke bonnets, which Hannah was not altogether sure entirely became her, and allowed herself to be shuffled through the door without protest.

Harry awaited George Hamilton's return with ill-concealed impatience, wondering at the same time why Eloise had not chosen to visit him today of all days, debating with himself whether or not to call upon her. Doubtless she would be suffering from the blue-devils, would not know of her father's plan to get the better of Craven and could be relieved of her concerns by the intelligence he had to impart on that score. But Sir Henry, reading his son's mind, recommended that he remain at Boscombe Hall. George Hamilton would return soon enough and it was surely his place to acquaint his daughter with his actions. Harry reluctantly acknowledged the truth in his father's words and settled down to await Hamilton's arrival with as much patience as he could muster.

George did not disappoint and presented himself at Boscombe Hall before even Harry had considered it possible. The euphoric expression which lit his features as he was shown into the drawing-room caused a huge weight to lift from Harry's shoulders and he waited to hear the particulars of Craven's downfall with a feeling of deep gratification.

'I take it matters went as planned,' he remarked with a smile, as Sir Henry handed their guest a glass of claret.

'Indeed they did, Harry, thanks to you, and far better than I could have anticipated.' He took a healthy swig of his drink and smacked his lips in appreciation.

'Tell us,' invited Sir Henry, as the three gentlemen seated themselves.

'The scoundrel arrived half an hour late for our appointment, which did not entirely surprise me,' commenced Mr Hamilton. 'When he did finally condescend to put in an appearance I retaliated by having my clerk keep *him* waiting.' Sir Henry and Harry chuckled their amusement. 'He sauntered into my office when I finally sent for him with a most unbecoming sneer gracing his features. He thought himself to have bested me, you see, and I amused myself by allowing that presumption on his part to continue into the start of our interview.'

'You cannot be blamed for extracting the maximum amount of revenge from the situation, George,' remarked Sir Henry.

'That was my opinion precisely. Unchristian though it might be, after all the damage he has inflicted upon our respective families, I would be less than human if I did not extract pleasure at his discomfiture.'

'So how did you broach the subject of his banishment?' asked Harry.

'I did not at first. Craven, arrogant as ever, had the temerity to enquire after the health of my family, if you can believe such hubris: he even went so far as to name Eloise. There was a most superior smirk on his face as he did so; rather as if he wished to emphasize his supposed control over us all.' Mr Hamilton lifted his chin, the light of battle glinting in his eye, and Harry could tell it was at this point that he had started to enjoy himself in earnest. 'He is not the first young man to suppose he could get the better of me. Anyway, since I offered him little in way of response to his enquiries he then dwelt at length upon the subject of Thomas's engagement to his sister; about how pleasant it would be to have a formal connection between the two families and how he trusted he could count on my good will in the future.'

'A remark which could only be taken as a warning of his intention to fleece you for all you are worth. It would appear that he unintentionally played straight into your hands,' remarked Sir Henry.

'Indeed, yes. As you can imagine, Harry, after you left me I gave much thought to the conduct of the interview and, aware now of just how full of conceit the man is, I concluded that he would not be able to prevent himself from boasting about his supposedly superior intellect.' Mr Hamilton smiled in spite of his obvious disgust. 'About the neat way in which he outsmarted us all: or so he thought.

'He eventually asked, bold as brass, why I had requested an interview with him and I took great delight in informing him that the requirement for his services as a broker between myself and the aristocracy was at an end.'

'That must have jolted him out of his smug demeanour,' suggested Harry.

'Not a bit of it; the man thinks far too well of himself to consider that he can be bettered by the likes of me. He merely shrugged, offered me a look of mild derision and informed me that the particulars of our contract protected his position until such time as all the shares in the mine were sold and that there were still twenty per cent unaccounted for.'

'How did you respond?'

Mr Hamilton grinned enigmatically: shades

341

of Eloise at her most mischievous apparent in the gesture. 'I informed him that lamentably his information was not up to the mark and that the remaining twenty per cent had been taken up. At last I had the satisfaction of seeing him look ruffled. He asked me who could possibly have the ready blunt to take such a large shareholding and why he had not been a party to the negotiations. I did not immediately satisfy his curiosity and he was too rattled to repeat his question, but I could see from his expression that he was manically assessing his options: eventually he decided to ask me to settle with him so that we could go our separate ways.

'I knew, naturally, that he would then become a stone around Thomas's neck, constantly trading upon my son's good nature and love for his future wife to gain his ends. It was the moment I had been waiting for and I told him then that I was not prepared to release him from his contract, since it still had over a year to run. He looked interested, suspicious and avaricious all at the same time and I confess that I amused myself by feeding upon his greed for a few minutes, outlining a most lucrative position that had unexpectedly arisen and for which I required someone on whom I could absolutely depend.'

'And he believed you?' asked Harry

askance. 'After all the callous suffering he has inflicted upon your family he still believed that you would offer him the time of day? I cannot begin to comprehend such ingrained conceit.'

'I had the satisfaction of seeing that conceit shattered into tiny pieces when I described to Craven the precise particulars of the position I had in mind for him,' responded Mr Hamilton, clearly relishing the memory. 'For the first time I extracted a genuine response from the scoundrel. He leapt to his feet, told me I must be out of my senses if I thought for one moment that he would demean himself by travelling to such a God-forsaken place and said I need not imagine that I could get the better of him through such underhand methods.

'It was then that I did as he had asked earlier and carelessly informed him that the methods were not of my devising but of yours, Harry, and that it was your family who had taken up the remaining twenty per cent shareholding in the mine.'

Harry and his father exchanged smiles: Sir Henry rising to refill their glasses.

'That must have afforded you great satisfaction, George.'

'I must confess to the truth in your statement, Henry. I have never seen anyone half so angry: he was speechless for two minutes together and his face paled so dramatically that I quite thought he might swoon in the fashion of some helpless female. He recovered himself eventually however, looked me square in the eye and said that neither I nor you, Harry, should make the mistake of assuming we had got the better of him and that he would have his revenge upon both of us. He then stormed from the room.'

'So you have deliberately made an enemy of the man by revealing your hand in the affair?' said Sir Henry to his son. 'Was that absolutely necessary?'

'I most particularly asked George to ensure that he knew of it, Father. Upon my honour, you can hardly expect me to pass up such a ripe opportunity for revenge, given the fact that the man tried to kill me.' Harry lifted his now slingless but still weak arm by way of demonstration. 'Besides, Father, we have bested him: not through physical violence but superior thinking. What could he possibly do to a family as powerful as ours to exact revenge?'

★ ★ ★

Harry discovered the answer to that question on the morning following the duchess's ball.

344

He was in the library with his father, looking over the papers George Hamilton had left for them to sign in respect of their shareholding in the mine, when the sound of an unseemly commotion in the hall alerted them to the arrival of visitors. The door to the library opened and Rogers informed the gentlemen that Lord and Lady West had arrived — the lady being in a state of some considerable distress and the gentleman one of agitation — and were desirous of an immediate interview. Sir Henry raised a brow in surprise and instructed Rogers to show them into the morning-room.

As soon as Harry and Sir Henry joined their unexpected guests Lady West jumped to her feet.

'Oh, Sir Henry!' were the only words she could manage before bursting into inconsolable tears.

It was left to Lord West, in a state of acute embarrassment, to inform his astonished audience that Lady Hannah had failed to return home following the duchess's ball. Upon being informed that the girl's bed had not been slept in and that her maid was nowhere to be found either, Lady West had searched her escritoire and discovered two letters: one addressed to her aunt and uncle, the other for Harry.

'She has eloped!' said Lord West, his voice conveying a wealth of dismay, humiliation and disgust at the girl's appalling behaviour. 'As we speak she is already well on the road to Gretna Green with her paramour.'

'But why?' asked Sir Henry, genuinely perplexed. 'And, more to the point, with whom?'

Lord West, standing in front of the fire, was unable to look Sir Henry in the eye when he responded. 'With Richard Craven,' he said abruptly, his eyes fastened on the burning logs.

18

Henry's first inclination was to laugh. He fought against the inappropriate urge to do so and focused instead upon Lord West's distraught features, his wife's state of near collapse, his father's expression of speechless shock.

Rapidly assimilating the enormity of the situation did little to quell Harry's desire to smile gleefully, even as a sense of unmitigated relief at his timely escape flooded through his person. His nemesis, supposing himself to have exacted the ultimate revenge, would be devastated to learn that he had, instead, done Harry the ultimate favour. He was quite unequal to suppressing a brief derisive smile at that thought, but quickly schooled his features into an appropriately grave expression: now was not the time for levity.

'Oh, sir!' cried Lady West, between earnest sobs, dabbing ineffectually at her eyes with a tiny square of lace-edged cambric that was totally inadequate for her purpose. 'I blame myself! I should have kept a closer eye on — '

'Compose yourself, Lady West,' interposed Harry smoothly. 'Can I offer you something for your comfort? Peach ratafia, or perhaps a glass of sherry?'

'You are too kind, sir, I deserve no such consideration.' Fresh sobs ensued. 'Oh, what are we to do? The disgrace, the humiliation; I cannot bear it! How could the wretched girl be so thoughtless?'

'Perhaps you should start at the beginning, Lady West, and tell us precisely what happened?' suggested Sir Henry, belatedly finding his voice.

Lady West sat up a little straighter and made a conscious effort to compose herself. 'Yesterday afternoon I drove in the park as usual. Hannah was in the carriage with me, as was my good friend, Lady Clancy.' Sir Henry nodded his encouragement and Lady West continued, 'Quite by chance we encountered Richard Craven, with a party of friends, walking in the Row. Naturally we stopped and exchanged greetings. Richard requested that Hannah be permitted to join his party on foot. Now, perhaps I should not have allowed it but it seemed harmless enough and, besides, I had a matter of a delicate nature which I was desirous of discussing with Lady Clancy and could scarcely do so in Hannah's presence, and so I permitted it. Richard's party stayed within sight of our carriage at all times,' she added quickly, 'and all the proprieties were observed. I would not have you think that I was in any way neglectful.'

'I am persuaded that you acted with complete propriety,' said Sir Henry with a smile.

'Well, I am sure I had no idea that Lord Craven could be so devious,' she complained with a dignified sniff, 'since it is now apparent to me that he sought us out with the deliberate intention of persuading Hannah to elope with him. If a gentlemen in his position is not to be trusted then I am sure I do not know what the world is coming to.'

'Was there any particular reason why Craven would single out my fiancée?' asked Harry, feigning innocence.

Lady West answered by launching into another tirade against Craven's duplicity, which was eventually cut short by her husband. 'You must be aware that they have an amatory history,' he said succinctly.

'No, sir. I was vaguely aware that they had known one another, but I am not party to the particulars of their relationship.'

'Craven pursued Hannah quite ruthlessly the year she came out,' said Lady West. 'Well, we thought nothing of that at first since she was an attractive chit, as well as being an heiress of considerable stature. But it soon became apparent that she preferred Richard above all her suitors and we considered it was but a matter of time before he offered for her. It would have been a splendid match and Hannah appeared quite determined to have him.'

'Determined to be a duchess one day, more like' said Lord West with ruthless honesty.

'Yes, my dear, but she was quite in love too; of that I am persuaded. Anyway, Richard went off on his Grand Tour with your younger son, amongst others,' she said, glaring almost accusingly at Sir Henry, as though Craven's behaviour could be attributed to him. 'And when he returned he was a changed person. Hannah was confident that things would be between them again as they had been before his departure: but they never were. She was quite distraught at the change in him: the more so since she had declined several advantageous proposals in his absence. I am unaware whether there was an unofficial understanding between them — I know not what was agreed on that score — but I do know that Hannah would look at no one else and was devastated when he showed no particular inclination for her upon his return. She would have it that she had been used abominably, jilted even, but of course we could not go about saying such things about the son of a duke.'

'And so when he paid attention to her in the park she was glad to have him notice her again?' suggested Harry acerbically.

'Oh, sir, I am sure it is not what you think. I cannot believe her capable of such wilful deceit.'

'Really! Then where is she now?'

'Oh, dear God, what is to become of us? The shame of an elopement! How will we ever live it down?'

'Calm yourself, Lady West,' said Sir Henry with a warning glance in his son's direction, 'and tell us what happened next.'

'Richard returned Hannah to the carriage after half an hour, said everything that was proper to myself and Lady Clancy and took his leave. I thought no more of the matter.'

'And last night you went to the duchess's ball.'

'Yes. Hannah had been vexed that you were still indisposed, sir, and unable to accompany her but, now that I think about it, since walking with Richard in the park she made no further comment about the inconvenience your absence was likely to be to her.'

'And so all of this was planned within a half-hour walk in the park?' queried Harry incredulously.

'We must assume that to be the case since Hannah recruited the assistance of her abigail, being quite devoted to the girl and incapable of looking after herself, and that could only have been done in advance.'

'How is it that she was able to escape your chaperonage in order to make good her escape?' asked Sir Henry. 'I believe you said you did not gain intelligence that she was missing until this morning.'

Lady West, having given way to a fresh bout of weeping, was incapable of answering and it was left to her husband to explain.

'As we were leaving the duchess's Hannah requested permission to go on to Lady McKenzie's ball in the company of some people we know well; one of Richard's married sisters amongst them. You know how it is in the height of the season; several events in one night are not at all uncommon and my wife is not strong: she often finds herself unequal to the task of traipsing from one crowded ballroom to another. That is why Hannah is sometimes entrusted to the chaperonage of trusted friends.'

'Yes,' put in Lady West, who had again recovered the power of speech. 'I am sure I have always done my best by the girl but it is not easy, you know, having a young person thrust into one's care at my time of life. But I hope I have done my Christian duty by my poor sister's child; much good it has done me, to be repaid thus for my efforts.' More weeping ensued.

'Hannah deceived my wife most cruelly last evening, for it is now apparent that she did not leave the duchess's assembly in the company of Craven's sister at all.'

'You did not think to check the arrangement?' asked Sir Henry gently.

Lady West bristled at the implied criticism. 'Indeed that was my intention, but then, oh dear, there was such a crush at the door and Hannah told me not to fret so and as she was standing beside Lady Beatrice at the time I did not see any need to intercede.'

'What explanation did she give for her conduct in her letter to you?' asked Harry.

'She begged our forgiveness and understanding, spouting on at length about her undying love for Craven and how she accepted his explanation for his recent behaviour.'

'Which was?' prompted Harry, when Lord West fell into an embarrassed silence.

'He would have her believe that his family suffered acute financial misfortunes whilst he was travelling abroad and that he had been concentrating all his efforts to put the matter right since his return; even going so far as to take a consultancy with your neighbour, and did not wish Hannah to imagine that he was offering for her simply to secure her fortune. But then, seeing her engaged to someone else, he claimed it reignited his feelings for her: feelings that would not be repressed and he was powerless to remain silent.' Lord West threw a sceptical glance at Harry and his father. 'Just the sort of romantic rot an impressionable young girl would believe. She assured us she was satisfied he had been genuinely in love with her all along, but doubted her constancy, and that she was incapable of resisting his overtures, and losing him again now that they understood one another properly; how, er — ' Lord West coloured and, looking uncomfortable, lapsed into silence.

'What more?' asked Harry mildly, suspecting he already knew the answer.

'Well, to be honest, sir, I hardly like to repeat it.'

Harry's brows snapped together and he gazed at Lord West in silent expectation. Clearly unnerved West recommenced speaking. 'Well, she said she did not consider that your feelings for her were all that they should be: that a minor riding accident should be insufficient to prevent you acting as her escort for such a protracted period and that you were using it as an excuse to avoid her company. It's all nonsense, of course, you know how women can be about such things. She also complained that you paid more attention to your neighbour, her horse and even her dog than you did to her.' Lord West, looking more uncomfortable than ever, lapsed into silence and resumed his seat beside his wife.

'I see,' said Harry. 'In view of what you have just told me perhaps I had better learn for myself what she has to say to me on the matter.' He stretched out his hand to Lord West, who reluctantly handed over the letter that Lady Hannah had addressed to him.

Breaking the wafer Harry rapidly perused two pages closely filled with Hannah's tiny script. She offered few apologies for her action and, much as Lord West had predicted, attempted to shift the blame onto Harry; siting his neglect of her as the root cause of her action. Harry conceded that she had a point. She had no idea that his injury had been so much more serious than she had been led to believe and, as for his attitude towards Eloise, on that front he had no defence to offer since Hannah, more perspicacious than he had given her credit for being, spoke no more than the truth.

If she really did love Craven as much as her aunt intimated, and if he had deliberately gone out of his way to be agreeable to her,

Harry had no difficulty in comprehending how easily she would have been persuaded to act out this romantic elopement. Craven's encouragement would be all that was necessary as well for her to absolve herself of all blame, placing it squarely upon Harry's shoulders instead.

'Oh dear!' lamented Lady West for the tenth time since entering the room. 'What is to be done? We shall be ruined. You must go after them, sir,' she said, brightening as she turned beseeching eyes upon her husband.

'I fear it is too late for that. They have already spent the night together on the road,' said Harry delicately. 'Besides, I would not push Lady Hannah to honour her commitment to me if the prospect is as odious to her as she implies.' Harry waved Hannah's letter in the direction of Lady West, who almost choked on a fresh bout of hysteria. 'I think,' he continued meditatively, 'it would be the best for all concerned if I were to announce that I had already released Lady Hannah from her engagement to me, the two of us being mutually agreed upon the fact that we would not suit after all.'

Lady West gasped her astonishment. 'You would do that, sir, after the way she has treated you? I cannot comprehend such goodness!' She turned to her husband, her eyes already devoid of the tears that had afflicted her since her arrival, a contriving expression replacing them. 'We could explain away the elopement as romantic nonsense on the part of a love-sick chit. I am sure the Eshers would be anxious to join forces with us on that score and then it will soon all blow over.'

'And she will be a duchess after all,' added Lord West, clearly not as averse to the idea as he tried to make out.

★ ★ ★

When Sir Henry returned to the morning-room, having escorted their guests to the door personally, he found Harry bent double, helplessly convulsed with laughter.

'It is no laughing matter,' cautioned Sir Henry, even though he too appeared to be afflicted with an overwhelming desire to smile.

'Yes it is!' choked Harry, speech almost impossible for him in the light of his mirth. 'Don't you see, Craven thinks he has scored the ultimate revenge upon me? But instead he has been of the greatest service possible in ridding me of Lady Hannah.' Harry choked on yet another bark of laughter.

'Yes,' agreed Sir Henry, 'even before Lady

West concluded her explanation I could see why he had acted as he did. He can no longer rely upon George Hamilton to fund his expensive habits and has no wish to be exiled to Southern Africa. His only other way out was an expeditious marriage to an heiress. He knew of one who was already devoted to him: one whom he could sweet talk in an instant and one who had the added appeal of already being engaged to you. A very satisfying solution to his problems.'

'Well, at least Hannah's fortune will solve Craven's financial difficulties and he won't be tempted to approach Thomas for assistance, causing more friction in that quarter.'

'Her fortune would be enough for a sensible man, given to making wise investments, but I fear Craven will revert to type. He is a gamester at heart and that will never change. I predict that Lady Hannah's fortune will go the same way as all the other funds that have passed through his rapacious grasp and she will then discover just what sort of man she has landed herself with.'

'She does not deserve that,' said Harry quietly. 'In spite of the way she has behaved I feel true regret that her romantic dreams will be shattered.'

'She will doubtless find other diversions,' said Sir Henry callously, 'in the way that ladies are wont to do. I wager that becoming a duchess will go a long way to atone for her husband's short-comings. Anyway,' — Sir Henry rose and poured them both a substantial measure of sherry — 'enough of what might have been. Time to discuss what should happen to you now.'

'Doubtless you have other well-bred heiresses in mind for my inspection,' remarked Harry drolly.

'Actually no,' responded Sir Henry, leaning back in his chair and regarding his son levelly. 'I rather thought that this time you might prefer to follow your heart.'

Harry's head snapped up abruptly. 'Do not jest about such matters, Father.'

'I was in earnest.' Satisfied that he now had his son's full attention, Sir Henry continued to speak. 'I knew almost immediately that I had made a mistake in persuading you into an alliance with Lady Hannah: I could see that neither of you had the will or the desire to adapt to one another and make the union work. But, of course, by then it was too late and I knew you would have to make the best of it.

'Then these matters with Craven cropped up and I found myself disgusted by his pride:

at the way in which he thought his family was better than just about everyone else's. I rejected out of hand the uncomfortable feeling that he was doing nothing out of the ordinary and was thinking in just the way that I do about our clan. It surely could not be the same thing at all?'

Harry sat forward in his chair; his gaze focused unwaveringly on his father's face. 'Go on,' he encouraged.

'When I realized there was little to choose between the two of us I felt thoroughly disgusted, but there did not appear to be anything I could do to rectify the matter. Then, on that dreadful day that will be ingrained upon my memory for ever, when I received the devastating news that you had been shot, possibly killed, I truly thought my world had come to an end.' Sir Henry's voice caught but he waved away his son's concerns and continued speaking. 'When I arrived at the Esher's dowager house and found you not only alive and in possession of your wits but also kissing the woman you love with a passion that would be impossible to feign, I knew you had been in the right all along and that I was the one who was misguided.' In response to Harry's incredulous expression, Sir Henry smiled fondly and clasped his son's uninjured shoulder.

'Go to her, Harry: go to her immediately and tell her what is in your heart. Tell her I would be honoured to have her as a daughter of this house.'

19

Henry saddled Sampson himself. Awkward still with his injury he was nevertheless in a tearing hurry, too impatient to wait for his groom to perform the simple task for him. When he arrived at the Staverley stable yard he found the object of his mission leaving the side door of the house and heading in the direction of the stables herself.

'I was just about to call upon you,' said Eloise, her smile tinged with a degree of sympathy.

'Ah, so you have already heard,' said Harry.

'Yes,' she said, reaching out to touch his arm. 'The Wests' first port of call this morning was naturally the Esher's town house; the purpose of their visit impossible to keep private for long. The house was in uproar and Emily knew of it at once. Thomas just rode from town to acquaint Father and me.'

'Good news travels fast then?'

'Good news? Harry, how can you say that?'

'Come walk with me, Eloise, and I will explain.'

Eloise allowed him to steer her in the direction of the grounds: more specifically the lake and summerhouse that was situated on its western bank. Seating her on a bench on its veranda, Harry took the place at her side.

'Harry, I know that you perhaps did not care for Lady Hannah in the way I consider a gentleman should look upon his future wife, but then I am given to romantic notions which I am well aware have no place in the real world. I cannot say, in all honesty, that I much cared for your choice of a wife either, but to have that wretched man snatch her away from you in such a shocking manner, just to get even with you, is despicable and will doubtless cause you considerable embarrassment within the *ton*.'

'Thank you for your concern, brat,' he responded lightly, 'but Craven cannot be accused of stealing Lady Hannah from me.'

'What, but I thought — '

'If you peruse tomorrow's *Chronicle* you will see that I had already released her from our arrangement.'

'I do not understand.'

'We had decided that we would not suit after all, you see; call it a case of fatal incompatibility, if you will. And so,' added Harry whimsically, 'she was quite at liberty to elope with whomsoever she wished.'

Eloise looked up at him through huge eyes rendered luminous with shock. Harry felt himself helplessly drowning in their fathomless depths and made half-hearted attempts to concentrate on the matter in hand. Her cheeks were flushed with surprise and he reached out to gently trace the outline of one of them; its colour deepening in response to the smoothness of his touch.

'Well,' she said in a voice that was not quite even, 'I suppose that puts a different complexion upon the matter but still, I cannot help but think she used you extremely ill, Harry, and I dare say you are quite vexed.'

'That is just your problem, sweetheart; you think too much.'

'Well, one of us has to,' she responded, appearing to snap out of her lethargy and regaining some of her customary spirit. 'What shall you do now?'

'Resort to my original plan, of course.' He took her hand in his. 'You were the first lady I proposed to, if you recall, so how about it? Will you marry me, Eloise?'

'Don't be ridiculous, Harry!' she snapped angrily, snatching her hand away and averting her gaze.

'Now stop being difficult,' he teased. 'I am entirely in earnest.' As if to prove the point he slid to his knees in front of her. 'Now do you believe me?' His smile was rakish; overtly and subliminally confident; full of sincerity and unmistakable admiration.

'Harry, get up and stop being so foolish.'

'Foolish, am I? Well, I seem to recall you saying that you enjoy my attentions; enjoy being kissed by me; enjoy — '

'Harry Benson-Smythe, how dare you repeat things I said in a moment of acute distress; a moment moreover when I considered you to be unconscious: at death's door even.'

'A moment when you felt free to speak the truth?'

She offered him a minatory look, sufficient in its intensity to discourage a less determined man. 'Stop playing games, Harry. I cannot marry you; I cannot marry anyone of consequence. You of all people should be aware of that.' She turned away from him but not quickly enough to hide the devastation in her eyes.

'Eloise.' He placed his hand on her shoulder and gently turned her to face him. 'We have always been honest with one another; let us at least not lose sight of that.' She offered a reluctant nod in agreement. 'And now, being completely honest, look at me and tell me whether or not you love me.'

'Of course I love you, Harry,' she said

quietly, 'you are like a brother to me.'

Harry's transfiguring grin was meltingly gentle. 'It is not brotherly love that I am in need of.' He pulled her towards him, into the circle of his arms, but she snatched her body free of him, jerking painfully at his injured arm as she did so.

'Stop it, Harry!' She rose to her feet and walked away from him. 'I appreciate that you are feeling usurped, but that is not sufficient excuse to dally thus with my emotions.'

'Eloise, what must I do to convince you that I am in earnest? Have I not just proposed to you, on bended knee no less? What else would you have me do, my love, you have but to say the word?'

'Harry,' she responded, pacing the veranda as she fought to contain her temper, the train of her velvet riding habit swirling about her ankles, in danger of tripping her up, 'it has been drummed into my head since the first day I entered this house, by a spiteful half-sibling and many others along the way, that I will never be a lady of quality and that all the money in the world cannot make amends for the misfortune of my birth.'

Harry watched her in astonishment. She had never revealed this side of her character to him before; never shown any outward resentment at the hand life had dealt her, which she had always appeared to accept with equanimity. Harry could see now just how much it must always have hurt her to be treated as a social outcast and, as a result, she had never appeared more compelling to him: a complicated minx whom he had never wanted more.

'Eloise, I — '

She silenced him with a gesture. 'Have no fear, Harry, I have long since become resigned to my position and would not have you discompose me now with half thought out proposals that have no place in reality.'

'Eloise.' Harry stood several paces away from her, not trusting himself to touch her: desperate for her to take him seriously. Kissing sense into her stubborn head was his first thought but, somehow, he knew it would not be the right way to resolve this impasse. Not yet anyway. 'I think I first realized I was in love with you when I encountered you in that oak tree attempting to rescue a kitten that was in no need of being rescued; wearing Thomas's clothes; berating me for interrupting you and then bestowing kisses upon Sampson, completing ignoring me.'

Eloise offered him the ghost of a smile: a smile which rapidly disappeared, along with his fledgling hopes. 'Even if that is true,

Harry, you cannot marry me; your father would never permit it.'

Fear and exhilaration fought for dominance within Harry as he sensed they had reached the crux of her objections. Harry understood now what should have been apparent to him long before: Eloise would not inflict what she had been taught to look upon as her inferior person where it was not welcome. Sensing victory at last he offered her a triumphant smile.

'I am here with my father's blessing,' he told her.

Eloise appeared stunned. 'Sir Henry would approve of me?' she asked in a daze. 'You really are in earnest, Harry, are you not? You honestly love me and wish to marry me?'

Harry knew the time had now come to convince her in the way that came most naturally to him. He closed the distance between them and took her into his arms, meeting with no resistance as he did so. As his lips descended towards hers, so her hands slid around his neck, her fingers buried themselves in the thickness of his hair and her delectable body moulded itself against his, fitting against him in perfect symmetry. He knew then that he had won her: her incredulous expression; the pulse beating wildly out of control at the base of her throat;

the light that shimmered in eyes that burned with love and happiness told him all he needed to know on that score. At last he kissed her, already sure what her answer to his proposal would be.

But it could wait until later.

THE END

We do hope that you have enjoyed reading this large print book.

Did you know that all of our titles are available for purchase?

We publish a wide range of high quality large print books including:
Romances, Mysteries, Classics
General Fiction
Non Fiction and Westerns

Special interest titles available in large print are:
The Little Oxford Dictionary
Music Book
Song Book
Hymn Book
Service Book

Also available from us courtesy of Oxford University Press:
Young Readers' Dictionary
(large print edition)
Young Readers' Thesaurus
(large print edition)

For further information or a free brochure, please contact us at:
Ulverscroft Large Print Books Ltd.,
The Green, Bradgate Road, Anstey,
Leicester, LE7 7FU, England.
Tel: (00 44) **0116 236 4325**
Fax: (00 44) **0116 234 0205**

Other titles published by
The House of Ulverscroft:

DUTY'S DESTINY

Wendy Soliman

When Felix, Viscount Western, discovers his father's shipping line is being used to smuggle ex-slaves, he is determined to put a stop to the evil trade. The man masterminding the scheme has a daughter, Saskia Eden, who is also suspected of being involved. Felix registers as a guest at her aunt's house and is astonished to find Saskia running the place virtually single-handed. Felix soon realizes that Saskia knows nothing of her estranged father's business and reluctantly accepts her help to get to the truth. But what he did not plan on was falling in love . . .

LADY HARTLEY'S INHERITANCE

Wendy Soliman

When Clarissa Hartley discovers her late husband's estate has been left to his illegitimate son, she fears she has lost everything. Only her godmother's son, Luc, Lord Deverill, suspects fraud. Compelled to work closely with the rakish earl, of whom she disapproves, Clarissa catches glimpses of the compassionate man lurking beneath the indolent façade. But, denying any attraction between them and ignoring his autocratic attitude, she takes matters into her own hands. Plunged into a perilous situation by dint of Clarissa's stubbornness, Luc must race against time if he is to rescue her. But can he succeed?

HIDDEN INHERITANCE

Emily Hendrickson

Beautiful Vanessa Tarleton accepts a position repairing tapestries for the Earl of Stone, knowing full well his reputation as a handsome rake. She had heard gossip about him during her London season, but when her father gambles everything away, she knows the offer is too good to reject. Nicholas, Lord Stone, faces his own dilemma. He must wed an heiress to restore his nearly bankrupt property and to keep a promise made to his grandfather — but is the beautiful and wealthy Mrs Hewit the right choice? Although forewarned about the dangerously attractive earl, is Vanessa forearmed to resist his charm?

GENTLEMEN IN QUESTION

Melinda Hammond

In the closing months of 1792, the terror of the French Revolution forces Camille, the young Comte du Vivière, to flee his homeland and seek refuge with his relatives in England. For Madeleine, the arrival of her handsome French cousin marks a change in her so far uneventful existence, and soon she finds herself caught up in a dangerous web of intrigue that also entangles Camille. But is he victim or villain?

A DISSEMBLER

Fenella-Jane Miller

When Marianne Devenish arrives in Great Bentley she expects to find her great-uncle in residence but instead meets the Earl of Wister, Theodolphus Rickham, pretending to be Sir Theodore Devenish. She is compelled to move in with Lord and Lady Grierson at Frating Hall. But what is their mysterious connection to the local smugglers? As Theo's dissembling leads to heartbreak, Marianne's tattered reputation forces her to flee. Ostracized by society, she seeks refuge at a small estate in Hertfordshire, but her life turns into a nightmare. Can Theo rescue Marianne before she is lost to him forever?

THE OTHER MISS FROBISHER

Ann Barker

Elfrida Frobisher leaves her country backwater and her suitor to chaperon Prudence, her eighteen-year-old niece, in London. Unfortunately, Prudence has apparently developed an attachment for an unsuitable man, which she fosters behind her aunt's back. Attempting to foil her niece's schemes and prevent a scandal, Elfrida only succeeds in finding herself involved with the eligible Rufus Tyler in a scandal of her own! Fleeing London seems the only solution — but Prudence has another plan . . . Elfrida yearns for her quiet rural existence, but it takes a mad dash in pursuit of her niece before she realises where her heart truly lies.